NADYA'S WAR

C.S. TAYLOR

A Tiny Fox Press Book

Cover design by Alfred Quitevis.

Library of Congress Catalog Card Number: 2016920778

ISBN: 978-1-946501-01-1

Tiny Fox Press and the book fox logo are all registered trademarks of Tiny Fox Press LLC

Tiny Fox Press LLC
North Port, FL

For Gramps

Chapter One

13 August 1942
Anisovka, Saratovskaya Oblast

WHEN I CLIMBED into my single-engine, low-wing fighter, praying to get my first kill, I never thought I'd fall in love with someone who'd have me shot.

I flew through my pre-flight checklist as fast as I could, verifying every setting and gauge in the cockpit. I was a last-minute substitution for a patrol near the Don River, and the added pressure of having to scramble put a tremor in my hands. I feared I would miss something that would prove deadly. A single overlooked item could be the difference between coming home in one piece and not coming home at all. And I had promised my little brother a game of cards when the war was over. I didn't want to go to my grave knowing a fourteen year old had cleaned me out the last time we played.

"Nadya! Slow down!" Klara Rudneva shouted as she hopped on my plane's wing. Her short stature and oversized male, khaki

1

uniform made her look childish, but her face looked anything but. She reminded me of the famous operetta star, Anastasia Vyaltseva, as they both had the same lively smile, sparkling dark eyes, and angelic beauty. Despite the urgency in Klara's voice, she gently slid a pair of goggles over my leather cap. "You'll want to have these, Little Boar."

I groaned as I set the trim and flaps to neutral in preparation for takeoff. "I wish you wouldn't call me that. I'm not a boar."

Klara was a mechanic at the airfield and had seen me off for all seven combat sorties I'd been on. She'd called me Little Boar since I'd arrived at the 586th Fighter Aviation Regiment regardless of my constant objection. She gave the gritty harness that held my parachute on my back one solid tug before tightening my lap belt. "Little boars are hot headed and charge fearlessly at their enemy."

"Boars are mean and ugly."

"You are far from ugly, Nadya," she said with a longing in her tone. "Not with those gorgeous cheek bones and golden locks of yours."

"And fat head," I tacked on. "You forgot to mention that, and you do think I'm mean."

"Only when someone teases you about your Cossack heritage," she replied, referring to an incident that had happened two days ago involving me and our commanding officer, and ended with me scrubbing floors for eight hours straight. "But if you are mean, be mean to the Germans. Be mean and deadly as my Little Boar should be."

The roar of two engines firing up on the airfield drew both our attentions. That was the start of the other Yak-1 fighters on this mission's flight. In moments, we'd all be in the air, eagerly looking to pick a fight with the German Luftwaffe. The time Klara and I had was short, despite my wishes to the contrary.

Klara leaned into the cramped cockpit and gave me a one-armed hug. She smelled of sweat and oil, and grease transferred from her face to mine. I didn't mind. "Come back to me safe, Nadya."

"I will," I replied. This brief exchange had become a ritual between us since our first pairing, twelve days ago. It was a moment in time I'd come to relish. It was our little space where nothing could harm us. Not Hitler nor his army looking to conquer. Not Stalin nor his fanatics looking to purge. It was a place where two friends could savor a moment before being thrust into the chaos of the Great Patriotic War.

"Now go and get your first kill," she said, squeezing me one last time before jumping off the wing.

Once she waved she was clear of the propeller, I gave her a light-hearted salute and started my plane's engine. I watched the needle on the oil pressure gauge climb and tried to calm my nerves. The Luftwaffe had dominated the air since the start of the war. Today would be no different, and I wondered how many more planes and pilots we would lose in defense of the homeland. My muscles tightened in my back, and I blew out a simple, hushed prayer. "God be with me."

As comforting as those words were, I hated whispering them, but over the last twelve years I'd learned to keep prayers to myself after seeing those who didn't be shot or sent to labor camps. I told myself I was being pragmatic, surviving, even if official persecution had been called off. Some nights when I tried to sleep, however, I considered it was more cowardice than anything.

I used the two wheels on my right to open the water and oil radiators, and then started taxiing the plane into position on the runway. I leaned out of the cockpit to see where I was going since the plane's nose blocked my view. The cool afternoon breeze carried with it hints of petrol.

The radio sprang to life. Martyona Gelman, my wing leader, spoke with calm authority. "Form on me after takeoff, five hundred meters. One circle of the airfield and we're going."

I slid my canopy over my head and locked both it and the tail wheel into place. The roar of the engine softened by about a third, but I felt as if its vibrations in the stick and the foot pedals were three times what they were. I soon became aware that the engine wasn't causing my controls to shake. I was.

"Easy, Nadya. You can do this." I told myself, double-checking the gun sight. Focusing on the crosshairs felt reassuring, as if I had control over my destiny. All I had to do was put my enemy in them and down he'd go. I could make a difference in this flight, in this war. A great difference. More so than any of the other girls? No. As far as I was concerned, each one of us in this all-female regiment would leave our mark in history.

"Red Eight, this is tower. You're clear for takeoff."

I pushed the throttle forward, and my fighter started down the runway. It built speed like a wild horse cut free from the pens, and I was along for the ride. I used the left rudder pedal to counter the plane's innate desire to hook right, lest I crash before leaving the ground. God, how embarrassing would that be?

Once the plane hit one hundred and seventy kilometers per hour, with both vehicles and buildings zipping by on the ground, I eased the stick back. My Yak-1 leapt into the air as if it were as eager to reach the sky as I was. An overwhelming sense of freedom washed over me, and I smiled while slipping into a V-formation with the two other girls. Flying was still as magical as I'd dreamed it would be when I had been a little girl watching hawks sail overhead.

I took my position flying wing for Martyona. I was off her right side by a dozen meters, and another girl, Kareliya Malkova, flew on Martyona's left. In the short time I'd known Kareliya, I had learned two things. First, she was as reserved as they come, and second, she had a vicious streak that hungered for her first victory against a German pilot like none I'd ever seen. I wondered if she'd beat me to it and secretly prayed she wouldn't.

Our flight should have been four, a pair of wing leaders and wingmen, but another girl's plane needed last-minute work on the landing gear, and even a dullard knew taking off with only one wheel ended badly. Normally, we would have waited on the repair, but the Germans had reached the town of Kalach-on-the-Don a couple of days ago and were now less than seventy kilometers from Stalingrad. We couldn't afford to let them reach that mighty city, and thus were forced to go up one pilot short. Our CO said we'd be fine. I dared to believe her.

Our trio headed south. On most flights we'd protect high-value targets from the Luftwaffe, such as railways, bridges, and depots, but with the pressure on Stalingrad, we were being sent to patrol a swath of area northwest of the city. Despite the Red Army Air's high losses, I was glad we were headed closer to the front as it let me be proud of my service and reinforced the notion we were all doing something important. That and guard duty was about as exciting as hours of pot scrubbing.

The Volga River flowed off to my left. I enjoyed the view of it from above as it reminded me that even in war, nature was beautiful. I also loved seeing the ships come and go from port—they looked so free—and enjoyed wondering what the little girls in the nearby fields thought when they looked up and saw us fly by.

"Everyone tighten up," Martyona ordered. There was a bite to her tone, not painful, but threatening, like a straight razor pressed against the skin. "Sloppy girls are dead girls."

I stiffened in my seat. Kareliya was in formation, but I had drifted off and dropped altitude, putting me outside and low of my slot by fifty meters. I slipped back into position with a combination of throttle, elevator, and rudder so we once again made a perfect V.

For the next fifteen minutes we flew in silence, and I was embarrassed at my rookie mistake. I was a Cossack, proud and true, and from a long line of warriors whose skill was only rivaled by our dedication. Thankfully, Father hadn't been witness to it.

I wondered when we'd encounter German fighters on the prowl. At our current speed, we'd reach their lines in about twelve minutes. As such, I kept a constant watch over the bright blue skies and the rears of the other girls' planes as best I could and trusted they did the same for me. Though rear visibility wasn't as bad as I heard it was with German fighters, our Yaks still had a blind spot.

I saw no planes other than the two dark green Yak-1 fighters to my left, and nothing shared the sky with us other than the late afternoon sun. That scared me more than anything. Ever since I'd come to Anisovka, Martyona had told me time and again most pilots were shot down by enemies they never saw. German aces came from unseen places, like monsters in the night every child fears. Luftwaffe pilots, however, were real and more lethal than any imagination.

The radio crackled, and our wing leader spoke. "I can see the Don. Change course to two-three-zero and look sharp. The fascists want to tear into us as much as we want to tear into them."

Her plane climbed with a gentle bank, and me and Kareliya followed suit. My mouth dried, and goosebumps rose on my skin. The past seemed to fade away, and thoughts of the future fell as well. All that existed was the moment.

I flipped the safeties to both the nose-mounted cannon and the pair of machine guns in the cowl. They should have been ready to fire after takeoff, but I'd developed the habit of waiting later in flight to do so. I was fearful of an accidental discharge, and the last thing I wanted was to be responsible for damaging—let alone destroying—another girl's plane.

"Stay with me and Kareliya, Nadya. I haven't lost a girl in almost twenty-four hours," Martyona said.

I chuckled nervously, her joke doing little for my nerves. Still, I tried to keep the air light and confident. "Don't worry. I'm not going to ruin your new record."

Kareliya didn't chime in on the conversation. She couldn't, as only a few planes in our regiment had RSI-3 Eagle radio transmitters installed. All Kareliya had was the RSI-3 Hawk receiver, thanks to some genius who thought the ability to talk during a dogfight was unnecessary. After all, who in her right mind would want to lug around a few extra kilos for the ability to say, "Check your six!" or, "I need help!" Idiots probably thought we'd talk about hair and makeup the entire flight, as if that's all us girls were capable of. They did promise us we'd all have two-way capabilities in the future, but I wasn't expecting that day to be anytime soon.

The Don River passed beneath us. I bit my lip in eager anticipation of a fight and the chance to prove myself. At the same time a knot formed in my stomach. I checked and rechecked everything. Water temperature. Clear tail. Oil temperature. Oil pressure. Clear tail. Fuel pressure. Manifold pressure. Clear tail. Gun sights. Fuel level. Clear tail. I did this entire routine four times before running my fingers over my leather cap and wondering what I was missing.

"I've got eyes on Luftwaffe, one o'clock low," Martyona said. "Four He-111s along with two 109 fighter escorts. Five kilometers away. Headed east."

I easily spotted the flight. He-111s were medium-sized, twin-engine bombers, and a staple of Hitler's war machine. Their lumbering bodies flew in a tight formation and bristled with machine guns to cover one another. Their green paint jobs blended well with the terrain, but their bulk made them stand out. The bright yellow noses of their Bf-109 escorts were even easier to see.

Martyona's plane accelerated, and my engine's pitch grew louder and higher as we followed her higher into the sky. The enemy planes stayed on course, apparently unaware of our presence. Even as a green pilot, I understood why Martyona didn't charge in. She wanted to have the advantage in altitude. Altitude could be traded for speed, and speed meant life. The only thing flying a low and slow plane would grant you in a dogfight was a condolence letter to your next of kin. The only letter I wanted written was to Father, telling him how his little girl scored her first aerial victory. I'm sure he'd celebrate for a week straight once he got that news.

"Stay fast and hit them hard," Martyona said. "Hit them for the Motherland. Hit them for all you're worth!"

The ferocity of her words ignited a fire in my soul. I narrowed my eyes and turned my anxiety into hate, hate for those who bombed our cities and razed our villages. I rolled my plane to the left and followed Martyona in a diving attack, vowing to make the fascists pay for flying half asleep over Soviet soil and thinking we'd been so beaten they were safe from our air force. Their audacity fueled the burning in my chest.

Though I was flying to cover my wing leader, I placed the last of the German bombers in my sights. I'd be able to make at least one firing pass on it while keeping Martyona clear of escorts. Once we shot by, we could reassess, maybe even engage the 109s if no one took damage from the tail gunners. Three on two were good odds as far as I was concerned.

Time stretched, and I measured each second by the heavy thumps of heartbeats. I used the gun sight to gauge the distance to my target. Once the bomber's wings filled the diameter of the sight, it would be about two hundred meters away.

The bomber drew near. Six hundred meters. Five. Four. I don't know if it was sheer luck or an angelic whisper that tore me away from my target to peek over my shoulder, but when I did, I gasped. Four German Bf-109 fighters bore down on us from out of the sun, their yellow noses filled with guns and cannons promising swift and certain death.

"Break! Break! Break!" I yelled.

Martyona snap rolled her plane and reversed direction with an inverted dive. I followed her as best I could, flipping my fighter and pulling back on the stick. The hard maneuver pressed me against my seat. My arms felt as if they had large bags of lead attached to them. I strained under the G's, gritting my teeth. My head grew light, and the world muted. I prayed I didn't black out under the maneuver, and I prayed it had been fast enough that the Germans couldn't follow.

"Nadya watch your six!" Martyona said as we came out of the dive and into a shallow, spiral climb.

Out of instinct, I rolled left. Tracers zipped by my cockpit, and I looked frantically over my shoulder. One fighter was peeling away, not bothering to follow me into a speed-bleeding maneuver, but I caught sight of another lining up from above. God, how did we miss them?

I jinked right, and a sound like gravel hitting a tin roof filled my ears. My controls became mushy. I glanced to my right wing and felt nauseous. Numerous holes were scattered across the surface, and my aileron was missing a fist-sized portion. Worse, I was also trailing a light brown mist.

"Nadya, you're clear but leaking fuel. Get out of here while you can," Martyona said.

I knew she was trying to sound reassuring for my own sake, but the tremor in her voice belied the optimism she put forth. I yawed my plane left and right, sliding the nose as far as I could without tumbling the aircraft so I could get a good view of what was behind me. The He-111s flew off in the distance, keeping their original heading, with the original two escorts flying loosely nearby. How smug they must have been, watching us play right into their trap.

Closer, some five hundred meters away, both Kareliya and Martyona fended off the Luftwaffe, but it was clear they were fighting a losing battle. The Messerschmitt pilots were taking turns making diving attacks, forcing my sisters-in-battle to burn altitude and speed to dodge the German's sights.

"Two thirds left," I mumbled, checking the fuel gauge mounted on the wing. That was more than enough to get me to Kamyshin where there was an auxiliary airfield we'd planned to refuel at on the way home. It was tempting to make a run for safety, but I didn't want to see a girl who abandoned her sisters every time I looked in the mirror, and that wasn't even considering what others would think of me.

I pulled on the stick and climbed, pushing past three thousand meters. With a gentle roll I brought my plane to bear on the dogfight. Martyona and Kareliya had sacrificed a lot in altitude and were making tight turns and staying together to keep each other clear. They didn't have much more height to burn, and once they were skimming the treetops, they'd be easy pickings. But if I got there in time, the three of us had a decent chance to all go home, maybe even send the Germans running if we flew well enough.

Two 109s from up high began another diving attack. I was too far away to stop it, and all I could do was scream. "Two more coming! Break! Break! Break!"

"Nadya, I told you to return to base!" Martyona shot back at me. "Do as you're ordered!"

I didn't.

I pushed the throttle as far as it would go. At that setting, the engine guzzled fuel and would be running on fumes in short order. I took aim at one of the 109s that had just started its dive, and even though I was about four hundred meters away, I opened fire with both cowl-mounted machine guns.

Orange tracers streaked through the air. They didn't come close to hitting their target, but since they flew in front of the German, they produced the desired effect. The 109 pulled out of its dive and rolled away to avoid my fire. I followed the enemy fighter up into a shallow and banking climb, spraying bullets once more. Most missed, but I managed to pepper the German's tail. Tiny pieces of fuselage broke off, and in my excitement, I pushed the trigger to my cannon.

The 20mm ShVAK cannon sprang to life, belching flame and large shells that could punch through an engine block or explode a fuel tank with a single hit. My plane shuddered from the recoil as I held down the button, hoping for a kill. The shots failed to connect.

Worse, I was about to overshoot my target and thus put myself directly into his crosshairs.

I pulled up and rolled my plane to keep my speed high, and then pulled the nose of my aircraft back down to meet him. Within a split second, my enemy realized what had happened and began rolling and pulling his nose into my maneuver. Over and over we went, like a pair snakes wrapping around each other in a corkscrew fashion, each trying to get the other to overshoot, each trying to score the kill. With every roll we made, our planes grew closer.

In a span of a few heartbeats, I could see every marking on the pilot's plane, from the red letter "U" with a set of wings on one side and inscribed in a shield that labeled the pilot as being part of the Jagdgeschwader Udet unit, to the bright yellow eight painted over the rear of the fuselage, to the white tallies on the tail. My breath left me when I saw those. There had to be twenty victory markers painted on the right side alone. Each one represented a plane he had shot down. I hadn't picked a fight with a fresh, scared pilot like myself. I'd picked one with a proven ace at least four times over.

Our planes continued to jockey for position. My rolls became slower and slower. The muscles in my arms and shoulders strained more and more. Each pass we made gave him an edge and me notice my life was now measured in seconds. I realized it wasn't only my inexperience that was about to get me killed. The damage to my right wing had given my enemy more than enough advantage for him to exploit, too. My plane wouldn't respond as fast as his no matter how skilled I was.

"Damn it, Nadya," Martyona said over the radio. "Why didn't you leave when you were told?"

I swallowed hard as the German ace and I rolled by once again. I could see his sharp, unshaven face this time as our canopies nearly brushed by. I could see the shark-like grin he wore. We both knew what was about to happen. "I'm a stubborn boar," I said. The calmness in my voice surprised me. At least I'd die a heroic death.

On the next roll, I overshot my enemy. I continued until I was upside down and then yanked on my stick for all I was worth. Pain erupted in my arms and back, and I was convinced the sinews were pulling themselves apart. The G's slammed me in my seat, and I held the tight maneuver as long as I could.

My vision darkened. Yells, orders, chatter on the radio faded to nothing. Exhausted, I let go of the controls. My plane leveled. My senses returned.

"Nadya break!"

Before I could react, my plane exploded.

Chapter Two

FIRE RIPPED THROUGH the cockpit like it was made of flash paper. Flames licked my leather jacket and pants, and found my hands and neck with glee. Thick black smoke poured from my engine, blinding me to everything. I choked on the billowing clouds, and even protected by my goggles, my eyes watered. Worst of all, the smell of scorched metal and burning fuel filled my nostrils.

My ears took in the shrieks of a woman desperate not to die. Momentum slammed me into the side of the cockpit as the plane spun out of control. I fought with my canopy and managed to get it open. The instant it slid back, I unfastened my lap belt and was thrown clear of the fire-trailing wreck.

My training kicked in the moment I kissed fresh air. I arched my body for all it was worth, and my fall stabilized to a belly-to-earth position. I pulled the ripcord to my parachute, and when my silk savior blossomed round, I was sitting in the harness less than three hundred meters above the earth. God that was close. A few seconds' hesitation and I would've made a quaint crater.

Descending, I knew I wasn't out of the woods yet. There were still plenty of ways to die before I reached friendly lines. I ignored the pain in my hands and neck as best I could and got my bearings. A large plume of smoke rose from the ground a little over a half a kilometer away, and I could see burning debris scattered around it. Above and to my right, a Yak-1 fought against a pair of 109s. Both groups exchanged tracers, but only the Yak streamed white coolant against the orange evening sky.

The chatter of machine guns came from behind. I twisted in my harness and saw another 109 with a Yak firmly latched on its tail taking shots as they both weaved left and right. The two planes flew by, and in that split second, I identified them both. Martyona was hot on the German ace's tail. My wing leader's aerial acrobatics rivaled any seraphim's, and I was thrilled to have front row seats for when she knocked him out of the sky. His plane was already leaking fluids.

The German climbed and rolled, and Martyona easily followed, but as she chased him into another tight corner, she suddenly overshot. My heart stopped as a burst of cannon fire spewed from the Messer's nose. Chunks flew from the tail and left wing of Martyona's plane. Her fighter tumbled, and before she could recover, the German fired yet again and sheared off her wing.

"No. No. No. Please, God, save her," I said, trying to fool myself into thinking if I prayed hard enough, I could stop her plane from spiraling in the ground. I felt small and helpless, as if a cruel Universe knew my every fear and brought them to life for its own amusement.

Martyona's plane smashed into the steppes below. The brilliant explosion of yellows and oranges was mesmerizing. Even from where I hung in the sky I could feel the heat from the blast. The sudden change in air pressure also put a thump in my chest and a ringing in my ears.

The Messer circled around me, and I could see the pilot inspecting his kill. An ear-shattering bang came from his plane.

Black clouds billowed from the nose of his craft and his prop stopped. As he leveled his plane, I hoped he'd lose control and crash, but I ended up cursing when I saw him bail and his chute open wide. I then prayed he'd break his neck on landing.

I slammed to the ground, the impact jarring my thoughts back to Martyona. I unbuckled my harness and let the rig fall from my back. Smoke rose from where my wing leader had crashed, and I stumbled toward it as fast as I could. Time was not on my side. My world view narrowed, and all of existence shrank down to me and her.

"Martyona! I'm coming!" I said. Somehow, she'd survived. I was a Cossack, a devout daughter of the Living God. He would hear my prayers. He had to.

My right ankle warmed, and within a dozen steps, I noticed I wasn't putting as much weight on it as I should. The rocky terrain added to the difficulty, but that didn't matter. I had to get to her and pull her from the plane before she burned to death, and then together we'd have to reach the other side of the Don before the Germans came. Surely they saw my parachute and were on their way to capture us both. Or at the very least, help their pilot return to his airfield.

I glanced over my shoulder toward the river. It was a kilometer or two away, which meant judging from the smoke rise, Martyona's crash was at least three kilometers from the water. I worried I wouldn't be able to drag her that far if she were wounded, but I told myself I could find a way to bring her across the river and all the way back to Anisovka if I had enough faith in myself.

A throbbing built in my foot, as if it might burst from my boot. When I crested a small rise, breathless and teary eyed, I looked down upon the wreck. Her plane was as scattered as my hopes were for her survival. The wings, tail, and part of the rear were gone— but the main body remained. My eyes widened. A fool's optimism sprang to life. Not only did the fuselage remain, but it looked like the cockpit was still intact.

"I'm here! I'm here!" I shouted, limping forward. I grunted and let the pain in my leg redouble my efforts. When I got to what was left of her Yak-1, I climbed it as best I could to get to the cockpit. Portions of hot metal seared my hands, but I didn't care, especially when I realized the cockpit hadn't been spared at all.

"God, no," I whispered. What I had thought was the entire fuselage was half of it turned on its side with a portion of the canopy still attached. Bits of controls, seat, pedals, and twisted metal were strewn around. I saw Martyona's body a few meters away, charred and torn in two, and fell off the plane. I vomited until my stomach had nothing left.

A gunshot cracked through the air, and dirt kicked up a few meters away. I scrambled forward, taking cover behind the remains of the fuselage. Drawing my Mosin Nagant revolver from its holster, I dared a peek.

The waning evening light made details difficult to see, but a German leaned around a small tree a few dozen meters away with a 9mm Luger in hand. By his light jacket, trousers, and boots—not to mention lack of rifle or submachine gun—I assumed he was the German ace I'd been fighting.

He rattled something off in German. I hadn't a clue what he said, but figured my response was universal enough. I answered him with a gunshot. I hoped it would take off his head, but all it did was dig a little hole in the ground some forty meters behind him.

The man ducked behind the tree. He laughed and called out to me. "Apologies. I forgot you probably don't speak German. So quick to shoot. Good for me your aim is as bad down here as it is up there."

He mangled his Russian and his accent was still as German as ever, but I could understand him. "Funny. You missed me, too." I replied.

"A woman?" I couldn't see his face, but I could hear the shock in his voice. "This world is full of surprises. But I missed on purpose."

I snorted. "Why? Wanting to court me?"

The man laughed again. "No, but I dare say you'd be interesting if we did. I wanted you to drop your weapon so we could properly talk."

"I won't let you capture me," I said, checking my revolver. I had six shots left, which meant I had five to fight with. The last one was reserved for me. I prayed it wouldn't come down to that.

"I guessed as much since neither one of our sides treats prisoners well," he said. "But I've never met any of my opponents. I've wanted to for a while now."

A stabbing pain built in my hands and arms, and it dawned on me that the adrenaline that had kept my mind off my injuries must be fading. I turned my head when I heard the engine of an approaching vehicle, and I knew I had to get out of there. I kept my weapon aimed at the tree, and retreated toward the Don. I saw the German peek at me once, but he said nothing else and he didn't try and stop me. Why, I hadn't a clue, but I was grateful to God for whatever protections He saw fit to bless me with.

My ankle protested each step I took as I hobbled. I heard Martyona's voice urging me on, one step at a time, and from it I took a cautious optimism I'd make it home. Up until that point, I'd always known life could be harsh, but never appreciated it would be harsh to me. My dreams as a little girl were always adventures filled with magic and travel, never terrifying. Nightmares happened to other people, yet there I was, part of the others. I told myself this wasn't the end, and I'd pass this story down to my children's children's children, to inspire them to never give up, to always believe in themselves. I'd like to think that's what gave me strength to carry on.

I also thought of my father, of his father, of my entire lineage of warriors who had fought and suffered throughout history. I told myself they had had it worse than I did and still pressed on. How could I allow myself to succumb to a few burns and a twisted ankle? And if that wasn't enough, I thought about what the Germans would do to me. I'd be lucky if they'd shoot me on the spot. There would be rape, torture.

Worse, if the Soviets liberated me, German treatment paled in comparison to what the NKVD would do. They would test me to be sure I wasn't a fascist sympathizer. I, like everyone else, was well aware of Stalin's Order 270 given last year. In it he'd said, "There are no Soviet prisoners of war, only traitors."

Vehicle sounds grew, and with them I heard the all-too-familiar squeaky noise of moving tank treads. At the top of the hill, I thought I could make out the outline of a German armored vehicle. It was hard to see now that the sun was gone and only a sliver of moon hung in the night sky, but with a full Panzer division in the area, there wasn't a lot of guess work to what it was.

I hobbled toward the Don, praying the darkness would cover my movements. I surprised myself at how fast I could go, injuries and all. Without warning, the ground gave way under my feet, and I toppled headlong down a steep incline. I twisted and bounced down the slope, crying out several times along the way. When I slid to a stop, fire ran through my hands, and I could barely move my right leg. I half thought it would feel better if I chopped it off.

"*Hier! Schnell! Schnell!*"

I bolted upright. The shouts couldn't have been more than fifty meters away, near the top of the embankment I fell from. God, how had they tracked me in such darkness? Had the German ace been following me, leading them? Or was I cursed and happened to tumble near a German patrol?

It didn't matter, and I didn't have the time to think it over. I pressed north in the darkness, heart pounding in my ears. Branches snapped and tore at my skin. Leaves crunched. German orders came faster, closer.

The foliage opened up, and I found myself at the edge of the Don. Sadly, I could only make out the first few meters of water from the shore. Darkness swallowed the rest. I had no idea whether or not it was a hundred meters across or five. I'd grown up in Tula and became a strong swimmer thanks to the Upa River, but my usual confidence at being in the water faltered as I worried my leg would betray me halfway across the Don and send me to a watery grave.

"*Hier! Hier!*"

It seemed as if they were shouting in my ear. I limped into the cool water and swam. The current pushed me and stung my hands, arms, and neck. My right foot became dead and useless to kick with. Water filled my leather jacket, dragging me down. I knew I couldn't swim much longer with it on, so I took a deep breath, let myself go under, and pulled the jacket off.

The jacket slipped from my arms with little effort, but returning to the surface was harder than I anticipated. My water-logged boots, like the jacket, gave me trouble. My left boot came off after a brief struggle with the laces. The right was nearly impossible to remove due to the agony racing up my leg every time I moved it. It took three submerged attempts to pull it off. When I finally succeeded, I shot to the surface like a champagne cork free from its bottle.

"Thank God," I said, feeling hopeful despite my injuries and predicament. "If you can get to the other side, Nadya, you'll be safe."

I found my spirit bolstered when I talked to myself. It was as if I weren't alone and someone with me knew things would be okay if I mustered the tenacity to carry on. I managed to pull myself across the Don with nothing to guide me but the stars above. I didn't know how far the current had pulled me once I reached the north bank, but I couldn't have cared less. I was out of the water and exhausted.

With my last bit of strength, I limped up the bank and into a tree line before collapsing on the ground. At least now when morning came, I told myself, the Germans wouldn't be able to see me from the other side. As vulnerable as I was, I cracked a smile as I thought about how frustrated the fascists must be to have been right on top of me only to lose my trail at the last second.

I lay for what must have been hours, too tired to move, too pained to sleep. I wondered what Klara was doing, thinking. She had to know by now her plane and her pilot were missing. She'd be worried—no, scared—for me I'm sure, and I wondered how much she'd hug me when I got back. I wondered how hard I'd hug her in return.

When I finally passed out to the distant thundering of artillery, I dreamed of scalpels filleting my hands and vices crushing my feet. At the edge of those nightmares, I was vaguely aware of voices closing in and looking for a downed pilot.

* * *

I woke and squinted at the mid-morning sun. I raised my hand to shield my eyes. That moment was the first time I could clearly see my injuries. The skin had peeled from my hands. Blisters raised across my swollen and red palms. Each hand had a small patch of skin that was charred and leathery as if they'd found the hot end of a blow torch and played a game of catch the flame. As ugly as they were, I hoped that in ten years the scars that would form would tell a story of courage and perseverance. But given the horrific agony racing through those wounds, I had half a mind to find a way to make a clean chop at the wrists. That had to be less painful that what I was currently enduring.

My dry tongue stuck to the roof of my mouth and my heart pounded against my ribcage as I started to panic over the severity of my wounds. Infection could kill as easily as any bullet, and there was no telling what I'd picked up on the way. I toyed with the idea of risking a wash back at the river, but with the Germans still in the area, I guessed I'd be shot in short order. Thus, I had to find water elsewhere. Sadly, I had difficulty remembering the maps of the area.

It took me a good five minutes to slow my breath and calm my mind enough to think clearly. I had a feeling that there was a small village to the northeast, so I limped in that direction. With a bit of luck, I could get some alcohol to clean my wounds and then stuff my face with food. On top of everything else, my stomach was gnawing on itself. At least I was safe from German infantry. They were headed to Stalingrad and wouldn't be on this side of the Don.

The uneven terrain made for slow progress throughout the morning. Rocks dug into the tender soles of my feet, and I stopped often to let the pain in my ankle subside. My hands still tormented me, but I found a way to hold them at my side I could suffer through. To keep my mind off my wounds, possible infection, and a painful death, I imagined a crystal-clear pond waiting for me at the end of my journey. The thought of letting my matted hair soak and watching the dirt wash away soothed my soul like a cool summer's breeze. I even smiled, more so when I added all the grapes I could eat to the fantasy.

By noon, my thoughts muddled and my breath turned raspy. I needed something to drink. My burns must have caused dehydration to set in, and the sun wasn't helping. I wanted to rest, but knew I couldn't. So I willed myself forward, one step at a time.

I turned to song for added relief. Song had been with me for twenty years of my life. My parents had sung to me when I needed it the most as a child, and now I would sing to myself for that same reason.

The piece I chose was "Snow, the time has come." Father used to say some people erroneously called it, "Snow, enough of you," and thinking about that made me laugh. I settled on that piece because it was one every Cossack knew by heart, one sung before battle, and one that strengthened the bonds of family.

I started the song slow, working the bottom of my register as the words stirred my soul. By the second verse, I imagined a chorus of brothers and sisters in arms traveling with me, each with their own burdens to carry, each one lending their own voice. When I reached the end of the first stanza, pride and energy coursed through my veins.

I ignored the scratchiness in my throat and sang on. Two stanzas. Three. The words came faster, stronger, as did my steps. I sang of life as a Cossack, of carrying on without fear and worry. I sang of dark woods and foreign lands. I sang of parents, family, and wine. I sang with all of my heart, teary eyed and broken, but not defeated.

I stepped onto a dirt road and took several steps across it before realizing its significance. This would lead to somewhere with people, with help. Maybe even to a friendly baker who had a plate full of turnovers and a pint of fresh milk in miraculous anticipation of my arrival. He'd also double as an excellent physician that could patch me up in no time.

I dropped to my knees to give a thankful prayer and rest my weary body.

A vehicle skidded by, clipping my left side. I spun to the ground. The back of my head struck hard, and my vision exploded in an array of colorful lights.

Shadowy forms loomed over me against a blown-out sky. Their words were muffled in my ears. I tried to sit up, but their firm hands kept me on the ground.

"I need to get to Anisovka," I said, my voice weaker than a chick's first attempt at flight. "And I need a bath."

The voices replied, but they were less intelligible than before. Pressure tightened under my shoulders, and my knees were lifted in the air. My surroundings became meaningless shapes of color and motion before I slipped into blissful unconsciousness.

Chapter Three

I DRIFTED IN and out of sleep as I was taken on a bumpy ride. I caught glimpses of the tan interior of a beat-up car, and occasionally saw the driver and the front-seat passenger. They both wore camouflage smocks and olive M40 helmets. They spoke from time to time, but I'd pass out before I could talk to either.

When I woke for good, I was lying on the ground next to a green GAZ-61 automobile, surrounded by three men. The tallest of the group was both muscular and aged. He wore trousers as grey as a stormy sky and a white cotton shirt with its sleeves rolled up to the elbows. His face reminded me of the infamous Kamchatka brown bear, and I guessed he was nearly as strong.

The other two I recognized as those who'd been in the car with me. The over-sized Soviet uniforms they wore combined with each of their young faces made it seem as if they were playing war in their older brother's clothes more than they were true soldiers of the Motherland. To that observation, I couldn't help but let out a stifled chuckle.

"She wakes," the tall man said, pointing two fingers at me. He kneeled at my side and put his hand on my shoulder when I tried to stand. "Stay on the stretcher," he said. "I don't want you to put weight on that ankle."

My face scrunched. "Who are you?"

"Doctor Grigory Rusak. You're at my field hospital," he said, gesturing to his side.

I glanced at the two-story farm house. Though it looked older than the Church, I was grateful for anything indoors at this point. "I could use some water," I said. "My throat is parched."

One of the soldiers produced a canteen. "Here. Drink slowly."

I sat up and snatched it out of his hand. Lighting shot up my arm, causing me to whimper. Still, I tried to take hold of the canteen but ended up dropping it as the pain intensified a thousand fold.

"Allow me," the doctor said, picking up the canteen and holding it to my lips.

The warm liquid coated my mouth and throat. It spilled from my lips while I chugged, dripped down my neck, and soaked my clothes. In that moment, I couldn't have been happier.

"Thank you," I said, once finished. "What happened?"

"I was hoping you could tell me," the doctor replied. "Soldiers Pasportnikov and Orlov were running supplies when you stepped in front of their auto. I'm guessing they're responsible for your concussion, but not your burns, nor the half set of clothes you're wearing."

"What kind of person rams another with their vehicle?" I asked.

"An accident, I'm assured. What can you remember?"

I looked at the two boys, hoping they would jog my memory. They looked away, shame and worry on both their faces. I laughed.

Grigory tilted his head and he looked at me like I was a curiosity in a museum. "What's so funny?"

"I called them boys in my head," I explained. "I dare say they're my age."

The doctor smiled. "Good. Your head isn't as cracked as I feared. How old are you?"

"Twenty," I said. I was pleased the answer came to me without hesitation. "I'll be twenty-one this October."

"You're wearing the trousers and shirt of someone in the Motherland's service," Grigory said. "Were you in combat?"

I looked myself over. Combat? I was in uniform, or half of one at least as I was missing a jacket and boots. Dirt encrusted my pants and tunic, but I didn't see any bullet holes. I wrinkled my nose at the smell wafting from my lower half. I needed a bath, preferably a foam one in a tub the size of a cargo ship with champagne and strawberries. And as long as I was daydreaming, a personal stylist—the kind the stars of motion pictures had—to tend to my ratted hair would be fantastic.

A plane flew overhead, and the previous day's events flooded my mind. I could smell the grease from Klara and relished the memory of her embrace. But then I saw the fire inside my cockpit, felt my frantic bailout, and heard Martyona's fighter explode when it crashed into the ground. My breath left me, promising to never return.

"Easy," Grigory said. "War is still fresh in your head. We'll talk later when you're able."

Pasportnikov and Orlov carried me inside via stretcher. They transferred me to a table inside a small room that smelled of alcohol and urine. After I was situated, they retreated from the room, and once they were beyond the doorway, I heard them begin to talk about me in hushed tones. Instead of trying to eavesdrop, I stared at a mildew-covered ceiling and thought about Martyona. Those thoughts consumed me in seconds, and I relived her death again and again. Each time I saw her plane go down I was reminded how powerless I was to stop it—how useless.

What did that make me? A failed pilot. A daughter from a long line of holy warriors who'd brought shame to her lineage, to her God. The Almighty, after all, protected His saints, answered their prayers, but did nothing for mine. I wondered what I'd done to warrant His scorn. For a moment, I wondered if He even existed. Immediately, I chastised myself for thinking such things. Saints had suffered more than I'd endured. Perhaps that was why they were saints and I was not.

"Good sprain on that right ankle," Grigory said, entering the room and holding an x-ray in my face. "Bones are fine, lucky for you. I'm still worried about your head. Any injury that affects thinking has the potential to be serious."

"So no head-butting my CO, and I should wait till next week for the marathon?" I said, managing a half smile.

"Don't take your condition lightly," he said. "The brain can be both resilient and fragile. I'm not sure which yours is. And that leg of yours has a lot of bruising and injured ligaments. You'll need to stay off it for at least two weeks," he said. "Light duty after that for another three or four. By then most of your burns should've healed. I think I can clean them well enough to stave off any serious infection."

"Most?"

"The majority are second degree, including the ones on your neck and thigh. They are painful, I'm certain, but not critical," he said. "Small portions of your hands and arms are much worse. You can see by the charred look they have. I doubt you're feeling much from them now, but they will likely cause you problems later down the road."

"My cockpit was on fire," I whispered. "After I bailed out, I searched through a wreck on the ground."

"You're a pilot then. I'd heard they'd put together a few female regiments. You're the first girl I've met from them."

"I was a pilot," I replied. With Martyona's death over my head, I didn't feel worthy of the title. She was a pilot. I was the person who got her killed.

"Are a pilot," he corrected. I suspected he hadn't a clue why I had said what I said because he tried to sound hopeful as he delivered his prognosis. "Your ankle will heal. I'll need to do some debridement on those burns once you're cleaned. They might hurt the rest of your life, but I believe you'll be back in the air sooner than you think."

"I hope so," I said, faking a smile. I didn't believe any of what he said, but his kindness touched me, and I thought the least I could do was make him feel as if he were making a difference. Men, boys, always tried to fix things, and what was wrong with me was nothing they could set straight. Thus I figured it was better to put on a show. I tried telling myself tomorrow would be easier. I almost believed it.

"You don't sound convinced," said a new voice. "Not what I would've expected from a pilot for the Motherland."

I craned my neck to see who had spoken. Near the entrance of the room stood a man in his forties. He wore a dark tunic with blue shoulder pads and piping. A leather belt was cinched across his waist, and on it he kept a Tokarev semi-automatic pistol holstered. His dark breeches were also piped blue and stuffed into high-top leather boots. I recognized him immediately as a commissar of the NKVD—the People's Commissariat for Internal Affairs—but I didn't need to see his uniform to know that. His devil eyes and cruel face told me enough.

"I have fought as I should, Commissar," I said.

"The flutter in your voice belies your claim," he said. "You're likely a deserter, or a thief who stole clothes. Possibly both."

"I'm no thief, and I'm no deserter," I said. I may have cost Martyona her life, but it wasn't because I left her to die. No one could call me a coward, and I wasn't about to let that positive bit of my character be stripped from me. And I would never, ever be a thief, so help me God. "I am Junior Lieutenant Nadezhda Buzina, assigned to the 586th Fighter Aviation Regiment at Anisovka."

The Commissar crossed his arms over his chest and smirked. "And pray tell, why are you so far from your airfield, Junior Lieutenant Nadezhda Buzina?"

"I was patrolling the Don, northwest of Stalingrad, with Senior Lieutenant Martyona Gelman. We intercepted a flight of bombers yesterday, and I was shot down," I said. My shoulders slumped. Though I wanted to stay strong in the face of this officer, the wounds to my heart were still fresh.

"So I can radio your unit and she will corroborate your story? She will tell me of your bravery and how you stopped the bombers at all costs? Or will she curse your cowardly retreat?"

A lump formed in my throat. "She'll do neither. She was killed."

"How convenient for you the brave one perished and you did not."

"Convenient? Convenient!" I shot up with fire in my blood. "Yesterday was the worst day of my life!"

"It was the worst day of her life," he said. "Stabbed in the back by a coward who should've been loyal to her to the end. You should've fought with every bullet you had and when they were gone, you should have plowed your fighter right through their cockpits."

"I fought until my plane exploded," I said. "And then I fought with one of their pilots when I crossed with him on the ground."

"Did you kill him? Or better, bring him back for interrogation?"

"No," I said. "I took a shot at him as he hid, but I had to escape when the panzers came."

Petrov snorted. "One shot and you ran. The story of a deserter and traitor. You should have beaten him to death with your hands if you had to. You shame your regiment and aren't even a step above those filthy Cossacks who betrayed the Motherland."

I tried to go after him, but Grigory locked his hand on my shoulder and kept me in place. "You have no idea who I am," I said, balling a fist behind my back. "Do the world a favor and play in a minefield."

The Commissar pulled his weapon and leveled it at my head. "I should shoot you on the spot and save myself the trouble of an investigation," he said. "You'd serve as a good example to the rest. Failing one's duties won't be tolerated."

Before I could speak, Grigory stepped forward with one hand outstretched. "If she's telling the truth, Commissar Petrov, there will be hell to pay," he said. "She would've been handpicked by Marina Raskova, and from what I hear she'll fight for all of her girls tooth and nail. You don't want her using her connections with Stalin against you if you act without proof."

Petrov lowered his pistol and stared at me the way I imagined a hungry shark would watch a wounded seal make it to shore. "Thank the good doctor," he said. "He saved your life. But talk to me that way again, and I'll end it without hesitation." When I didn't do as he told, he set his jaw and motioned toward Grigory. "I said thank him."

"Thanks," I said, not daring to take my eyes off the Commissar.

"I'll leave you be for now," Petrov went on. "But I will investigate your loyalty. When I find you in want, not even Major Raskova will be able to protect you. I don't care how much of a national heroine she is."

"You'll not find me in want," I said. I prayed the lie was good enough, not only because deep down I felt I'd failed on patrol, but also because my family had ties to the White Army during the Revolution years ago. If he found out, he'd label me an enemy of the state and execute me on the spot.

Petrov left, and for the next several minutes Grigory washed my lower right leg and wrapped my ankle in a tight bandage. When he was finished, he broke the silence. "For your sake, I hope you fly better than you mind your manners. Picking a fight with a commissar is like picking one with a king cobra. You can only hope he doesn't want to waste his venom when he decides to strike."

"He started it," I said, despite how childish it sounded. "Why is he after me?"

"The Germans march on Stalingrad," Grigory said. "We've lost the gains we made last winter, and though no one wants to say it, that city is going to be a last stand we may lose. But don't worry. If they shot every pilot who'd lost his aircraft, we'd have airfields of planes with only ghosts to fly them before the month was up. He'll move on to other things."

"I hope you're right. It's not easy to relax after staring down the barrel of a gun."

Despite the doctor's optimism, I couldn't shake the feeling the commissar's fixation on me was far from over. We didn't discuss the matter any further, and after being given a crutch, I was escorted by a soldier into a room where yellow paint peeled from dirty wooden walls and piles of laundry were stacked everywhere.

A nurse named Sofia entered and shooed my male escort out. She looked older than my mother by at least ten years. Countless wrinkles had set into her round and stoic face, and I found myself jealous of her shoulder-length, curly hair. She wore the hair of a girl. Mine was a boy's cut, chopped short the day I arrived at Engels to train as a fighter pilot.

Sofia said little as she bathed me with a wash cloth, large bowl, and pitcher. My hair was so grimy that she worked it with her fingers like a baker kneads dough. When she tended to my burns, however, she traded her rough touch for a compassionate one rivaling the angels. Once finished, she handed me clothes and my mood lifted. Funny how something new to wear could do that.

"You carry a lot of guilt for someone so young," she said, giving me another shirt as the first had been too long. "You'll put yourself in an early grave if you don't learn to let it go."

At first I wanted to deny it all, but I could see it in her eyes. She knew. "How can you tell?"

"I've nursed more soldiers than I can count," she said. "I know the look they bear and why they have it."

My eyes glistened. I couldn't deny she had hit the mark, but I couldn't speak of it either. All I could do was sit there and wonder if those she'd seen had the same regrets I did. This conversation hurt worse than any I could have had with the commissar. Eventually, I managed a question, curious if we had similar experiences and she had some secret she could pass on to help. "How many of them have died in your care?"

"Too many for my likes," she said as she found me a pair of trousers. "These are probably too large, but they are the smallest clean ones I have."

I took the pants and put them on, trying my best not to aggravate my ankle. "Did you lose ones you should have saved?"

"We all have, dear, but there's a saying I've taken to: Life is life."

I grunted, and my face soured. "I hate that saying. It's so hopeless, as if the world is out of our control."

Sofia laughed, but quickly recomposed herself. "The world is out of our control," she said. "That doesn't make it hopeless."

"How's that?"

"You always control your own actions," she replied. "You can make your own purpose and worth, find your own hope."

I chewed on those words. I could make my own purpose. Right now, I was the girl who let Martyona die, but I could change that. I could find that German ace, bring him down, and show the world how good I was. As strong as that conviction sounded, though, I doubted my abilities as I thought about how easily the man had out flown me. Would our next encounter be any different? I'd have to find a way to ensure it didn't, otherwise I'd always be a failure. I managed one last question, one that haunted me in the shadows of my thoughts. "What if the future doesn't cooperate?"

Sofia shrugged and with a half-smile, winked. "Life is life."

Chapter Four

A WEEK LATER, I was riding in the back of another GAZ-61 and on the last leg of my journey back to Anisovka. Doctor Grigory had cleared me for travel, feeling my burns had healed enough for me to return to my own unit. Despite the windows being down, my shirt stuck to my chest and beads of sweat lined my forehead. It wasn't only the mid-August heat making me sweat. My hands ached more than they had when I was shot down.

Watching the scenery distracted me from my wounds. Large grass fields stretched out on either side of the road and were dotted with firs. They brought back memories of climbing similar ones as a child and using them as shields during snowball fights in the winter. Those were times I longed for, where friends stayed forever and I was naïve to the cruelty of the world. But life is life. I grinned at that last thought, realizing the saying had taken to me despite my objection.

The bumpy dirt road brought us by several small farms and villages. The inhabitants went about their busy, seemingly normal lives, but a keen observer could tell things were anything but. There were no able-bodied males to be seen. The ones out were either decades past their prime or shorter than their mothers' hips. I wondered how long the villages would stay that way, or worse, what would happen when the front reached them. I hated that it was a real possibility, but resolved myself to help ensure Stalingrad would not fall. If we could hold the Germans there, these towns—these children—would never have to truly see what had claimed their fathers and brothers.

It was early afternoon when we reached Anisovka. I was eager to see everyone again, Klara the most. I couldn't wait to share a meal with her, especially since eating back at the field hospital was boring at best and depressing at worst on account of all the injured.

We parked next to a beat-up ZIS-5 truck, painted the standard olive green and sporting wooden railings for the flatbed in the back. Bullet holes ran through the side and the top of the cab, and I cringed at the sight. At least in my plane I could fight back. Whoever had been driving the truck was a big, slow target. Maybe it had been hit while parked and no one had been in it. I latched on to that story as I exited the car.

"Shall I walk you in?" my driver said, motioning toward the single-story brick building that served as the airfield's HQ.

"I'll be fine from here on out, thank you," I said.

My driver saluted. "Then I'll take my leave, comrade pilot. I've orders to return as soon as possible."

I returned the salute and sent him on his way. I wondered when such military protocols would feel normal. Here I was an officer, albeit a junior one, and so many soldiers looked up to me, saluted me, and even waited for my instruction. Any other time in history I would've been seen as barely an adult. Secretly, I didn't feel like I knew what I was doing, but I was good at faking it. Sometimes that's all that counts.

I hobbled toward the command building, disappointed no one had come out to greet me. I couldn't blame them. It's not as if I'd given an itinerary on when I'd arrive. That and flights still had to be planned. Patrols still had to takeoff. We were in a war that hadn't stopped because my flight was shot down. I thought I'd do well to remember that.

Though my eyes misted at Martyona's memory, I smiled as a Yak flew overhead. The roar of its engine gave life to my heart like the Harrowing of Hell gave life to the dead. The old me had died, or must die at the least, and a new me would rise like a phoenix from ashes, brighter and stronger than ever before. Too bad I wasn't a red head.

The door to the command building opened. Out stepped my commanding officer, Tamara Kazarinova, limping from an injury she'd suffered long ago during an air raid in Grozny. She wore a peaked service cap, leather boots, and a dress for a uniform. God! An actual dress! Had we finally gotten clothes tailored for women?

As soon as her eyes met mine, surprised flashed across her face, and her usual stoic features softened.

I stiffened and offered a salute. "Major," I said. "Junior Lieutenant Nadezhda Buzina reporting for duty."

"It's about damn time you got here," Tamara said with a glare, but her hardened façade melted in a flash. She ran up to me with a smile and gave me a hug. "Glad to see you're safe, Nadya. When no one returned, we feared the worst."

Tamara had always been stiff and cold in all she did, as if she were trying to mirror her older, masculine counterparts. I wasn't prepared for her sudden warmth. "Kareliya didn't come back?"

"No. We found her body at the crash site a few days after the mission. I'm sorry."

I knew she'd died, even if I hadn't seen it. She'd faced too many Messers and at least one ace for there to be any other outcome. I stood silent for a moment, wondering how long she had lasted before they tore her apart. "I should have flown better."

Tamara pulled away. I caught a glisten in those dark eyes of hers, one I wagered few had ever seen before. "Luftwaffe pilots are incredibly skilled, even if the brass doesn't want to admit it. I've said time and again you girls need more training before being sent into combat. If anything, we failed you."

"I don't know . . ."

Tamara squeezed my shoulder and added, "I do. Think nothing more of it. That's an order."

"Yes, comrade major," I said. Though I agreed to her orders, I was certain I'd have better luck getting away with shooting a commissar in broad daylight than not blaming myself for that failed mission. Ultimately, I knew I couldn't change the past. But I could redeem myself. I picked my next words carefully. "I'd like to start flying again in a day or two, comrade major."

"Are you sure?"

"Yes," I replied. "If I don't, I'm afraid what little nerve I have left will be gone for good."

Tamara took in a long, slow breath before straightening her uniform. Compassion faded from her face and the characteristic wrinkle across the bridge of her nose took form. "You do seem eager," she said. "But I'm concerned about your wounds."

"They're better," I said. "Give me a few days and I'll be okay."

"You've got a bad limp. You won't be able to use the pedals much," she said. "I dare say your burns won't allow you to pull hard on the stick either. I know you want to defend the Motherland, but if you get back in the air, it won't be in a few days."

"If?" My heart skipped a beat. I swallowed hard, and words poured out of me like water from an upturned pitcher. "Every night I see Martyona's face. I hear her calling to me on the radio. I have to avenge her. I have to kill the bastard who shot her down and make sure no one else dies at his hands, otherwise I'll always be the girl who got her killed."

"Steel yourself, Nadya," she said. "Before this war is over, more girls will die—some who you'll have known longer than Martyona. It's an ugly fact there's no getting around."

"Should I pretend Martyona never mattered?"

Tamara shook her head. "Of course she mattered, but don't let your grief get the better of you. You must move on. If you can't control yourself here, how will you be able to in the air where it counts the most?"

My head swam. Her advice seemed impossible and dishonoring, and her unyielding tone made me wish for the commander I'd caught a glimpse of moments ago. "I can control myself," I said, though I didn't sound convincing even in my own ears. "Let me back up so I can put that man into the ground."

"I intend to make them pay. I promise," she said. "Now go get some lunch. Once you've had your fill, I'm putting you to work."

"Doing what?"

"Our 4th tank army suffered heavy losses, and the Germans are fifty kilometers from Stalingrad. You can help with managing supply for the city's defenses. There's also plenty of admin, inventory, and inspection you can do."

"But you won't let me fly."

"That's the last of it, Nadya," she said as her brow knitted. "Bravery may win a battle, but logistics wins a war, and right now I want to help win the war. When the doctor says you're fit to go up and I'm convinced you can, we'll discuss it again."

I was hurt at how final it all sounded as she left. I clung to the idea that one day soon I'd be allowed back in the cockpit. Until then, I decided I could refine my dogfighting skills in my head by analyzing every possibility and engagement I could think of so the next time I encountered the German Yellow Eight, I'd be the one doing the killing.

With a rumbling stomach, I went to the mess hall. The building was made of wood and painted blue with a brown slanted roof that looked like the butcher shop near my family's home in Tula. Mice scattered from the entrance as I approached. The airfield had been infested by the rodents all summer, and I reminded myself to watch my step, not so much for the mice, but because I didn't want to risk turning my ankle if one ran under my boot.

Inside the building I received a warm reception by those inside—kitchen staff as well as some of the pilots and ground crews of other planes. I appreciated their kindness, but their words and hugs put me on edge. I worried that if they knew what had happened that day, they'd blame me for Martyona's loss.

I took some bread and a small bit of kasha for lunch. The foremost was stale, but I was hungry and didn't care. The latter was delicious. Usually the grain porridge was bland and at times undercooked, but this time it had salt, onion, and a touch of beef broth. In our world, such food was considered a slice of heaven. I shoveled the food in my mouth, occasionally having bits go flying or stick to my mouth and chin. More than once I wiped my face on my sleeve. Though unladylike, we were all used to eating in a hurry. Once finished, I tossed the small metal plate it had been served on onto a nearby counter and left posthaste.

I didn't get far before I heard a familiar, frantic voice from behind.

"Nadya?"

I turned around the second Klara dropped the wrench she was carrying and lunged after me. "It's me! It's me!" I said, laughing.

Klara wrapped me in a bear hug so strong I was certain she'd pop a rib. She eased her grip as I wheezed, and she nestled her head between my neck and shoulder. "My Little Boar," she said. "Why did you take so long to come back? I should sock you in the head for making me worry."

"I misplaced your plane and had to walk home."

"They said you were shot down."

I nodded. "By misplaced I meant turned it into a burning wreck that tried to kill me."

"Why would you do such a thing?" she said, an edge of anxiety in her voice.

"I . . ." Grief hit me like a wild kick from a mule, and I found I couldn't even start the story. In the short time I'd been at the Anisovka, Klara had become my best friend, and she looked up to me more than she should. She'd also been good friends with Martyona, and I feared her reaction if she knew how I'd failed.

To my surprise, Klara backed, pain and horror on her face. "Oil was ejecting from the gear valve again, wasn't it? I'd meant to have it re-checked."

I grabbed her tightly by both shoulders, grimacing as a stab of pain shot through my palms. She had a touch of paranoia that could swing out of control if not caught fast. "The plane flew fine. I did not."

Klara bit her lip. She picked up her fallen wrench and studied it as if some defect would present itself. Finally, she looked at me and said, "Promise I didn't miss anything?"

"Promise."

"Did you ram one? I know they told you to do that if your guns jammed."

I laughed. "If it came to that, I don't know if I'd still be here."

"Probably not, so try not to," she said. Creases formed in her brow. Her voice turned vengeful. "I hope you find the men who killed Martyona and Kareliya. They deserve an early, painful grave."

In full agreement, I nodded. "I actually met the one who shot down Martyona," I said. Klara's eyes widened, and I explained. "He had to bail when his engine gave out. We met on the ground."

"Tell me you killed him. What was he like?"

"A heartless butcher," I spat, thinking how he tore Martyona apart. As fast as those words came out, that image jarred against my encounter with him on the ground. That experience left me perplexed as to who he was since I couldn't understand why he hadn't killed me or taken me prisoner. All I knew was I hated the man, that and one other thing. "He's also a terrible shot with a pistol. He took a pop at me and missed."

Klara shuddered. "I'm glad he is. When do you fight again?"

"Kazarinova didn't say. She's worried about my injuries."

Klara's face soured, and she snorted. "Figures. If I were you, I'd make friends with the doc and get as many girls to support you as you can."

"What for?"

Klara glanced around. The nearest group of people was a ground crew fifty meters away loading ammunition belts into one of our fighters, but despite the distance, Klara spoke in hushed tones. "Father always said gambling was wrong, but if I had to, I'd bet against you," she said. "Kazarinova's a bitter pill. If her wounds are keeping her grounded, she'll do the same for you. She won't have a lower officer showing her up."

"No, she's not like that," I said. "I know she's hard, but she was sweet when I first arrived."

"All for show," Klara said with a dismissive wave of her hand. "Kazarinova's been in trouble recently from some of her decisions. Losing Kareliya and Martyona added to the fire. She's not going to risk more girls getting killed if your injuries are a problem."

"She wouldn't replace me," I said. Even as I spoke the words, I didn't believe them. Two dozen Yak-1s sat on the field, and a thousand times that many girls were scattered across the country yearning to climb in one. Tamara would have no trouble filling my spot.

"Something else," Klara said. "Liliia and some others have asked Major Raskova to remove Kazarinova from her post. If Kazarinova goes down, I can see her taking some of us with her simply out of spite."

I gave her an incredulous look. It was unheard of to jump the chain of command and petition Major Raskova directly about anything. "They say they milk chickens, too."

"I'm serious, Nadya. It's not a rumor. They've gone to Raskova twice now."

The image I had of Tamara crumbled like a childhood fantasy crushed by the hammer of reality. Liliia had been flying since she was fifteen and was an instructor prior to the war. She'd never struck me as someone who went at things lightly or rebelled against senior officers. I wondered what Liliia knew about Tamara that I didn't. Then again, maybe I didn't know Tamara well at all. "If that's true, I'll have to convince the Major I'm better in the air than on the ground."

"You make it sound easy."

"I don't know about easy. After all, without effort you won't pull a fish out of a pond," I said with a growl. I turned and started for the command building, intent on saving my wings. I would not let my identity be forever fixed on being Martyona's killer. I'd die before ever having to go home with such a thing hanging around my neck. So help me God I would prevail, and woe to anyone who tried to stop me.

"Come back to me safe, Nadya," Klara called out after me. When I glanced over my shoulder, she shooed me on and gave a devilish grin. "Now get going and get your first kill."

Chapter Five

EVERY DAY FOR two solid weeks I argued with Tamara to reinstate my flight status. She kept insisting I had to heal before she would give me further consideration, and I kept hammering the topic, saying I was ready. The first few times I ended up with cleanup duties in the kitchen for insubordination, but after that, I respected her warnings—sometimes merely a set jaw or dip of the head—and dropped the matter until the next day.

When I wasn't scrubbing pots or hauling trash from the mess hall, Tamara had me working with her from sunrise to well after sunset, pushing papers, taking inventory, and scheduling flights, repairs, and resupplies. She had a large map of the war's southwestern front stuck with pushpins on the wall of her office. Each day those pushpins would move as reports came in, and each day I saw the Germans advance toward Stalingrad. Nothing seemed to slow them down, and a last stand at the city seemed inevitable. At least when they reached the city, Tamara would need every pilot for its defense. She'd have to put me back in the air, and then it would only be a matter of time before I'd cross paths with Martyona's killer.

Each day I'd also comb over the reports, desperate to find any sort of intel on who that man was. To my dismay, nothing came up, not even when I sent telegraphs to other regiments trying to track him down. It was as if he'd vanished from the war, a ghost never to be seen again. I began to wonder if I'd seen his number wrong and that's why no one knew who he was. Was it really an eight on his tail? Maybe I'd gotten the color wrong, too.

On the fourth of September, I was walking back from the airfield with dozens of papers from the morning fighter inspection stuck to a clipboard. My steps were brisk, and the pain in my hands and arms had dwindled to a manageable throb in the background.

I sang *The Birch Tree* as I went. The traditional song had been stuck in my head the past few days, and it reminded me of how beautiful Father's voice was when he'd sing it. Also, I enjoyed the range of tempo and emotion in the piece, and the lyrics were something I could identify with. The birch had lost its leaves and lost who it was. Exactly how I had. Despite connecting with such words, deep down, I felt flight was more of a possibility than ever before. Maybe that's why I sang it. I wasn't afraid I'd lose my wings forever.

I entered the command post and found Tamara sitting behind her cluttered desk of daily paperwork and a week's worth of plans on top. To her side stood my squadron commander, Evgeniia Prokhorova—Zhenia for short. Her posture was perfect, and though her brown field shirt hung well on her athletic build and the male breeches she wore looked tailored to her body, Zhenia's large chin and short, fat neck gave her a comical appearance—something she herself would poke fun at from time to time.

Zhenia was loved by all the girls, myself included. She trained all of us in the air as much as she could, and when we weren't flying, she always gave instruction on the ground, even if it was only a tidbit during a quick passing. Most important, since I'd returned from my ill-fated mission, she'd helped boost my hope I'd fly again.

Given the confrontational look on both their faces, I sensed I'd interrupted something important. "Should I come back?"

"No, there's work to be done," Tamara said.

I went to my little space of mundaneness without word, a small desk in the corner, and hoped the two would continue whatever it was they were doing before I entered.

"Do you have anything you'd like to add, Zhenia?" Tamara said. At this point I faced away from them and didn't dare look over my shoulder, but by the Major's annoyed tone, I could imagine the sour look on her face.

"Only to remind you this escort you need is short one pilot," Zhenia replied. She spoke in a cultured voice, but her R's never came out right. "Olga is still ill from last night, and I'd like it noted I've brought this to your attention."

"So it shall," Tamara said. "We're out of pilots today. You knew this coming in, and I want the matter dropped."

Silence filled the room, settled on my shoulders like a heavy wet blanket. Inside I screamed my name over and over, hoping, praying either Tamara or Zhenia would see the willing—and desperate—girl in the corner, begging to fly.

"As you wish-" Zhenia started, but that's all she got out.

I leapt to my feet, heart pounding in my chest and sending paperwork flying off my desk. "I'll go."

Again, the two stared at me. Tamara looked shocked due to my sudden interruption that might have bordered on insubordination. She had, after all, told Zhenia to drop the subject. I told myself I wasn't included in that order, so I should be okay. Zhenia on the other hand, with her back turned to Tamara, grinned and gave a wink.

"She'll do, Major," she said, facing Tamara once more. "She could use a simple flight after being grounded so long."

"I can do simple!" I said, bounding forward.

Tamara grunted. She made tight fists and placed them behind her back. "You think you're ready?"

"I'll be fine. See?" I hopped back and forth on one leg a few times, showing off the strength I'd regained in my ankle. It warmed under the strain, but I kept a smiling face. I had to be strong. I had to seize this opportunity, an opportunity that could only have been divinely orchestrated. Olga's sudden illness was proof enough for me.

Tamara remained skeptical. "And your hands?"

I held them up and flexed my fingers several times. Lighting shot through my forearms as I did, but I'd been expecting it and hid it well under a guise of excitement and confidence. "Couldn't be better."

Tamara walked over and outstretched an open hand. "Let me see."

I placed the back of my right hand in her palm. My skin warmed under my collar, and I did my best to keep an even breath as she gently inspected the wounds.

"They do look healed," she said.

"They are. I promise."

"Communications are hinting that tomorrow is a big day," she said, leaning over my wounds and tracing them with a sharp fingernail. "We might be called to help keep the skies clear of Luftwaffe over the front. Do you think you're fit to assist?"

"Absolutely."

Tamara clamped down on my hands and drove her thumbs into the scar tissue. Unprepared for the attack, I screamed in pain and doubled over. She let go a second later. "She's not ready."

With tears in my eyes, I stood back up and gasped for breath. "That wasn't fair!"

Tamara's cold stare cut through me. "Neither is combat."

Zhenia put her hands in mine. "Grip them." When I hesitated, she said it again with a growl. When I complied, she added, "Tightly."

I set my jaw and summoned all of my strength and squeezed. I squeezed until I thought the bones in both of our hands would break. Fire ran through my arms, but I did not yell. I did not cry. I fought the pain with anger. Anger at my one shot at returning to the air being stolen from me.

"Now pull," Zhenia ordered.

I pulled against her hands so hard I yanked her forward a few steps. I let go, confident the point had been made. Beaming, I looked at them both.

Zhenia shook out her hands in the air. "She's got an iron grip. She can fly."

"No, she can't. She's still in pain."

"As squadron commander, I have the right to pick my pilots for a flight. She will be my responsibility."

"Absolutely not, Lieutenant," Tamara said with bite. "She is my responsibility. Her plane is my responsibility, and the success of your escort is my responsibility. I'll not risk multiple lives and multiple fighters because she's overeager."

"But you'll risk multiple lives and multiple fighters sending us on an escort short one plane. One plane can turn the tide of a dogfight, if it comes to that. Hell, an extra plane can stop a dogfight from even happening if the fascists don't like the odds. Do you want to explain to Marina why you lost a VIP when you didn't send the proper number of fighters?"

Tamara crossed her arms over her chest. Her jaw was set like a vice. I held my breath, waiting for her reply. She was considering it. She had to be. What else would she be thinking about? I bit the inside of my lip, not knowing if I should say something or if I would be better served to keep quiet.

"Fine," she said. "You'll have another pilot."

"Thank you!" I said, shouting with glee. Tamara held up a hand, and though I quieted, I couldn't stand still. I was too giddy.

"Not you," she said.

My heart skipped a beat. "What?"

Zhenia's face scrunched. "If not Nadya, who?"

"Take Klara," Tamara said. "I think she's due for her first combat sortie."

"What? You're taking a mechanic over me?" I said. My face flushed. My muscles tightened in my shoulders and back. Fire raced through my arms. "She can't even fly!"

"She's got almost three hundred hours flying in an air club before the war," Zhenia said with a downcast face.

"And you've been training her for three weeks," Tamara added. "You said yourself you thought she'd make an excellent pilot one day. If Nadya doesn't heal, I'll need a replacement."

"You can't do this to me!" I said. My body trembled. Tears ran down my cheeks. A large part of me wanted to throttle Tamara where she stood. The other half wanted to grab the wooden chair behind me and smash it over her head. My rage built ever more as she looked at me without the hint of compassion. "You can't ground me forever! I fought with Martyona! I swore to avenge her!"

"Nadya, this isn't up for debate," Tamara said, glaring. "You will recompose yourself this instant or you'll rot in the box for two days. Choose your next words carefully."

"You might as well send me to the grave if you're clipping my wings!"

"Have it your way. That's two. Want to make it two more?"

"Make it a goddamn week for all I care!"

And so she did.

Chapter Six

THE GUARD JABBED the barrel of his PPSh-41 submachine gun into the small of my back. I stumbled into a tiny room with a curse under my breath. He'd hit me in the same spot for three days straight now, and the bruised area was tender to the touch. Though we were an all-female regiment, there were a few boys that had been stationed at the airfield since the start, and more had trickled in over the last few days, helping with construction and logistics. Rumors had it even more boys were coming. If they were all as gentlemanly as this one was, I had a suspicion I'd turn my own wings in just to be free of their company.

My prison was a small wooden shack with a dirt floor and no windows save for the tiny one in the door. A single beam ran underneath the pitched ceiling from which a rusted lantern hung—a leftover from when the structure had been a storage shed. The air smelled of mold and sweat, the latter coming from myself. My only regular visitors were the guards, whoever brought me food and water, and a handful of mice that scurried in through a hole near the corner and would serenade me with squeaks from time to time.

Twice a day I was allowed to use the latrine and receive my meager rations and water, once in the morning and once in the evening. The rest of the time I was forced to quietly stand. I'd run combat scenarios in my head until ten o'clock at night, at which point I was permitted to lie down and sleep, giving much relief to my aching legs.

I felt the punishment was tough, but fair. I did mouth off to my commanding officer. I had no one to blame but myself. It could've been much worse. I could've been sent to the labor camps, stripped of rank and honor, and I was thankful I hadn't. Still, I was irritated Tamara hadn't put me on escort with Zhenia and wondered when my mouth would land me back in here.

Occasionally my thoughts turned to Martyona and why the world was cruel and unfair. She had done everything right, yet I was the one who survived. I wondered if it would be worse that no god existed or one did who allowed evil to not only exist, but thrive. A god who let horrid things happen was confusing at best, and truth be told, I wasn't sure which of the two possibilities I would've preferred. I never came up with an answer. The best I could hope for was she'd gone home, her eternal one, and one day I'd see her again.

I wasn't always so gloomy when thinking about that terrible flight. Several times I managed to think about it objectively, trying to learn as much as I could, and I came away with two things. First, the unseen enemy was the deadliest. I had known that in theory before, but the German who'd killed Martyona had shown what it looked like in practice. Second, which played off the first, bait was both simple and lethal. I'd need to be mindful about taking it and skilled at offering it, especially where an ace was concerned.

Occasionally my mind focused on that nameless German ace as it tried to piece together who he was. He had to have been toying with me on the ground. What other explanation was there? I could see him now, reclined in a leather chair, cigar in one hand and brandy in the other, laughing with his fellow Luftwaffe pilots about how he'd knocked me out of the sky and then played God with me at the crash site. Maybe he felt shooting me in the back wasn't sporting enough. Or maybe he simply wanted to score another aerial victory on me so he could paint another kill tally on his tail.

It was frustrating not having an answer.

On the third day of my incarceration, I heard the guard outside talking to another. "Can't speak to her," he said. "Leave it and go."

The exact time eluded me, but I thought it was mid-morning, which meant breakfast had arrived. There was some muffled commotion, and then the guard chuckled. "Fine. One minute and you're done."

The door creaked open, and Klara walked in, holding a torn hunk of bread in one hand and a canteen in the other. Despite being parched and hungry, I scowled at her arrival. "Put it on the ground. I'll eat later."

"Look, I don't have long," she said after she wiped her mouth as if she'd tasted something repulsive. "But I have a couple of things you need to know."

"Such as you replacing me as a pilot?" I tried to come across as if her actions hadn't hurt me, but as I spoke those words, I could feel her knife in my back twist. My throat tightened, and a torrent of emotion pushed against my ruse like backwater on a failing dam. At that point, I stopped pretending. "How could you? I'm struggling enough to keep my sanity and you come along and steal my slot."

"It's not like that," she said, handing me my breakfast. "I don't want to stay on the ground, but I'm not after your slot. I swear it. I'd die before betraying you."

I snorted. "No one else is grounded. Hard to think otherwise. Why didn't you tell me?"

"I wanted it to be a surprise for when we flew together for the first time." Klara's voice dropped to a whisper. "If I were in your shoes, I'd think the same, maybe worse, but believe me when I say this. Changes are coming, and no one is supposed to know."

"Sure. No one knows but you."

"A few days ago the 24th and 66th Armies attacked the XIV Panzer Corps. Brass hats are trying to cover up the disaster, but word got out and the Germans are at the southern end of Stalingrad," she said. "Everyone is afraid the city is going to fall, no matter how much they say otherwise. If it does, there's no stopping the Germans. Kazarinova is transferring over a half dozen pilots to help with the defense."

I chewed on her words, unsure how to take the news. Had she been training with Zhenia in the hopes of moving to a new regiment or to take the place of someone leaving? Or had she been trying for my spot all along and this news was a convenient cover story?

"Twenty seconds or I'm locking you in," the guard called out.

Klara's face turned worried. "There's more. There's a commissar named Petrov with Kazarinova right now. He's asking about you and not in a good way."

My gut tightened. "How?"

"He thinks you left Martyona to die. Please tell me you didn't."

"You know me, Klara. Of course not."

She blew out a puff of air, but her body was still tense. "I believe you, but he sounded so sure—said you were a spy for the Germans and that I shouldn't talk to you at all. He said you didn't kill one of their pilots when you had the chance."

"He's on a witch hunt. Nothing more." While part of me wanted to shoot the man, most of me wanted to cry. Not because Petrov was hot on my heels, but because Klara was taking a risk in telling me what he was up to. I had no doubt he'd label her as a traitor too if he caught wind that she'd tipped me off to his investigation. "I'm sorry I doubted you," I said, hugging her. "You're nothing but a true friend."

She snuggled into the embrace with a sigh. "Thanks."

"Hey! I said you could talk! Nothing else," the guard shouted. "Now get out."

"Be strong," Klara said, disengaging.

"I will," I said, convinced I could even if my hands felt as if they were on fire. The hug aggravated the injuries, but it might have been the stress from everything else as well. That was another thing I'd noticed while standing in the box. The pain from my burns was an excellent barometer to my anxiety.

Once she'd gone, I ate my breakfast of bread and water. The bread tasted like a brick of sand, but it might as well have been manna from heaven on account of how hungry I was. I nursed the canteen as I ate, careful not to spill any of the precious liquid inside. It would be all I'd get until supper.

My cell door opened an hour later and in strode Petrov. His eyes reminded me of a wolf who'd spotted a wounded deer, and he wore a uniform straight from the front lines: a peaked field cap, a waterproof jacket with rank diamonds on the collar, and field breeches tucked into his boots.

I shifted my weight from one leg to the other out of unease and offered a salute. "Commissar."

Petrov stopped a couple paces away. In his hand he carried a lit pipe with a black stem and dark wood for the bowl and shank. "Why am I not surprised you're here? But I guess it's one step closer to swinging from a tree."

I lowered my hand after it became clear he wasn't going to return the salute. I suppose he could have nailed me for that as well, but given my aching arms and weary body, I hadn't the desire to play games. I wanted this conversation done. "Can I help you with something, Commissar?"

"So polite. So direct," he said, bringing the pipe to his lips and taking a puff. He walked around me, eyes never leaving my body. "I came to tell you I'm going to enjoy having you with me at Stalingrad where I can keep a close, personal eye on you."

"Comrade commissar?" I cocked my head to the side while my heart pounded against my chest. I had no idea why I was being transferred. Surely I hadn't angered Tamara that much. Maybe he was simply toying with me.

"When I heard Kazarinova was sending off the troublemakers, I'd hoped you were in that group," he said. "And then I was disappointed to find out you weren't. But can you imagine why I was so delighted to learn you were no longer fit to fly?"

"I haven't the foggiest."

"Because as a simple administrative clerk, you're no longer crucial to the 586th's readiness. Transferring you is a simple matter as you're no longer under Major Raskova's wing."

I crossed my arms over my chest and balled my fists. I knew he was trying to get under my skin, but it was all I could do to not punch him in the face. "Why are you telling me this?"

Petrov stopped behind me and leaned in close. He took a long drag off the pipe and blew the smoke to the side. As he spoke, his words were soft, petrifying. "Fear brings out the truth, and I want you to know from this day on you'll be under my careful watch. So run if you want. It'll only make this all the more enjoyable."

A shiver ran down my back. My mind raced in a thousand directions thinking about what he could do. Hard labor. Starvation. Rape. Those were the tip of the iceberg concerning methods to extract confessions. I'd heard stories of people whose feet were crushed multiple times, and others had various portions of their bodies scalded over and over with boiling water. Trying to escape was tempting, even if it ended with me being shot. But that's all it was, a temptation. "I'm not running," I said as strongly as I could muster. "And I'll always be a pilot."

"We all have our delusions," he said as he walked out of my cell. "I look forward to seeing your face when I come to pick you up."

Chapter Seven

THE MOMENT COMMISSAR Petrov left, my mind raced to find a way to secure my flight status. Even if I somehow dodged or survived serving with Petrov, losing my wings meant I'd never find Martyona's killer and redeem myself.

To get back in the air, I needed Tamara's unwavering support, but I couldn't gain it. At least, not on my own. I'd have to have someone else on my side who said I was fit to fly. My own desires to prove myself were not enough. Zhenia's wishes were also not being listened to and she was flight commander. That left me with two options as far as I could tell, and I was skeptical either would succeed.

The first was to work my way up the chain of command and petition someone with higher authority to let me fly. Tamara would have to listen to her superiors, and the first logical choice was to speak to Marina Raskova. Major Raskova was the one responsible for not only forming my regiment, but the other two all-female aviation regiments as well. Her word was law when it came to us girls, and I liked to think I'd made a favorable impression upon her when I'd met her at Engels during training.

Unfortunately, it would take some time for me to get a letter to her and have her reply, assuming I even could. By then, Petrov would've had his fun with me, not to mention ample opportunity to intercept any such communication. It's not as if they granted me a radio to speak to her in this cell. I also didn't know to what lengths Marina would go to save me, let alone listen to me. As such, the Major was out, which left me with the regiment's doctor, Ivan Burak.

I'd seen Ivan Burak a couple of times since my return about my injuries. He didn't offer much other than to see him in a few weeks if the wounds turned ugly, and the exams were brief. The latter was on account that his eyes stared more at my body than my arms, and everything about the encounters had me shifting in the seat and wanting to get out of there. Despite that, I needed his help. A medical condition was holding me back, threatening my life. He could fix it all with Tamara if I could get him on my side.

I leaned against the door and cleared my throat to get the guard's attention. The soldier, eighteen by my guess, shot me a glare out of his icy blue eyes. Another ten years and he might have been intimidating, but his baby face wasn't much to fear. "I want to see the doctor," I said.

"Shut up and get back from the door," he said. He unslung his weapon from his shoulder and rested his finger next to the trigger. "You can see him when you're out of here."

"This is a minor infraction," I said, knowing my rights. "And as an officer, I'm entitled to see the doctor for treatment when I demand it."

"Treatment for what?" he scoffed.

My burns ached more than usual, and I realized his balking was raising my anxiety. I decided to put pressure on him and play the resentful type. I couldn't afford delays. "Listen, private. You're doing your job well, but I am an officer, and I will be out of here in a few days. Do you want to be on my bad side when that happens?"

The guard hesitated before calling another soldier over. The two had a quiet conversation, and though I couldn't hear the words, their gestures and glances told me it had to with the claims I'd made. After a short while, the soldier ran off and the guard returned. "I'm fetching the doctor, but if you try anything queer, I'll shoot."

I waited patiently, pleased at the authority I carried. Funny what a uniform and attitude could do. Had I neither, I'd have been merely another twenty-year-old girl saddled with despair and stuck in a cell.

It took about a half hour for Doctor Ivan to come. He walked in with his hands in his trouser pockets and an old stethoscope hanging around his neck. His hawkish eyes locked on to me, and a tight smile spread across his face. Without looking back, he waved the guard away. "You can wait outside, soldier."

"Comrade doctor, I must-"

Ivan cut him off with a scowl. "I said you can wait outside. Now close the door."

I enjoyed seeing my overzealous guard run off, but as soon as the door shut, I wished he had stayed. The air about Ivan felt off, as if it couldn't settle in his presence. My gut told me to tell him I was feeling better and he could go, but I told myself I was being paranoid. "Thank you for coming," I said, managing an appreciative smile. "I could use your help."

"I might be able to," he replied. "What's wrong?"

I rolled up my sleeves and outstretched my arms, palms up. "My burns are giving me trouble."

"We've been over this before," he said. "Such terrible wounds can cause pain for a lifetime, even if they are small. Living life is not like crossing a meadow."

"I'm not expecting life to be easy or the pain to go away. All I want is for you to tell the Major I can fly."

"If you can't work the controls safely, I'm afraid I can't."

His dark eyes looked regretful, but the slight drawing back of the corners of his mouth said otherwise. There was something on his mind, and it wasn't relief for me. I dreaded asking the next question, but I didn't feel I had any other choice. "There must be something you can do, yes?"

"A small dose of morphine could take the edge off," he said. As soon as my eyes reflected my hope and I leaned forward, he added to his comment. "That would still take you off flight status. The Major would be concerned your brain would be muddled."

"I could handle it."

"I'd like to let you try," he said. "But I have to document all I do. Not to would be . . . risky."

There it was, the unspoken request. My stomach tightened, and the room chilled worse than any Siberian winter. I forced the question he wanted out of my mouth. I had to fly. I had to avoid Petrov at all costs. "What could I do to make things easier?"

Ivan closed the distance between us. His fingers toyed with my hair before trailing down my shoulder and side. "Where's the fun in spelling it all out?"

I considered the offer, even though I loathed myself for doing so. I hadn't a choice. It would be the lesser of two evils, I told myself. The doctor was only in his thirties, so there wasn't a huge age gap between us. And I might have found him handsome if he hadn't been so creepy.

Ivan touched my shoulder and leaned in close. "My room then, in the evening, when Kazarinova says you're done in here. Do freshen up first."

His words echoed in my ears. I felt myself withdraw deep inside my body as I pictured what spending a night with him would be like. I even dared to hope it would be a one-time event as well.

"I-" I stopped once I caught a whiff of cologne come from his neck. I cocked my head when I noticed his chin was freshly shaven as well. Muscles tightened. He'd planned all of this before he even spoke to me. My hands made fists, and I stepped back. I hated him for thinking so little of me, but I hated myself for even tiptoeing around that path, even if it was on account of how badly I needed to be in the air. "Get away from me."

"Throw your life away then," he said. "In four days you'll be gone, and no amount of begging will get me to save you now."

The cell door slammed shut so hard I could feel the shock though my feet. I paced around the room like a caged animal looking to break free. No, like a wild boar ready to charge head long through whoever stood in my way. I could catch them by surprise. I could steal a gun, a car, or a plane if I had to. Even the darkest creatures from the gates of Hell would not be able to drag me back to him, and certainly the Almighty would not condemn me to such a fate. I could break free. I would break free.

"I won't break free," I said, sighing. "Think, Nadya. Think."

I put one hand in the other and squeezed. My wounds throbbed and my head floated, but I squeezed harder, hoping to train my mind to accept the pain and move on. If I could master my body, I could show Tamara I could climb back in that cockpit.

I pulled my hands against each other for a quarter hour until I was dripping with sweat. I knew my twisted face and trembling body wouldn't pass Tamara's inspection, but I told myself I was on the right track to building tolerance. All I needed was more time.

I looked around the room hoping to find something. Since this was a cell, however, there wasn't anything to work with. When I looked up and saw the single wood beam above me, I grinned.

"How about this for a good pull demonstration," I said, feeling clever.

I jumped up and grabbed the beam with both hands. Fire raced through my arms as I pulled my chin over the top of the beam and held it. In my head I counted, determined to reach thirty seconds. Sharp stabs pulsated from my wrists to my shoulders, and I fell off before I reached the count of ten.

I hit the ground with a thump and spent a few minutes there, arms wrapped around my midsection, and I rocked until I felt strong enough to stand. Five minutes later, I worked up the courage to jump up again, only to fall once more. And so I repeated the process well into the night until my shoulders and back muscles were sore and my palms tender and red. I spent the next day doing the same, and the day after.

On the morning of the fourth day since Doctor Ivan's visit, the last day of my incarceration, I waited patiently for breakfast, thinking about how lovely a dip in the river would be. The door opened, and it wasn't breakfast coming through the door, but Marina Raskova. I could scarcely believe my eyes, and I'm sure I looked stupid gaping at her. She strode in with her dress uniform adorned with medals and blue piping, signature short-styled hair, and radiant charisma. I'd looked up to her ever since I was thirteen and she became the first female navigator, and even though her usually bright face bordered on infuriation, she was such a beautiful sight I almost didn't notice Tamara following her in.

"Do you plan on saluting me Junior Lieutenant, or do you want to dig your grave even deeper?" Raskova said.

I snapped to attention at her cutting remark and gave her the proper honors. "Apologies, comrade major."

Marina wrinkled her nose and took a half step back. "I suppose I can overlook your hygiene at the moment, given where you are, but you will clean up once we are done. Understand? You're filthier than a herd of swine stuck in a bog."

"Yes, comrade major."

"Now then, you have some explaining to do." Her expression changed to one of disappointment, and I loathed her next words, more so than if she'd simply been angry with me. "I expected much more out of you since your graduation at Engels. I want to believe in all my girls. Empower them. Defend them. Exalt them. Your recent actions don't make me want to do any of that with you."

"I don't know what to say, comrade major," I said. My eyes went to my dirty feet. I wanted nothing more than to shrink away into nothingness, but since I knew I couldn't, I prayed I could salvage my image with her. "I was upset at losing my flight status, and I lost my bearing with Major Kazarinova."

"Do you think she's a capable commander?"

I straightened, surprised at the question. A glance to Tamara showed she was caught off guard as well. Was Marina truly asking my opinion on the matter? There wasn't but one reply to make, was there? In all truth, I didn't feel qualified to make such a judgment call, despite the gossip I'd heard, so I said the one thing I felt I could. "Major Kazarinova has always been fair and capable, comrade major."

"Yet you challenged her authority in the most shameful of ways, in front of another pilot, no less."

"I have no excuse, Major," I said with a wavering voice. Marina was set against me, and my identity as a pilot was slipping away.

"And what of this business with Commissar Petrov?" she asked, folding her arms over her chest and looking more displeased than ever. "My girls aren't cowards. They don't betray the Motherland. They fight with honor and courage. It hurts me even more to think you'd abandon everything we stand for. Do you know how many girls are out there who would die to sit in your plane and fight the fascists?"

My sorrow turned to anger at the mention of Petrov's name. Throughout all of my days, I might have been as stubborn and hot headed as a boar, but I was no coward. "Petrov's accusations are lies," I spat, putting in as much venom as I could. Such comments and attitude could land me in front of a firing squad, but I wanted Marina to know without a doubt my words were true. "I nearly died trying to save Martyona, and I scoured her crash site, hoping she'd somehow lived. Only when I found her body did I work my way back to our lines. All I want to do today is get back in the air and shoot down the man who murdered her."

Marina exchanged a look with Tamara, and from what I could tell, neither doubted my claims. That said, Marina asked me to recount the entire day, and so I did in vivid, emotional detail. When

I was done, she sat on my words for several tense moments. "I believe you," she said. "But if you can't fly, you have no place as a pilot in the 586th."

"I can fly," I said, clearing my eyes. "My burns hurt from time to time, yes, but I'm more than capable of doing my duty."

"I know you want to," she said, this time with a sweet smile and eyes filled with compassion. She put a gentle hand on my shoulder and squeezed. "But both Major Kazarinova and Doctor Ivan think otherwise. I won't overrule her decisions, especially since by your own mouth she's a fair and capable commander. You can find service to the Motherland elsewhere."

I set my jaw and refused to be hung with my own words. In a flash, I jumped up and caught hold of the wooden beam above me. My two superiors watched in silence as I dangled, and I dare say they both looked impressed. I fed off their reaction, used it to anesthetize myself from the burning coursing through my limbs. When I dropped sometime later, proud and assured of my spot, I smiled. "I can fly."

The corner of Marina's mouth drew back. "Major Kazarinova, what say you?"

Tamara's face turned stoic. "I have an empty billet for one pilot. I have two girls wanting it. One is healthy but lacks experience. The other has some experience and is questionably fit at best."

"I'm not questionable," I said, trying to keep my rising anger under control. I brought back the edge to my voice as much as I could before going on. "I'll hang there as long as it takes. I'll show you my wounds won't interfere."

"We'll see," Tamara said. She called for the guard, and he darted in the room like a dog coming to its master. "Fetch me Klara Rudneva, and be quick about it."

He left as fast as he came, and we waited a bit for him to return with Klara. Marina held an inquisitive look, but didn't ask questions. I suspected she wanted to see where this was going without any influence on her end. I stayed quiet out of fear as I wasn't sure what was happening.

"Comrade majors," Klara said, entering the room and giving her proper salute. "I was called?"

"Stand next to Nadya," Tamara replied.

Klara came to my side with trepidation. She bit a small portion of her lower lip and fidgeted with her hands behind her back. "Am I in trouble?"

"No," Tamara replied. "You want to fly in my regiment, yes?"

Klara hesitated. "I do, comrade major."

"You are aware there is only one slot available, yes?" she said. "The two of you are going to compete for it. When I say jump, you both will pull yourselves up on the beam above and hang. Whoever hits the ground first stays on the ground. Understand?"

Klara started to object, but whatever she was going to say, she cut it off at the first syllable and instead gave a short nod. "Yes, comrade major."

"Good. Now jump."

The order caught me off guard, and I nearly slipped off the beam the moment I hit it. My muscles protested at the demand I put them through once more. I shifted my grip a few times, trying to rid myself of the stabbing sensation in my palms. But anywhere I held on, it felt like I was driving nails through my wrists.

For the first couple dozen seconds, I stared straight ahead and tried not to focus on anything else but hanging. Klara grunted and drew my attention. Her dark eyes met mine, and though she spoke no words, I could've sworn she was apologizing to me. For what, I didn't know. Sweat trickled in my eyes. My body trembled, and all the while her athletic figure looked as if it hadn't a smidge of strain upon it. Then I realized she was apologizing because she knew she'd outlast me without trouble.

A lump formed in my throat. If I didn't fight harder, my life would be over. I thought about what Petrov would do and tightened my grip. I shut my eyes and counted the seconds. Five. Ten. Fifteen. Thirty.

My grip weakened, and I pictured that devilish German ace, rolling his Messer around me, taunting me with his wicked grin, and then pictured the look of shock on his face when I'd turn the tables and blast him apart. The only way I'd see that day is to hang on longer. That final confrontation would be far harder than hanging off some silly beam. I would do it. I had to.

When my arms threatened to rip themselves apart, I thought about what the commissar would do to my family. If they were lucky, they'd be sent naked to a work camp in Siberia and be met with a swift, frozen death. Those thoughts helped me galvanize my body to bend to my will, and the pain faded.

I peeked at Klara. Though she was sweating, she still looked like she could go on for an hour. I shut my eyes and told myself to only worry about my own performance, my own strength. In that moment, my hands gave out, and I crashed to the floor.

Chapter Eight

"I SUPPOSE IT had to end at some point," I heard Klara say. She sounded both disappointed and amused.

I opened my eyes and looked up at them. I was shocked to find Tamara offering me a hand up.

"Congratulations, Nadya. You're still flying," she said. "But if those wounds cause issue, Klara permanently takes your seat."

Confused, I twisted my mouth and glanced to my side. Klara stood next to me, arms wrapped around her midsection.

"You beat her by about a half second," Tamara said, hand still out. "I'll be honest, I thought she had you licked."

"So did I," I confessed. I winced as I took her hand, and she pulled me up.

Tamara turned my wrists and stared at my palms. "What on Earth did you do to yourself?"

I looked at my hands. The insides were rubbed raw and covered in broken blisters. I smiled sheepishly. "Practice, comrade major, over the last few days."

Marina laughed and squeezed Tamara on the shoulder. "I can't begin to tell you how impressed I am she wants to fly this badly," she said. "I think you can give her a day to get cleaned up and rest before tossing her back in the cockpit."

"Agreed," Tamara said. "Nadya, you've got twenty-four hours. I'm putting you on the first patrol for tomorrow night."

"Yes, comrade major."

Marina and Tamara left. The moment they were gone, I jumped up and down, screaming like a little kid who'd opened up her perfect present for Christmas. "Oh God," I said, stopping and abhorring my behavior. "I'm so sorry. I'm such an ass for acting like that."

"It's fine," she said. Her arms hung limp at her side, and her eyes stared out into the distance like a bit of her soul had gone away, never to return. She turned her face to me and gave a smile. "I should get back to work before I end up here."

She left, and I latched on to her words. Everything was fine. I'd kept my flight status. She was moving on. It wasn't like she couldn't take another slot when it opened up. More importantly, I was going to fly! I would redeem myself, avenge Martyona, bring honor to my lineage and earn respect from my peers. God, the day was a miracle!

I ran out the door and twirled. I longed for a dance partner, and I found Valeriia Khomyakova, deputy commander of my squadron to fill that need.

Valeriia had the face of a cherub with dark eyes that at first glance were playful and inviting, but if one held their gaze long enough, there was a dangerous glint to them. It made me think of her as a lioness who'd smile at someone who could be her next friend or next meal. I'd always thought that look was perfect given what we did. We were fighter pilots, a pride of huntresses, warm to each other but lethal to others. And though she had me by eight years, she barely looked twenty. Secretly, I hoped I aged as well as she did. To my delight, she never saw me coming as I snatched her up, spinning and laughing.

"Nadya!" she yelled, eyes wide. She pushed away out of reflex but didn't pull herself free from my grasp. "Have you gone mad?"

"I'm flying! I'm flying!" I said over and over. I pounced on her like a cat on a mouse and squeezed her tight. She was taller than me by a few centimeters, and thus hanging off her neck came easy.

"Okay, okay," she said, laughing. This time she squirmed out of my grasp and used her hand to keep me at bay. "For all that is holy in the world, Nadya, you need a bath. You reek."

I sniffed myself and gagged, but feigned ignorance. "Not that bad. Surely you jest."

"Come off it, Nadya," she said. "Don't try and pull that on me after a week in the box."

I curtsied and failed to keep a straight face. "I apologize if I offended you."

"At the moment, you nauseate me more than offend. When's your first flight?"

"Night duty, tomorrow," I replied.

"On patrol with me then," she said. "That ought to give you enough time to be presentable, yes?"

"Maybe," I said. I staggered toward her. "I'm feeling faint. I think you'll need to help me."

I lunged at her, laughing even more now, but she was quick, always had been both in the sky and on the ground. Before I could smear my sweaty arms and face on her, she slipped away. "Don't you dare come at me again," she said. She leveled a stern finger, but her voice was as light as a schoolgirl playing games in the classroom when the teacher was away. "I mean it Nadya! We're hunting in less than an hour. I need to get ready, not fetch a change of clothes. I don't want the Germans finding us on smell alone."

"Fine," I said, crossing my arms over my chest and sticking my tongue out at her. "You really know how to suck all the fun out of a good celebration."

Valeriia waved her hand in front of her nose and rolled her eyes up in her head. "Your odor did that long before I did. Now go."

"I shall take my leave then," I said, curtsying once more.

I headed off for the Volga River, about a ten-minute walk from where I was. I made a quick stop to my dugout. It was my glorified hole in the ground where we slept when it was either too cold or too wet to sleep outside, but I'd taken to it enough to call it home. There I grabbed a change of clothes and a ratty towel. I thought about trading my soiled uniform for a new one right there, but I was so filthy, I didn't want to get my clean ones dirty the moment they touched my skin.

When I went back outside, I ran into Petrov as he came out of the command post. The perturbed look on his face intensified when he spied me, I'm certain on account of my upbeat attitude.

"Major," I said with the proper salute. "I thought you should know I'm still a pilot."

"So I've been made aware," he replied, but instead of a look of disappointment, he had an amused look in his eyes, one I was sure the Devil had when he started a new game with one of us mortals. "Don't think this changes anything. We'll be spending a lot of time together in the near future."

As unsettling as his words were, I kept my face straight, refusing to let him get to me. "I'll be looking forward to it, comrade commissar."

"No. You won't."

He flashed a predatory grin before sticking his pipe into his mouth and leaving. I hurried to the Volga to clear my mind of him, and a private driving an olive mail car picked me up as I headed out of the airfield. When I got in, I realized that from afar he must have thought me prettier than I was, for his eyes went wide when I got close. He said little to me, other than asking me where I'd like to get dropped off. Maybe he thought I was crazy. My matted, wild hair looked the part.

He let me out near the banks of the river, and I trotted to a secluded area where the grass grew high and trees shielded me from prying eyes. I shed my clothes and slipped into the slow-moving water. Goosebumps raised on my skin, and despite the chill, I savored every moment rubbing the grime from my body.

I dipped under the surface and washed my hair. I managed to get some of the tangles out in the water using my fingers, but I'd need a brush for the rest. So I floated on my back and watched the few clouds in the sky drift. A fresh scent in the wind helped me relax.

I daydreamed about finally being able to soar above them once more, and wondered how long it would be until I encountered the Luftwaffe again—a specific member of the Luftwaffe—and all the ways I'd become the victor. I wondered if I'd kill him while he was still in his plane, or if he bailed, I wondered if I'd come around and shoot him hanging in his harness. Pilots abhorred such behavior on both sides, but if I were presented with that scenario it might be one of the few times I truly wouldn't care what others thought.

Klara interrupted my daydreams with a sharp whistle. She stood near the river's edge, holding my towel. "Having fun exposing yourself to the world? The Major wants to see you."

"Not much left of me to expose," I said, noting I could stand to gain a few kilos. "What's going on?"

"Kazarinova's bumping you to a new flight," she said. "You're launching with Valeriia in less than an hour."

I swam over, scrambled up the steep bank, and grabbed the towel. "What happened? Why so sudden?"

"Escort mission for a VIP," she said. "Guess she's too short on pilots after all the transfers."

I dried and dressed as fast as I could. "Who was transferred?"

"Liliia, Ekaterina, Klavdiia, Raisa and four others." Klara replied. "Almost everyone who challenged Kazarinova's command."

"Do you know where they went?" I asked as sadness struck me at their loss.

Klara nodded. "To the 437th. They're based east of Stalingrad now."

"I can't believe so many are gone. Wonder how that will affect the rest of us. We're thin enough."

"The 437th doesn't even fly the same fighters as we do. It's a logistical and training nightmare. If I didn't know any better, I'd say she's trying to screw things up on purpose."

Despite the seriousness of the conversation, I chuckled. "Like a spy?"

"I know she's not," Klara replied. "I'd shoot her myself if I thought she was. But you have to admit, the whole thing is bizarre."

"Bizarre doesn't begin to cover it," I admitted. "But we should get back before she counts us as deserters and has our heads."

With brisk strides, we walked back to the airfield, making awkward small talk and dancing around this morning's events. She seemed unaffected at losing her chance to fly, and she never brought it up. I was sure it was a façade. I knew firsthand the sucking hole in the chest that formed and never healed when dreams were snatched. I wanted to stop and beg for forgiveness and promise I'd fight for a pilot billet for her every chance I got. I didn't, and I'd like to say it was because she wouldn't let me have such a conversation, but in reality I was too scared to start it as I didn't know what she'd say.

Klara returned to the field to prep the planes, and I ran into the command post to get briefed on the mission. It was what Klara had said it would be: a simple escort. Valeriia would be leading me and Alexandra Makunina, a new pilot I'd not met. We'd rendezvous with the VIP near Tolyatti, a city about two hundred and fifty kilometers to the northeast. Once we had him, it was a short flight to Kazan where we would all land. We'd refuel and come home, and he would go inspect whatever plant he needed to. It was going to be a sleeper of a flight. I'd sooner bet on Stalin becoming a capitalist before I'd bet we'd encounter any Luftwaffe as we'd be flying deep within our own country. Despite the constant reassurance by everyone of the same, as I left the command post and headed to my fighter, my stomach turned sour and my arms ached. All I could think about was how hot the flames must have been that engulfed Martyona's plane.

"I did the complete pre-flight check," Klara said, snapping me out of my daze. I'd walked the entire trip across the airfield and hadn't even noticed. "You're all set."

Instead of replying, I gaped at the plane standing in front of me. Metal skin, smooth as glass, wrapped the fighter and was free of holes and patch jobs. The olive paintjob didn't have a single chip in it, not even where the canopy slid back or on the wing roots where we often put our feet. Without even starting it, I knew the engine's purr would resonate with my soul like no other.

"Fresh from the factory," Klara said. "She's barely past her break-in."

"I'm almost scared to touch her."

Klara laughed. "Well don't be. You're going to love having a new plane. This one will take care of you."

"She's more than a new plane," I said. "She's a new me."

The fighter was exactly that. With it, I had a new identity and a new future I could shape. No longer would I be tied to that awful thirteenth of August. I would rise again, like a mighty phoenix birthed from its ashes. I would take to the sky and bring swift retribution to those who hurt me and my sisters.

"Are you okay?" she said. "You look like you're about to throw up."

I shifted my weight. Now that she mentioned it, emptying my stomach sounded like a half-decent idea. My now-spinning head didn't help any either. "I'm fine," I lied. "Nerves, I guess."

"You'll be fine, my Little Boar."

"Please don't call me that."

"I didn't-"

"No," I said. My voice felt weak, and it could barely get by the lump in my throat. For the life of me, I couldn't understand what was going on with me. I latched on to the one thing I thought it could be. "About this morning-"

Klara closed the distance between us and held up her finger. "It was always your spot."

"You wanted it as much as I did. I don't know if I deserve it more."

"If I'd taken your spot, Petrov would've taken you away," she said. Her eyes misted, and she searched for somewhere to stuff her hands, but apparently, everywhere she put them wasn't the right place. "At least this way you can still be alive, and we can still be friends. I don't think I could live with myself knowing I was the reason I'd never see you again."

"You knew about that?"

Klara nodded. "I pay attention."

"Did you drop on purpose?"

She nodded again, but this time, she didn't say anything.

My knees weakened. I wasn't sure what her actions meant, other than they were bigger than anything I could come up with. "Why didn't you tell me?"

"I didn't want you to feel as if you didn't earn it," she replied. "I didn't want to take that away from you."

"Then why are you telling me now?"

"Because I don't want you puking in my aircraft because you feel guilty," she said. "It was my choice to fall, even if morally it was the wrong thing to do. Not exactly Soviet-like of me, was it? Anyway, you have no idea how hard it is to clean these cockpits."

Her explanation soothed me on some level, but I also felt heavily indebted to the woman. That wasn't a bad thing as she was my friend, but I had no idea how I could repay her. She saved my life in more ways than one.

Feeling better with the conversation behind us, I climbed into the cockpit and prepped for takeoff. But as I read each dial and checked all the gauges and switches, tension mounted in my chest. The sidewalls closed in on me, and the air became scorching. Sweat beaded on my forehead and ran down my back. Air hunger built in my lungs, and no matter how large and fast of breaths I took, I couldn't get enough.

Klara grabbed me by the shoulders and pushed me back into the seat. "Nadya. You're okay."

I gritted my teeth and shut my eyes. The sequence of Martyona's burning plane spiraling out of control played over and over in my mind with painful detail. I could hear the flames crackle, smell her burning flesh. My chest imploded as my heart broke each and every time I watched her smash into the ground.

I shoved Klara away and unbuckled as fast as I could.

"What are you doing?" she said, fighting with me over the seat belt. "You three are about to fly."

"Not me," I said. The moment the words left me mouth, my heart slowed. It was the peace of Death settling over me, peace that only came when a loss was fully acknowledged. "I'm not flying. Never again."

Chapter Nine

"**D**ON'T BE STUPID, Nadya," Klara shot back, eyes full of fire. "You're flying. I gave up a dream for you. I won't let you ruin my sacrifice."

Despite her short stature, she packed a lot of muscle in her lithe frame, and she kept me in my seat regardless of my attempts to get out. I shouldn't have been surprised at her strength, given the sheer weight of all the equipment she had to lug around all day. Hell, the cylinders full of compressed air we used to start the planes were at least sixty kilos each.

I gave up fighting her and slumped against the seat. "I can't go. I'm a total wreck."

"You're a fantastic pilot, Nadya," she said. "Take a few deep breaths. It's a panic attack. Nothing more."

"Maybe I'll be better tomorrow, but not today."

Klara cackled like a mad woman. "Are you daft? You leave now and Kazarinova will never let you up again."

She had me there. Still, even though I was in the cockpit and talking to her, my mind continued to latch on to the final moments of my last sortie. "I can't get her out of my mind," I confessed. "All I see is pain, and terror, and Martyona dying over and over."

"Find something beautiful about it."

The unexpected response snapped me back into the moment, and for what felt like forever, I stared at her, thinking she had to be making an awful joke. "You can't be serious."

Her eyes told me she was. "There's beauty in every moment," she said. "If you can find it, you can survive it, react to it."

"Are you sick? There's nothing beautiful about watching someone burn to death," I said with venom.

"Not in her death, no," she said, quietly. "But there can be colors you like, maybe the way the wind felt if it was cool. Maybe grab on to the fact she stuck with you until the end."

"She did do that," I said, my voice trailing. Though it was a sliver of light in an otherwise pitch-black moment in my life, to focus on that and nothing else felt like I was cheapening things, as if I were pretending it never happened, or worse, she wasn't worthy of being grieved over. And if I convinced myself of that, I feared one day I'd forget her completely.

Klara took her hand off my shoulder and eased away. "It still hurts, I know," she said. "But you're already better. I can see it."

The tremble in my hands lessened, and I could think clearly enough to takeoff. "Clear the propeller."

Klara leaned in and gave a brief hug. "Come back to me safe, Nadya."

I smiled at our ritual. In my panicked state, that was something beautiful to cling to, a friend at my side. She dropped down, and I started the engine.

A few short minutes later, I was cruising my fighter a thousand meters over the landscape. Valeriia had the lead, and the new girl, Alexandra, flew on the opposite side of me in our V-formation.

Even though all three of our planes had two-way radios—something I was grateful for this time around—the three of us spoke little during the flight. Valeriia gave the occasional altitude and heading adjustments, and Alexandra gave the acknowledging reply. I think astonishment that I was actually up in the air kept me quiet more than anything else.

The rendezvous with our VIP near Tolyatti occurred without a hitch. The major was being flown in a PS-84 transport craft, which was an American DC-3 built in a Russian factory. Its fat, white fuselage and giant wings made it an easy target should it ever fall prey to the fascists, and the lack of defensive armament demanded an escort at all times. But neither machine guns nor fighters were required to see the plane safely to Kazan. We landed at the city without incident, and after we refueled, I dared to think this would be an uneventful day.

That changed when we returned home, refueled, and launched again.

"Tighten it up, ladies," Valeriia said once we were in formation. "We're going hunting."

I knew this day would come, but as we climbed thousands of meters above the earth, I wished it would have come later rather than sooner. Valeriia's plan was to head southwest, patrol along the Don, and refuel at a secondary airfield before coming home. For anyone else, it would have been a standard—though extended—mission. For me, however, it felt like the same, ill-fated flight Martyona had taken me on.

As we flew, I checked my six and scoured the sky for any sign of the Luftwaffe. Thankfully, the clouds were few and we could see all around us. The tips of my fingers went numb in the cold, and my arms ached. I alternated sitting on each hand to try and warm them up, but it didn't help. The more we traveled, the worse the pain grew, and the more it grew, the more I feared I'd get Valeriia and Alexandra killed by not being able to fly. I wanted to dive away and run from this stupid war.

I snorted, disgusted with myself for such thoughts. I could hear my grandmother now, telling me over and over how God saved me, put me back in the pilot seat for a reason, and all I had to do was trust in His plan. Years ago I wouldn't have questioned such beliefs—even a few months ago. Yet here I was, barely able to function, wondering how terrible things were about to become and how ridiculous it was to think any of it was part of some grand scheme.

"Contacts, ten o'clock low," Valeriia said. "Looks like a flight of three Stukas."

"Vis," Alexandra replied. "I see two escorts above them, five hundred meters."

"God, don't let this turn out like last time," I whispered, leaning forward for a better view.

The pair of Messers flying escort had their unmistakable bright yellow noses that somehow felt brighter and angrier than last time I'd seen them. The Stukas that were under their protection were single-engine dive bombers, painted an olive green with an inverted gull-wing design. The planes were known to be slow and able to take a beating, but they were most famous for their sirens' wail during an attack. I'd never heard one, but from all accounts, the noise terrified those on the ground, for it meant hundreds of kilos worth of explosives were being dropped.

"Nadya, do you see them?" Valeriia said.

"Copy. I have vis."

"Alexandra, hit the bombers and stay fast," she ordered. "Get them to jettison their loads. Nadya, you're on the 109 on the right. I'll take the left. Diving runs only. I don't want anyone bleeding speed in a turn."

Valeriia rolled into a dive, and the two of us followed. My fighter cut through the sky as it dove toward our prey. I sighted my enemy and prayed he would remain oblivious to our presence. Though I was too far to see his number, I wondered if the man I was attacking was Yellow Eight and if this would be the day my metamorphosis from failure to avenger would be complete. As hopeful as I was, I was equally terrified it was him and this flight would end worse than my last on account of how many kills he had to his name.

Four hundred meters away from the Messer, I eased my thumbs over the triggers. At three hundred, eagerness at my first kill took over, and I fired.

Tracers flew from the barrels of both machine guns and my 20mm cannon. My rounds zipped harmlessly through the sky. I'd given too much lead. The Messer jumped to the side, dodging my aim. I swore as I pulled the stick back and climbed into the sky to set up for another pass. I looked over my shoulder to see what my opponent was doing. He'd already brought his plane back on course, but he couldn't take a shot. I was too high and too far for him to risk it. If he nosed up, he'd lose speed, and when he lost that, he'd be picked apart by the three of us, exactly how those fascist bastards had picked apart Martyona.

"Good job, Nadya," Valeriia said. "Bring it around and keep them busy."

Though I'd blown the attack, I smiled at her praise. It was nice to have a voice complementing rather than criticizing me. "Pulling into a hammerhead now."

At my command, my Yak-1 pointed its nose at the heavens and climbed until it ran out of speed. The plane shuddered as the engine could no longer hold it in the air, at which point, my fighter stalled. I kicked my pedals, giving maximum left rudder. The nose of my craft slid sideways, allowing the engine to pull the plane nose first toward the ground.

It was a suicidal maneuver if someone had sights on you, for it left you as a fixed target hanging in the sky. Our enemies, however, were over a thousand meters below and had no hope of getting a shot on me. Thus, they could only watch in fear, I hoped, as I set up for another diving pass.

I didn't wait as long as I had on my first attack to open fire. Once I lined up my target, I let loose with both machine guns. I didn't expect a kill, but I wanted him to stay on the defensive and force him to roll out of the way, which he did. Seeing pieces of metal fly from his left wing was an added bonus.

"No tight turns, Alexandra!" Valeriia yelled. "That's an order."

"They haven't jettisoned any bombs," she protested. "I need to put more pressure on them."

I couldn't see her until I'd climbed and rolled my plane upside down. Alexandra was in the middle of a high-G yo-yo, a maneuver where a pilot follows a slower, tighter-turning plane in a curve by combining a steep climb with a sharp turn. It's done to keep from overshooting a target and to conserve as much total energy as possible, but it still bleeds speed.

The Messer I was responsible for banked right, setting himself up to intercept Alexandra's attack. I slammed the throttle forward to the stop and dove. "My guy is setting up on you!" I yelled, machine guns blazing.

I didn't ease off the trigger until I blew past the Stukas and started climbing once more. Tracers flew past my cockpit. When I looked behind me, I saw all three Stuka tail gunners firing on me.

"Alexandra, make another pass," Valeriia called out. "Nadya, clear her six when that fighter moves in on her."

I craned my head back, searching the sky for Alexandra. Valeriia kept the other German fighter on the defensive, circling above him, making feints and snapshots as she could. I pulled back on the stick, rocketing my plane upward for a better view of the battle below.

I found Alexandra barreling through the Stuka formation with the fury of a Valkyrie, machine guns and cannons blazing. Her rounds punched through a wing on one of the trailing bombers. Brown mist poured from the damage, and the Stuka fell out of the group. I screamed in delight as three bombs dropped from its fuselage a split second later.

"One jettisoned," Alexandra said as she peeled her plane left and entered a shallow dive. Unlike my own ecstatic state, she sounded calm, as if she'd done this a thousand times over. "Now if you'd rid me of this 109, I'll get you a nice bar of chocolate."

The German fighter followed her, and I pulled on the stick for all I was worth. Lightning shot through my arms, and I clenched my jaw as tight as I could to stave off the pain and keep from blacking out. When I let go, I was trailing both Alexandra and the Messer by at least four hundred meters.

"I'm too far to make a shot," I said. "If you circle, I might be able to get him in the turn."

"I'll do you one better," Alexandra said. "I'll set him up for the perfect kill."

My brow knitted. I wasn't sure what she was about to do. Then I saw her drag the fighter into a tight U-turn before shooting upward. My mouth ran dry. She was flying a hammerhead, and the enemy fighter was following her into it. They'd both be helpless in the sky. The question was, who would be shot down, Alexandra or the Messer?

Time slowed, and I held my breath. My heart thundered in my chest. My vision tunneled to where all I could see was the perfect image of the German fighter in my gun sight, climbing, aiming . . . stalling.

My heart prayed for guidance as my thumbs hit the triggers. Once again, the nose of my plane erupted with flame and smoke. Tracers slammed into the enemy fighter with bright flashes of light, tearing large chunks off its skin and internals. Black smoke poured from its engine, and I exhaled.

"Nadya, I love you!" Alexandra yelled.

Her exuberance filled me with pride, and I'm sure my face glowed brighter than any halo. "Circle back," I said, forcing myself to abandon the celebration and refocus on the mission. "There are still more."

"Negative," Valeriia said. "They're running. Form on me. We're leaving."

Perplexed at the order, I put my plane into a lazy circle and watched with an equal mix of frustration and disappointment as the German planes ran to the west, including the one smoking like a chimney. Though I knew it wouldn't last, I wanted the others, too. "We could chase them down."

"Negative. I'm low ammunition," Valeriia replied. "And despite what brass says are sound tactics, I have no intention of running this plane into another when my guns are dry. Besides, you'll be famous when we get home, Nadya. You scored not only your first kill, but the first victory for the entire regiment. You should be eager to get back."

I sank back in my seat and turned her words over. I didn't need the fame coming, but I was excited to write home and let them know what I'd done. Father would be proud of me, and I certainly would appreciate the acknowledgement by others that I was a damn good pilot. If I got enough of it, I thought I might believe it myself.

We cruised back to Anisovka, a few thousand meters high. We'd barely left the Don behind us when I heard the light thumping of rounds hitting my plane and saw tracers zip over my canopy.

"Break!" I yelled, instinctively I jamming my stick forward and putting the plane in a steep dive. My body lifted off the seat and my belt cut into the tops of my thighs. Plummeting toward the earth, I looked over my shoulder and saw two Messers hot my tail. We'd gotten sloppy with excitement and never saw them making the intercept.

"Nadya where are you?"

Valeriia sounded stressed, but at least she wasn't calling for help. Maybe these two were the only Messers around.

"Diving northwest," I said. I banked right, two thousand meters and falling, and made such a hard reversal that I knocked my head on the side of the canopy. I pulled out of the dive and checked my six, praying I'd thrown my enemies off my tail. I saw one extending away from me, but the other was unaccounted for. I weaved left and right a couple more times and wondered where he'd gone.

"Nadya, we're clear up here," Valeriia said. "Head northeast and we'll regroup."

I turned back toward my flight, and as I did a Messer dropped from the sky and saddled up next to me. There couldn't have been room for more than a single train car between our wingtips. I stared at the 109 in shock, and felt my mouth hang open when I spied the bright yellow eight painted on its tail.

"What the hell do you want from me?" I yelled, smacking the canopy as hard as I could.

The pilot waggled the wings to his plane and followed it up with a salute before peeling away, leaving me feeling confused and helpless all the way home.

* * *

"You can't be serious!" I shouted. Tamara stood a pace away in the command post, scowling. Her skin was flush, and her jaw set. I didn't care.

"This is your one and only warning, Nadya," she replied, leveling a finger at me. "I will throw you back in the box. I don't care how many pilots I need."

"I saw the shot firsthand, comrade major," Alexandra said. "She tore him apart and saved my life."

I turned and beamed at my newly found friend. Alexandra stood next me, her posture relaxed and her hands stuffed in her pockets. Other than her black hair parted down the middle and wrapped snugly in a bun, there wasn't a tight thing about her. I was astounded at her care-free attitude and wondered if it would work against me as Tamara always commanded with strict discipline, but at the moment, I didn't care. Someone was fighting for me, someone who didn't want to see me robbed of my accomplishments. "See?" I said. "There's your verification right there."

Tamara grunted with indifference. "You didn't see the plane crash, did you?"

"No, comrade major," Alexandra replied.

"Nor did you see the plane catch fire or the pilot bail out."

"No, comrade major."

My hands balled into fists at my side. "The plane was smoking worse than a barn fire," I said. "There's no way it didn't go down."

"I'm sorry, Nadya," Tamara said, and for the first time since we started this conversation, I thought I heard some regret in her voice, though there wasn't a hint of it in her posture. "If no one saw the plane crash or the pilot hit the silk, the best I can say is it was damaged. If our boys on the ground find the wreckage, then that will change. I'll even see to it you get your bonus."

"Bonus? What bonus?"

"There's a thousand-ruble bounty on fighter kills," she said. "Two thousand for bombers. I'm not saying you're lying, but there are some who would for the money alone."

A thousand rubles. God, what would I do with that? Send it home, I wagered, maybe donate some as well, but not before I bought some chocolate and a nice bottle of wine. Sadly, those were both luxury items and cost a fortune themselves. I stopped daydreaming when I realized I didn't want the money. "Keep the bounty," I said. "I want credit for the kill. That's all."

"No, Nadya. My decision stands."

"This isn't fair! I nearly got blown out of the sky coming back. The least you could do is say you're glad I'm alive and here's a little reward for your effort."

"I'm glad you're alive, but war isn't fair and hopefully this will be a lesson on always watching your six," Tamara said, taking a seat behind her desk and pulling the night's scheduled assignments from a nearby folder. "Go rest. I'll be pairing you and Alexandra together from here on out. If it's any consolation, I'm sure the two of you will bring down another fighter. You two work well together."

At this point I knew the conversation was over and that fueled my frustrations. I deserved that kill. I needed it. Not for my ego, but for my sanity. I had to show the world—myself—Martyona hadn't died in vain and had saved someone who could do more than get shot down. "I don't want a consolation. I want that kill, and I want the victory painted on my plane."

Tamara slammed the desk with both hands and shot up from her seat. "You had your damn warning, Nadya. You're spending the night in the box."

I stood there, gaping at her, not so much because she'd come down on me, but because she was being so stubborn about it all. It was one lousy kill. "Why are you doing this to me?" I said. "Is it the end of the world if you credit me with a downed German?"

"First of all, I don't have to justify myself to you," she said, walking up to me and jabbing two fingers into my chest. "But to shut you up, it's protocol, and everyone has to play by the same rules. If it's not confirmed, it doesn't count."

"Or maybe you're jealous I'm flying after my injuries and you're not."

Tamara's jaw dropped almost as far as Alexandra's did. Both of them looked as if they'd been clipped in the head by a wing tip, totally stupefied. Tamara was the first to regain her composure. "God, Nadya, you just don't learn, do you?" she said. "You really are a dumb Cossack."

I growled and wished I was the kind of person who would drive a fist into her teeth. I wasn't that brave. So I did the next best thing. I let my tongue loose. "At least I'm a flying Cossack and not some bitter cripple stuck on the ground."

Chapter Ten

TAMARA HIT ME in the side of the head with a right cross. I remember that much. The next thing I knew I was on my back, staring at the box's wood ceiling. It seemed damper than last time I saw it, but I was having trouble focusing and hoped it wasn't a head injury causing the new look. Alexandra was kneeling at my side, stroking the top of my head and singing a lullaby. She was so out of tune, I wanted to jab a screwdriver through my eardrums.

"That must have been some blow," she said, stopping everything she was doing. "Maybe you should have the doctor come."

"No," I said, sitting up. "I'll be fine."

"You don't look fine. You look worse than my brother when he got kicked by a mule."

"Well, if I blackout again you can call him." I groaned as I touched a tender knot on the back of my head and again when I felt the side of my face. While I had doubts about my own prognosis, Doctor Ivan was not someone I wanted giving me a physical. "How long was I out for?"

"Long enough to make me worry," she replied. "She hit you. You hit the floor. They dumped you here."

"Do they know you're visiting? If they catch you here, you'll be in trouble too."

Alexandra grinned. "I'm not a visitor."

I couldn't help but giggle like a schoolgirl who'd gotten trouble with a best friend. "What did you do?"

She shrugged sheepishly. "When she socked you, I had a few choice words for her. I think it redirected some of her rage at you to me. Valeriia let fly, too, but more respectfully than I'd managed."

"Sorry."

Alexandra shook her head. "Don't be. I owe you my life. Sharing the box with you for a few days is the least I can do, especially if it means you not being sent away."

"Away where?"

She shrugged. "Nowhere good, I imagine. Kazarinova's first words when you hit the floor were something about you never flying again. That's when I had to set things straight."

My thoughts ran in a thousand directions. I wanted to dig more into what Tamara had said, but I feared my imagination paled to whatever she wanted to do to me. And all of this started from a dogfight that instead of being a celebratory one had made things worse.

"That was a huge risk you took when we were fighting," I said. "I could have missed."

"But you didn't."

"But I could have," I said with a bite. My shoulders slumped, and I exhaled. "I'm sorry for snapping, but if he'd got you before I cleared your tail, I wouldn't have been able to live with myself."

"I wouldn't have been able to live at all," she said with a grin.

"Not funny."

Alexandra tilted her head. "Why don't you trust yourself more?"

"Why do you trust me at all?" I asked while brushing the dirt off my back and shoulders.

She laughed as if the answer was obvious. "Because you're one of the few women here out of thousands and thousands who wanted to be a fighter pilot. That must mean you're an amazing flyer."

I was a capable flyer, yes, but this last month had taught me learning acrobatics in a flying club and surviving combat were completely different animals. I did appreciate her faith in me, and her sincerity helped. "Still, I should have been torn apart at the end."

"Because they snuck up on us afterward? You still slipped away."

Her words, though an attempt at comfort, shivered my soul. "I didn't slip away," I said. "That ace—the one who shot down Martyona—let me go."

"Only because he couldn't catch you. You fly better than you give yourself credit for."

"No. I ditched his wingman, but he came along side me before saluting and peeling off. He could've had a letter sent to my parents if he wanted."

Alexandra's face paled. "Why do you think he didn't shoot?"

I shrugged. "I think it would be easier to bite your own elbow than understand the twisted mind of such a man. I considered his guns might have jammed, but that's too convenient of an answer. The man must be toying with me."

"To what end?"

I shrugged again. "No idea." A headache formed, and I rubbed my temples. "I'd rather not think about it anymore. It's not helping my mood, and I'm still irritated Tamara didn't give me that kill."

Alexandra beamed as if she'd stumbled on a mine full of diamonds. "I have the perfect fix, if you're interested."

"What's that?"

"How about a dance?" she asked. "Always makes me feel better."

"Do you waltz?"

"Is Kazarinova a bitter cripple stuck on the ground?"

I laughed, hard. Before I could say anything, there was a heavy thud on the door, and the same guard from before appeared in the window. "Shut up and stand up."

I took to my feet without word, though Alexandra and I shared glances and stifled giggles. Maybe it was the absurdity of it all or the delirium from being tired and beaten, but whatever it was, I couldn't help but find the entire ordeal hilarious.

The guard turned away, and Alexandra nudged me with her elbow. "We should waltz out of here when they let us go," she whispered. "Imagine their faces if we did."

"I can imagine us getting flogged for it," I said. The corners of my mouth drew back and I gave a curtsy. "But I can think of nothing lovelier than if we did."

* * *

Days came and went. We were supposed to have been cut free after a full day, but Tamara caught us both laughing and enjoying ourselves far too much that second morning and gave us another forty-eight hours to think about life, our contribution to the war, and whether or not we wanted to stay assigned to the fighter regiment. I'm sure she wished she had another cell so she could separate us, but this was the only one at the base.

From the time she left, we played our part, and we played it well. Whenever the guards looked in on us, we kept straight and somber faces. The reality was, however, we both became exceptional at keeping our eyes on the door, looking for any stray shadow or sign of movement, all the while entertaining ourselves to no end during the day. And for an hour or two at night, we waltzed in the dark, taking care to avoid the small sliver of light from outside and letting our bodies relish the movement.

Alexandra was a fantastic dancer. She kept a perfect rhythm and never once had a misstep or lost her balance, despite our pitch-black surroundings. She made me take the lead, insisting it was proper since I was the wing leader. It was a little awkward, given she was taller and larger than me. I was jealous of the latter, as it was clear she'd eaten well all her life. I kept those thoughts to myself, and we stopped when exhaustion took over or the cold made my hands unbearable, at which point she'd massage them enough for me to fall asleep.

Without a doubt, I would've preferred my freedom those three days. Alexandra's company, however, made the experience pleasant enough, and when Tamara walked into our cell on the third day to release us, a small part of me was sad the private bonding time I'd had with my new wingman was coming to an end.

Tamara looked us over, and once she'd sent the guard away, she addressed me. "I believe you have something to say."

"Comrade major?" I said, caught off guard. Tamara stared at me expectantly, and it clicked a second later. "I do," I said, straightening. "My behavior was uncalled for, comrade major, and any punishment was both fitted and warranted. I hope my actions will not adversely affect my flight status."

I'm not sure how much I believed those words, but they rolled off my tongue enough to sound sincere. I did want to get back in the air.

"And you?" Tamara said, turning to Alexandra.

"The same, comrade major," she said, lighter than I had. "I spoke in the heat of the moment, as Nadya had just saved my life."

"I'm aware of that," she said. She looked over her shoulder, I'm guessing to ensure no one was around, and then came back to the conversation with quieter tones. "I know you're frustrated, Nadya. When I couldn't reliably fly in combat, I was nearly robbed of my command, and it still angers me to this day."

"I had no idea."

She gave a half smile. "You suspected," she said, and she was right. Everyone did. Her limp was obvious, and aside from the occasional, non-combat flight, she never took a plane up. "That said, I won't tolerate insubordination, no matter how much we may have in common. You're both out of second chances from now on. I will replace you and strip you of rank. Understood?"

"Yes, comrade major," we replied in unison.

Tamara sighed and shook her head. Her posture foretold of the disappointment in her voice that came after. "I wanted to give you that kill, Nadya, just like I wanted to give one to Martyona."

"You still can," I said, hoping I wasn't stepping over any lines.

"No, I can't." she said. Her brow lowered and she grunted. "The 586th is under terrible scrutiny. The boys think we can't fly, and we're a joke. Whoever gets awarded the first kill is going to be examined like no other. Every aspect of every report has to be perfect, understand? There can be no question whatsoever."

I couldn't doubt the sincerity in her voice, but I had a hard time wrapping my head around her words. "Surely everyone wants us to succeed," I said. "Who would try to discredit our regiment?"

Tamara snorted. "They already have. Did you hear what happened with Liliia yesterday?"

I shook my head. Obviously being stuck in the box, Alexandra and I hadn't heard anything. I didn't think it wise to point that out to Tamara.

"She shot down two planes over Stalingrad," she said. I could hear it in her voice. She was both proud and disgusted. "Two planes! A Ju-88 bomber and a Messerschmitt fighter. Can you imagine?"

"That should be a good thing, no?" Alexandra said.

Her words mirrored my thoughts. "I don't understand why that's an issue for us. Good for her."

"Yes, good for her," Tamara replied. "Liliia is now the first female pilot in the country to earn a kill. But did they credit us? Did they award those victories to her regiment?"

I knew the answer. We both did. Tamara's passion seeped into my blood. "Who else would they give it to?"

"They awarded credit to the 437th," Tamara said, hitching a thumb south. "Not to us. To them. To that stupid, male regiment that begged us for help."

"Bastards," Alexandra said. "All of them."

I arched an eyebrow at my wingman's remark. Her words should never have been said about top brass, but in this personal moment shared between the three of us, a large part of me was glad she did. I hoped Tamara felt the same.

"Exactly," Tamara said. "So you understand that I have to run things tight. I can't cut corners. I can't award probable kills, especially for the unit's official first."

I nodded solemnly. The idea of me being a pilot equal to a male, dulled. "I understand. Thank you for telling me, and I'm sorry I've been pig headed."

Tamara shook her head one last time and then straightened her uniform. "We can only move forward at this point," she said. "There's one more thing I should tell you. We've identified the ace you encountered with Martyona. His name is Gerhard Rademacher, and he's part of Jagdgeschwader Udet. That unit has claimed two thousand victories now. They are not a foe to underestimate."

"Damn," was all I managed to get out. I appreciated having a name to attach to the plane Yellow Eight, but the total kill count of the unit was something I could have done without. Their experience against our lack thereof almost guaranteed we'd be on the wrong end of the shooting gallery whenever we met. No wonder Tamara hadn't thought we were ready before.

"He's a dangerous adversary, but not an immortal one. If you focus on your training and work together, I'm confident you can bring him down," she said. "Now get out of here. You're on flight rotations for four days starting tomorrow."

Alexandra looked at me, grinning, and held out an expectant hand. I took it with my left hand and put my right along the small of her back as she put hers up on my shoulder. "And here I thought you'd forgotten," she said.

"You are not dancing out of my box," Tamara said. She tried to be stern in it, but her amused face belied her cutting tone. When the two of us looked at her, poised like toddlers testing their parents, she cleared her throat and found her unyielding look. "I mean it," she said. "Save it for the airfield, but if you waltz out of this box, you'll be waltzing to the penal brigade before the day is up."

I let Alexandra go. We'd flirted with disaster enough. "On the airfield," I said to her.

Alexandra nodded and smiled back. "On the airfield."

We didn't wait until the airfield, but we did wait until we were far enough away from Tamara and the box that it didn't come across as insulting to our commanding officer. We made a run to the mess hall for breakfast, which we knew would still have some scraps left over from the morning line. When we reached its doors, we waltzed in, guzzled frigid water and tore into stale hunks of bread, and waltzed out. Some of the other girls lingering inside looked at us as if we'd come out of an asylum while others seemed to find our antics funny.

We were halfway down the airstrip when an infamous voice from behind stopped my heart and me dead in my tracks. "Tsk. Tsk. Nadya. Mouthing off to a commanding officer like that. You're making this too easy."

I turned to find Petrov standing nearby. He had a long combat knife with a black handle and an S-shaped guard in one hand, and in the other he lightly tossed an apricot. "I thought you were in Stalingrad," I said, my eyes never leaving the point of his blade.

"I was in Stalingrad, but now I'm here," he said. "And I'll be staying until I get what I want."

"More apricots?" Alexandra said, taking my arm. "My mother makes a fantastic apricot pie. I could see how you'd want them."

I shouldn't have cracked a smile at her smartass comment, but I couldn't help it. Sadly, her moment of levity was short lived.

"All I need is one," he said, slowly digging his knife into the fruit. "I intend on splitting it open so everyone can see exactly what it hides." He sheathed his blade and pulled the apricot in two. Its seed fell to the ground, and he then dropped the halves. "It's easy to get to the center when you know where to cut, isn't it? I wonder how long the flesh will take to rot."

I didn't have an answer or anything remotely snappy as a reply. Alexandra tightened her grip on my arm, telling me she didn't either. Thankfully, Petrov left without further word, but my skin still crawled from the encounter.

"Do you think he's here to stay?" Alexandra asked.

"Yes," I replied. "He was too sure of himself."

"Maybe Kazarinova can help."

"Maybe, but I fear the only thing I can do is pray something else gets his attention."

We started walking again, heading toward the fighters parked on the ground. About a dozen meters from the nearest plane, Klara spotted us. She dropped a belt of machine-gun ammunition off her shoulder and came barreling toward me.

"Shut your eyes, Nadya," she said, trying to cover my face with her hands. "I swear, if you spoil the surprise I'll clobber you with a wrench."

"Okay bossy lady, they're shut!" I said, happily following her orders. Her energy and upbeat attitude pushed all thoughts of Petrov from my mind. Next thing I knew, I had a dirty rag around my face that acted as a blindfold. "God, Klara. This thing smells terrible."

"And you smell about as good as my little nephew's diaper," she said, taking my hand and leading me away. "I suspect that's right for another three days in the box. I can't believe you said that to her."

"Me either," I said with a laugh. "You should've seen her face when I did."

"I can imagine. For the record, I would have sent you away for a week and stripped you of rank."

Klara's sudden seriousness put me on edge, and I half entertained the idea her surprise wasn't a good one, probably due to my recent encounter with Petrov. "Where are we going?"

"You'll see."

Alexandra cleared her throat behind me. "Since I'm still here, are you going to introduce us, or do you want to continue being rude?"

"Sorry, yes," I said. "Klara, my mechanic, meet Alexandra, my wingman."

"You're the one Nadya saved," Klara said, sounding impressed.

"I am. She's quite the shot."

"So I've heard. It's all everyone's been talking about. Well, that and Liliia shooting down a pair of fascists." Klara grabbed me by the shoulders and manhandled me into place. "Okay. This is it."

I smiled when she let out an excited little eep as she untied my blindfold. I had to blink a few times to square my eyes against the sun, but once they adjusted and I saw what she'd brought me to, words failed me.

A small, cartoon boar was painted on the side of my fighter's nose. It was charging forward, head down, tusks leading the way and dust trailing behind. That was cute, likeable even, but inscribed around it were the words, "Fighting for country and Stalin." My stomach tightened, and had there been a bucket of paint nearby, I would have tossed it all at the wretched thing. Though I was fighting in that man's air force, I would never fight for him. I fought for myself, my own kinsmen, and my own land. Not some paranoid, power-thirsty madman with the blood of countless innocents on his hands.

"Isn't it great?" Klara said, hanging off my arm. "I had a lot less to do the last few days since your plane wasn't going anywhere."

Thankfully, Alexandra spoke first. "It's a boar."

"Because Nadya is Little Boar."

"No, I mean, it's a boar," Alexandra said. Disdain dripped from her words, and her face soured. "They're ugly, stupid animals. Why would you ever call her that?"

"They're fast and dangerous," Klara said, tripping over her own reply. "It's nothing bad. I've called Nadya 'Little Boar' since I've known her."

Alexandra looked at me incredulously. "You let her? Surely not. It's the stupidest nickname I've ever heard. You're not a beast meant for slaughter. You're majestic and deadly, a bird of prey who has found her talons."

I liked the sound of that, a bird of prey, and the imagery was a thousand times more graceful and meaningful than a dirty pig. It was fitting for a Cossack, as such birds were free to roam where they saw fit, something we as a people had always done. More important, it gave me a way to attack the words around it without branding myself as a traitor. One does not request to strike out such things and live.

"You don't like it," Klara said, eyes glistening.

"I have asked you not to call me that," I said. With every word I spoke, I could see the proverbial dagger twisting in her gut, and I hated what I was doing, but I had to. I couldn't live with myself if everything I did was being dedicated to him. "And the colors are bright. I don't want to be easily spotted."

Klara's face and shoulders fell. "I understand," she said. "I'll have it painted over before you go up tomorrow."

"Good," Alexandra said, wrapping her arm around my shoulder and leading me away. "Glad to see that disaster was avoided."

I looked over my shoulder at Klara to say goodbye and assure her we'd catch up later, but the pained look in her eyes froze my tongue. She mouthed four little words. "Come back to me."

Chapter Eleven

A WEEK AND a half blew by. Petrov had taken residence in one of the nearby homes. Tamara had said he was temporarily assigned to the unit for an undetermined amount of time. She wouldn't say more than that, even when I'd pressed the matter on why our own regiment commissar wasn't enough (Olga Kulikova was her name, and what little dealings I had with her were pleasant enough). While I was thankful Petrov and I hadn't had any more face-to-face encounters, he seemed to always be nearby, watching me.

Alexandra and I had been on twenty-something sorties together at that point. I wish I could've said they were exciting, but they weren't. They all entailed flying lazy circles around a handful of rail stations and the only bridge at Saratov to keep them safe from enemy bombers, but not a single Luftwaffe came. I became frustrated at our lack of engagements and wondered if I'd ever see them again since our assignments kept us far from the front. How was I supposed to shoot down Rademacher if we weren't going to be anywhere near him?

To pass the time during guard duty, Alexandra would talk about her fiancé, Yuri, or her father's work as a surgeon back home and how he only had eyes for her mother. In the lulls of conversation, she'd occasionally sing to herself off key, but for the sake of my ears, I'd snap her attention back on our mission. I didn't have the heart to tell her how bad she was.

On the twenty-fourth of September, I was lying on my back on my bed in my dugout, trying to figure out what I was going to do with myself for the next hour before I was slated for night watch. The straw mattress was lumpy and cold, but far more comfortable than the damp dirt floor beneath. The evening sun cast a warm glow through the entrance but did little to affect the chill in the air.

We didn't have the luxury of sleeping in buildings since they were more susceptible to explosions during an air raid. Our earthen homes could survive a near miss by a five-hundred-kilogram bomb, whereas a typical wood dwelling would be turned into splinters by similar blasts. Some nights, however, when water stood on the floor and the mice took home in our covers, I would've been willing to risk being turned into a crater for a proper room and a clean bed.

Alexandra slept on the bunk next to mine, something I wished I was doing but couldn't. My arms hurt from the cold, making rest elusive. Worse, when I shut my eyes, I saw Klara's face and heard her last words to me over and over, haunting my soul. Sure, we'd spoken some over the last week and a half, but she spoke at me—giving at best factual, short statements. She no longer spoke to me as a friend or confidant. Our friendship had become threadbare at best, and I didn't know what to do.

"God help me," I muttered. I was so weary from it all I didn't even care when Alexandra stirred at my comment.

"What was that?" she said. "You're not turning religious on me, are you?"

I let out half of a chuckle. "Yep. And I'm taking you with me."

"I'd rather stick my head in a prop."

"Well if you do, don't do it to mine. I don't want the mess all over my plane," I said, trying to keep things light even though her remark stung.

Over the past week and a half, I'd learned a few things about Alexandra, most of them good. First, she loved Russian art and literature. Alexei Savrasov's *Winter* was her favorite painting, and she could rattle on for hours on anything written by Tolstoy. Second, she was incredibly sensual. She loved chocolate, pleasing aromas, beautiful sunrises, heart-felt songs, and exceptional rubs on the shoulders and neck. I couldn't provide the first three, but I could sing, and after some instruction, could give "decent enough" massages to help her work out the kinks in her neck from time to time.

The last thing I learned was Alexandra was a life-long communist who had no room in her heart for religion, but at least she wasn't violent about her opposition like some. Even so, I kept my beliefs to myself. When she'd asked me about them, I dodged answering, much to my shame. I suppose I wanted acceptance, and I didn't want her looking down on me for any reason.

I sat up at the sound of a dog barking and welcomed the distraction. "Oh damn. He's back."

Alexandra groaned. "Already?"

"Unfortunately," I said. "I don't think he's stopping anytime soon."

A mutt weighing five kilos soaking wet had taken to begging for scraps at the mess hall. This wouldn't have been an issue if the little fur ball hadn't also started chasing away Zhenia's cat named Bri. The cat was a lean, black and grey tabby that was cuddly when the mood suited her, and otherwise was a meowing, clawing, need machine that had no problems drawing blood when petted the wrong way or ignored when she didn't want to be. Basically, she was a typical feline.

Zhenia had taken in Bri from the nearby streets to be a mouser on account of her phobia of all things rodent. Zhenia had chased the dog off the other day, swearing if she ever saw it again, she'd shoot it dead. The dog's barks drew closer, and I tensed in anticipation of an ear-shattering, dog-silencing shot.

"Make it stop, Nadya," Alexandra whined. She rolled over and pulled her jacket over her head.

Bri rocketed into the dugout. Fresh on its heels was the mutt. The two darted around the room, under and over bunks, knocking over boots, books, tin cups and anything else in their way, before leaping onto Alexandra's bed.

"For the love of all!" Alexandra shouted, flying out of bed. She grabbed a boot from the floor and readied it for a throw, but before she could launch it at either animal, they both took their chase back outside. For a moment, she stared at the door, ready to cream whatever four-legged monster dared to come back.

"Rise and shine, beautiful," I said. Alexandra shot me a disapproving look, and I shrugged. "What? Could have been worse, right?"

"Only if I was thrown into a dungeon with the two of them."

Valeriia charged into the room, panting and face flushed. "Get to your damn planes, now!"

Before either of us could reply, she was gone. Alexandra and I exchanged looks of confusion and dread before snapping into action. I grabbed my leather jacket, cap, and goggles from the foot of my bed and raced out of the dugout. Alexandra followed, cursing about how she hated night flights as she tried to put her gear on.

Only a faint golden glow crested the horizon, but even in the low-light conditions, I could see the airstrip was a beehive of activity. We raced to our planes, and once I reached my Yak-1, Klara thrust my rig into my chest. "No time to lose," she said. "Your plane is warmed up."

I fumbled with the parachute as I slid it on my back and fastened the straps. "What's going on?"

"They spotted bombers and your fighters are the only ones ready."

"Good God." I jumped onto the wing and into the cockpit. Klara's hands were in there a split second later, making sure I was well situated inside. I craned my head around her. "Where's Alexandra?"

Klara growled and pushed me into my seat. "Damn it, Nadya, could you not think about her for a few seconds and get in the air? Zhenia's already taxiing."

The sharpness of her words left me speechless. I stared at her dumbfounded as she hopped off the wing and looked back at me expectantly. Only when she gestured at me with both hands did I kick into gear. I started the engine, motioned for her to pull the chalks, and taxied on to the runway.

"Red Eight, you're clear for takeoff," the tower called to me.

"Copy," I replied, easing the throttle forward at the same time as I tried to ease my nerves. I didn't like flying at night, especially under combat conditions. There were no lights on the runway to keep it from being easily bombed from the air. We only had the stars to use as reference points. My plane picked up speed, and I prayed it was headed in the right direction. My eyes hadn't adjusted to the dark yet either, and so I was effectively flying blind and on feeling alone.

My plane shuddered, jarring me in my seat. I punched the right rudder, realizing I'd drifted off the runway. The correction was too much, however. My plane tipped left as it slid. With a death grip on the stick and working the pedals with my feet as furiously as I could, I somehow kept the plane from flipping over.

I bit down on my lip hard enough to draw blood. When I guessed I was around a hundred and seventy kilometers per hour, I pulled hard on the stick, knowing I was about to run out of runway. The plane launched into the air. It wobbled and started to roll on its side. Immediately, I dropped the nose and used a side lever to extend the flaps. Once I had the plane stabilized and was no longer convinced I was about to die, I raised the landing gear and offered a silent prayer of thanks.

"Wow, that was close," I said over the radio, leaning back in my seat with a heavy sigh. "I think I almost carved a path through the maintenance shed."

Zhenia responded first. "Cut the chatter. Stagger altitudes and head to Saratov. Alexandra, fifteen hundred meters. Nadya, two thousand. Valeriia, you've got twenty-five. I'll be at three."

I leveled off at the prescribed height. Despite the five hundred meters of separation, I was still nervous about a collision. One plane colliding with another never ended well.

"We're looking for Ju-88s, ladies," Zhenia said. "ETA is under two minutes, and we'll probably only get one shot at them. Call your targets before you engage."

My eyes strained trying to pierce the night sky in search of the bombers. Unless the search lights below found them, we didn't have a prayer to make the intercept. Also, unlike the He-111s we'd caught before, the Junkers Ju-88s were built for speed. They could drop thousands of kilos' worth of explosives and be gone before anyone made the spot. If that happened, dawn would usher in slews of new orphans and widows.

I clenched a fist and hit the side of my canopy. I hated the pressure I faced. Though it was never said, everyone on the ground expected us to stop a raid in the dead of night. Correction, they demanded we girls fly blind and save countless lives. The truth was we had no control of what was about to happen, and this night would shape who I was and what I was worth. The whole thing made me want to vomit.

I rolled my shoulders a few times to try and loosen up and relax, but my body didn't cooperate. My tongue stuck to the roof of my mouth, and my breath hung in the air, reminding me the ache in my arms would soon become throbbing. Nothing about this flight was good.

My stomach knotted as the Volga River passed below us and we flew over the city of Saratov. Klara's words about finding the beauty in a moment came to me, and I looked for something to latch on. Inside the cockpit everything looked worn and shrouded in shadow. Outside wasn't any better. The night hid our enemy, and the cold air wracked my body. The moon illuminated my olive wings in a soft glow I found pleasing, but I couldn't stay focused on it as the fascists were closing in.

Then I found it. My brain tied combat with my paint job, and I thought about how Klara had taken it upon herself to give my plane custom nose art. Yes, she'd made my skin crawl with what she encircled it with, but now, slicing through the night air at nearly half the speed of sound, about to engage in mortal combat, my objections seemed so trivial. Moreover, her actions seemed so beautiful, made her so beautiful. I swore I'd mend the damage I'd caused between us the instant I could.

"Spotlights are up! Look for targets!"

Zhenia's voice ripped me out of the moment. Beams of light coming from the ground crews cut through the darkness. For a half-minute we circled, waiting for one of the enemy planes to be caught in the lights. All I could do was gnaw on the bottom of my lip and pray for His guidance.

One of the lights jumped and caught a Ju-88 dead in its beam. Zhenia was the first to call it. "On him," she said. "Mind your distance. Find his friends."

A couple seconds later, two more enemy bombers were hit with the lights. They were farther west than the first and moving fast, but well within range to intercept.

"Alexandra, take the bomber on the left," Valeriia said. "Nadya, shadow the right and engage after I've made a run."

"Copy, lining up now," I said, setting myself up for an attack on the bomber's rear. It flew a little lower than I did, so once I made my final turn, I also ended up in a shallow dive. Rademacher might have been willing to let his enemies go from time to time, but I wasn't.

Using small corrections with aileron and rudder, I kept the plane dead in my sights. At three hundred meters from the target,

I cut my speed to keep from closing any farther as I didn't want Valeriia to accidentally shoot or ram me. She knew I was trailing the bomber, but at the speeds we flew, half blind in the dark, there wasn't a lot of room for error.

Valeriia made her attack from above. Her tracers danced through the sky. Some found their mark, but most flew wide. "Damn it, I overshot," she said over the radio. "Nadya, don't let him get away."

I pushed my throttle forward, eager for the kill. "Engaging. Five o'clock high."

My hands tightened around the controls. I forced myself to be patient as I closed the distance. I didn't want to shoot early like I had with the 109, only to miss and have the plane take evasive maneuvers. When it looked massive in my gun sight, I closed one eye to preserve my night vision in it and pushed both triggers.

The muzzle flash lit up my cockpit, blinding me to all that was happening. I had to trust my aim was true, and I kept firing. The enemy tail gunner returned fire with his twin, rear-facing machineguns in the back of its cockpit. The flames from his barrel filled my view, and only then did I realize I was about to plow through the bomber.

I yanked the stick for all I was worth to avoid the collision.

"Fantastic!" Valeriia called out.

I twisted, pressed back in my seat from the steep climb, and looked over my shoulder. Even with one eye ruined for flying at night, the small fire erupting from the bomber's starboard engine was easy to spot. It turned the plane into a comet. No, an easy kill.

"Coming around now from his eleven," Valeriia said. "Get clear."

"Already done," I said, positioning myself high for a follow up to Valeriia's second attack, but it wasn't needed. She raked the poor bomber from nose to tip. It turned on its side and fell from the sky like a falling star. When it hit the ground, the explosion lit up the sky.

"One down," Valeriia said with pride.

"Stay focused. It's not over," Zhenia said. "Find the others and call your targets."

I scanned the area. The darkness was disorienting. Even with the searchlights shining, at times it was hard to tell where my plane was going since I was half blind, and I worried I might fly straight into the ground. Sadly, the night vision in my right eye wouldn't return for another twenty or thirty minutes.

I'd like to say we downed more, but our luck ran out. Each of us tried to make attacks on other bombers caught in the lights, but they would drop their bombs and peel off into the darkness before any of us caught up to them. I could only hope they were jettisoning their ordnance to get away and weren't hitting their targets.

A few minutes came and went in silence, other than the occasional request by Zhenia to report our location to avoid collision. My hands ached, and the cold made it worse, despite the fleece-lined coat, wool sweater, and leather gloves I wore.

I wanted to land, to find a fire and warm my arm and stop the pain, but I knew I couldn't. To distract myself, I pulled out a penlight and checked the gauges on my instrument panel. Everything was where it should be, except the engine temperature was climbing. I tapped the glass in front of the needle, but nothing changed.

"I'm running hot," I said. I looked over my shoulder, but saw only dark. "I can't see anything, but I must be leaking coolant."

"Head home, Nadya," Zhenia replied. "We can take it from here."

I kept a nervous eye on the temperature gauge as I flew back to the airfield. The needle continued to climb, but I was confident I had enough time to land before heat seized the engine. I stuffed the penlight back in my jacket and concentrated on flying.

Pain intensified in my right arm, and my eyes watered. Basic flying became a monumental task as every move on the flight stick shot fire from my wrist to my elbow. My vision wobbled, and my stomach threatened to empty itself.

I tucked my right arm against my midsection to fight the cold. This left me flying with my left hand, and it became obvious I couldn't work the throttle and keep the plane level at the same time. I flew on with one hand, regardless, as my right was still too painful to use.

I crossed the Volga River, about a thousand meters above. Despite the darkness, I could still pick out the airfield. It was a blot of shadow with a smoother texture compared to the other black patches of landscape. Had we not trained for such things at night, I never would have been able to find it. A night landing still frightened me, however, and I found it funny that downing a bomber had been relatively easy, but coming home safely was anything but.

"Tower, this is Red Eight, requesting emergency clearance to land. I'm running hot," I said.

"Runway is clear, Red Eight," replied the tower. "You can light up on final."

When I guessed I was two kilometers away, I made a couple of gentle, ninety-degree turns. The first put me on the base leg of my pattern, which ran perpendicular to the direction of the runway. The second put me on final approach and five hundred meters above the earth. At that point, I flipped the switch for my landing light and prayed ground control would see it well enough to direct me in.

"Heading looks good, Red Eight, but you're low about fifty meters."

I cursed under my breath and made the correction. At least the area had few obstacles and I was pointed in the right direction.

My plane slid to each side as I attempted to work the throttle with my left hand while keeping the stick in place with my knees to land. My fighter nearly snapped rolled into the ground, and I snatched the stick with my right hand to keep it steady. It felt like someone was twisting a blade deep in my wrist, but I held on to that stick as hard as I could.

As I touched down, a crosswind jostled my fighter. I tried to correct, but my arm didn't respond fast enough. My wing tip dug into the runway, ripping metal and leaving a sickening crunch in my ears. I kicked my right pedal and pushed the stick hard to the side. The fighter bounced twice on its wheels before settling. I chopped the throttle and eased the brakes, careful not to hit them too hard and tip the plane over.

Once I stopped at the end of the runway, elation hit me. We did it! We shot down a bomber and sent the others running, hopefully with enough holes in them that some wouldn't make it back home. On top of all that, I even managed to land with a crippled arm and not die. God, that was close. Had I been a little slower or in a little more pain, I don't think I would have walked away from that landing. Next time I'd have to be more careful.

That's when I realized winter was drawing near, and the real cold had yet to come.

I looked down at my hands and cried.

Chapter Twelve

THE FOUR OF us, myself, Alexandra, Zhenia, and Valeriia, all stood in the command post, grinning ear to ear as Tamara finished our debriefing. Thankfully, I'd regained my composure before climbing out of the cockpit as I didn't want Tamara questioning my fitness. Zhenia, on the other hand, still had puffy eyes from tears born from anger and frustration. Apparently, her guns had issues near the end of her flight, and two other bombers had gotten away from her that shouldn't have. I probably would have come down bawling too if that had happened to me.

"To be clear," Tamara said once she'd finished scribbling a few notes, "Valeriia, the Ju-88 you downed was the same one Nadya set alight?"

"Without a doubt, comrade major," Valeriia replied.

"Do you feel she contributed to the kill?"

Valeriia looked over at me and smiled. "Nadya tore into it like a lioness on a gazelle. It might not have made it back regardless of my pass."

My heart soared. I could be credited with half the kill the way this was going. We'd both be decorated, or at least recognized publicly, for earning the regiment's first kill—a kill at night no less. Certainly it wouldn't be as impressive if one of us had brought down an enemy plane unassisted, but-

Damn. My shoulders fell, as did my smile. "The fire wasn't big," I said. "It could have gone out."

"Nadya, that's nonsense," Valeriia said.

"No, it's not."

Tamara eyed me with surprise. "I think she's trying to share it with you," she said. "There's no need for modesty. You'll both split the bounty."

"Thank you, Major, but I stand by my words," I said, fearing I'd hate myself the next day for giving it up. I knew I helped with the victory, but I didn't finish the bomber off. It could have made it back, and moreover, I was content with my part and didn't want false praise. "My part was small and the regiment's first victory should go down as unassisted. Valeriia earned that honor far more than me. She deserves it."

"So be it," Tamara said as she jotted down more notes on an after-action report. "Since Nadya is pushing it, that's how it will be recorded. Valeriia, congratulations on not only your first kill, but the first official kill of the 586th. You do us all proud."

"Thank you, comrade major," she said.

"That said, I'm changing statements," Tamara said. "I don't want any doubt this kill was Valeriia's and Valeriia's only. I'll not have the boys thinking us girls need extra help. Nadya, Alexandra, you're out. As far as anyone else knows from this day forward, Zhenia and Valeriia were the only ones up tonight. It'll keep questions about who shot what at a minimum. Understood?"

We all nodded. Silently, I already questioned my actions. God, what had I been thinking? What if I never made another kill? What if my share of the two-thousand-ruble bounty was needed back home? Before I could think it through any further, Valeriia's arms found my shoulders and neck and squeezed. My worries were swept away by a deluge of happiness. Bolstering our friendship was infinitely more important than some silly downed bomber. Besides, the only kill that mattered to me was Rademacher.

"Thank you, Nadya," she said. "I'll never forget this."

Tamara filed the report away and sat behind her desk. "I'm giving the four of you the day off tomorrow. You've earned it. But be ready for action after that. It won't be long before we're moved closer to help keep Stalingrad clear of Luftwaffe. Brass doesn't have a choice if they don't want the city to fall."

"It's about damn time they committed us to the front," Zhenia said. "Limited engagements aren't doing the girls any good, and our boys on the ground are dying for more air cover."

"Perhaps, but I'd still prefer everyone had more training," Tamara replied. "That said, the war doesn't care what I think. Now everyone go get some sleep. Nadya, I'd like you to stay a moment."

The three other girls left after a short goodbye, which left me standing there, confused and worried as to why I'd been held back. "Is something wrong, comrade major?"

"I hope not, Nadya," she replied. Her eyes held mine, and my soul shivered as if she could scrutinize its deepest secrets. "You'd tell me if there was, wouldn't you?"

"Always."

"Then what happened with your landing?"

I cursed in my head. Of course she knew. Everyone had to know by now as near wrecks fueled gossip like oil in a bonfire. "As I said in my report, the plane was running hot and I was afraid the engine would seize," I said. "I came in faster and more worried than I should have. A crosswind caught me by surprise."

"And you want me to believe battle damage was responsible for your takeoff as well?"

"No, comrade major," I replied. "That was one hundred percent my fault. I spooked myself at launch. Never been fond of flying at night."

Tamara sighed and shook her head. "That's not a whole lot better than what I'm worried about. If the dark scares you, that doesn't bode well for your future as a pilot."

"It won't happen again, comrade major," I replied.

"How's your hand? You've had it tucked across your stomach since you came in."

Damn. I thought it, but I didn't say it. I don't think I showed it either. I held it up and flexed it twice for her to see. "Still works," I said. "It hurts now and again. I wouldn't lie about that. But I can fly. I assure you. After all, I did light up that bomber."

Tamara's face softened, and for the first time in this conversation, I managed to relax—right up until she spoke again. "I appreciate your honesty, Nadya," she said. "But all the same, with winter coming, I'm going to have to periodically evaluate your abilities. I don't want the cold costing the regiment a plane and you your life."

Damn. Damn. Damn. Damn. Damn.

"Yes, comrade major," I said with a rock-hard face. "I wouldn't expect anything less."

"Very good, Nadya. You're dismissed."

Damn. Damn. Damn.

I nodded, went outside, and threw up.

* * *

The next morning the regiment celebrated Valeriia's kill with vodka and watermelons. Alexandra enjoyed both, though she said she would've preferred wine, which wasn't something we had lying around. I stuck to eating the treats, however, as the alcohol didn't sit well with me.

Four days later, we were in the second week of fall, and the temperature during the night was close to freezing. I slept layered under blankets in my dugout, although a few times after the sunset I had to venture out on duties. Thankfully, they were of the logistic and briefing kind, and I hadn't been pulled for another midnight watch. But I knew I would eventually, and I prayed I'd be able to do my duties when the time came.

On the morning of 30 September, I sat on my bed while Alexandra massaged my right wrist and forearm as she'd done for the last week. I don't know if it gave any long-term benefits, but her help eased the pain for at least a few hours. As she worked on my burns, Zhenia sat nearby, studying the most recent reconnaissance maps and frequently pushing Bri off her lap.

"You should see the doctor about this," Alexandra said, eyes focused on her work. "Every day you wince more."

I grunted and scowled. "I saw him already. Besides, I'd rather swallow hot coals."

"I don't like him either, but you should try again. Maybe he's got something new. Or I could write my father. Maybe he would know something that could help."

"No. I'll be fine."

Alexandra stopped and looked at me with concern. "You're not flying as well as you used to."

My stomach turned. I knew I hadn't been at the top of my game, but I had no idea it was so obvious to others. And if it was obvious to my fellow pilots, it was obvious to Tamara as well. Still, I dared to hope otherwise.

"Have I?" I said, feigning surprise and giving an awkward chuckle. "I didn't think I was that bad."

"I've seen first-time students wobble less," Zhenia chimed in. "And yesterday you couldn't stick on Alexandra's tail to save your life. You used to be able to outfly her in your sleep."

"Maybe I'm getting better," Alexandra said, sticking out her tongue.

"You are," Zhenia replied. "At the same time, she's getting worse. Luftwaffe won't cut us any slack."

Zhenia didn't look up from her maps for any of the exchange, and so I couldn't get a read on her face. That heightened my paranoia. "If I don't bounce back soon, I'll see him," I said, hoping to placate them both. "The massages are helping."

I had no intentions of seeing the man. Thinking back to the day he suggested to give me morphine in exchange for . . . favors . . . still made me shudder. I continued hating him for ever trying such a thing, but I hated myself even more for keeping the offer tucked away as a last-ditch resort to retain my flight status. I'd do anything to stay a pilot, to redeem myself, to bring down Gerhard Rademacher, and I prayed I wouldn't be forced to go through such humiliating lengths to do so.

"You okay?" Alexandra said.

"Quite," I lied. "I was trying to remember when Valeriia was coming back."

"From Moscow? In five more days, I think," Zhenia replied. "She'll probably sleep another three once she returns. I imagine they're wearing her out parading her around as the next war hero, not to mention showing off her Order of the Red Banner. But I agree with Alexandra. You should get looked at."

"Fine. If it'll get the two of you off my back, I will. Any news from the front?" The first part was another lie, and the second was bait I hoped Zhenia would take so the subject would be dropped. To my relief, she did.

"We struck against the Romanians a few days ago. They're keeping the flanks of the German assault on Stalingrad secure, but I think they're the weak points." She paused for a second to push Bri away for the umpteenth time. "The new Yak-9s and La-5s are also coming in."

I perked, scooting to the edge of the bed. "Better fighters? Dare I hope we get them?"

Zhenia's face twisted with irritation. "Don't even dare to dream. The boys will be playing with them long before we do. Be glad you're in a Yak and not the Kukuruzniks the girls in the 588th are stuck with. The top speed on those biplanes is slower than your stall point."

From then on all talk of my wounds and the need to see the doctor vanished. Instead, we chatted about mundane things. Once Alexandra was done on my arm, I excused myself, saying I had some things I wanted to look at with my aircraft. What I said was true, to a degree, but I didn't mind that neither wanted details nor offered to come with me. What I was actually doing was going to try and fix things with Klara, and I didn't want an audience for when I ate humble pie.

I found Klara by my plane. She had the cowl off and was working on the engine. I know she saw me coming, but she kept her attention on her task at hand and didn't acknowledge I was there until I spoke. "Do you have a minute?"

"I'm trying to get your plane serviced for tomorrow, comrade pilot," she said. She threw me a passing glance as she traded a wrench for a screwdriver and sighed. "What?"

"I thought we could talk."

"About?"

"The nose art you painted."

"I'm sorry I didn't ask you first. You made your point, and I'm okay with it."

I raised an eyebrow. "Are you?"

"Yes."

She painted over the hurt I'd caused with a mask of indifference, and I knew she'd said such things because she had no other option. As I was an officer, she couldn't let me have it for ruining her gift.

"I'm not okay with it," I said. I took a tentative step toward her, unsure of how she'd react to what was about to be said. Hell, I didn't know how I'd react either. "I should've been more appreciative, and I'm sorry."

The screwdriver slipped from her grasp. It hit the ground with a quiet thud. She didn't go after it. "Why are you telling me this?"

"Because I miss you," I said. "I miss our chats. I miss you wishing me off each flight. I miss you ordering me to come back safely. We've drifted apart, and I hate it."

"What's done is done. There's no changing the past."

I shook my head. "No, there isn't. But I was thinking maybe you could paint something else on the nose instead."

Klara snorted as she picked up her dropped tool. "Something else? Like what? Whatever stupid bird Alexandra has picked out for you?"

"I'm no bird," I said. I stuffed my hands into my pockets and stared out into the sky, feeling as if I were about to make confession to a priest. "I'm a stubborn, stupid, little boar that's deadly to friendships."

"At least you're honest about it."

I caught her smiling back at me, and couldn't help but grin as well. "Am I forgiven?"

"I don't know," she said. "What do you want painted? I don't want to make an effort to give you something again and you throw it in my face."

I wanted to ask for the iconic cross from the Knights Hospitaller. I'd always admired their tenacity and dedication to the Living God, but I didn't think she'd paint it as she had less room for religion than Alexandra had. Furthermore, a cross would attract unwanted attention, from Petrov especially. Shame clawed at my heart as I continued to hide such an important facet of my being, but what could I do?

"I was thinking about another boar," I said, "but not so cartoony. Have you seen what the Americans have done with their P-40s? They paint shark teeth on the lower cowl. Could you do something similar, but with razor-sharp tusks coming out?"

"You want something fierce."

"And deadly," I said. "Something to strike fear in the fascists every time they see it. I want them to know exactly who shot them down every time."

Klara laughed, and for the first time in our encounter, she felt close again. "Getting a little ahead of yourself, aren't you? You haven't even gotten your first kill yet. Besides, I thought you said you didn't want to be noticed up there."

"I changed my mind," I replied. "And I'll get my first kill soon enough. Once I get enough of them, Martyona's killer will come looking for me."

Her face grew somber. "So this isn't about you wanting to make amends. I guess it's true. Only the grave will cure a hunchback."

I took hold of her hands. They were slick and covered in oil. "I'm making amends. I swear. The last bit is an added bonus." When she hesitated, I said the first thing that came to mind. "You asked me to come back to you. Here I am. It took me longer than it should have, but I'm not going anywhere. Never again."

Klara stepped away. "I'm glad, but . . ."

"But what?"

"But I don't want to get attached to you again," she said. "Not yet at least."

"I'll earn your trust then if I must."

She shook her head. "No, it's not that. I overheard Kazarinova talking. She's grounding you on account of your burns and performance lately. Once she does, you'll be gone, and I'll be alone."

"She'll want to test me first," I said, setting my jaw. "Or at least see how I do on one last mission."

"Why? Because you've got a fool's hope?"

"Because she would have grounded me already otherwise." I said it as confidently as I could, but I knew I was grasping at straws. I had to believe I still had a shot to control my destiny.

"Even if you're right, your wounds still interfere with your flying, and there's nothing you can do about it. The only right thing to do is replace you."

My body numbed, and it felt as if I was smothered in a thick blanket. "No," I said. "You're wrong. There's one thing I can do."

Chapter Thirteen

THE NEXT DAY I learned I was slated for one mission, a simple patrol deep in our own lines, and I had nothing lined up for the remaining week aside from drills and mock combat with Zhenia and Alexandra. Tamara said the schedule was as such because she hadn't decided what everyone's assignments were. I knew that was a lie as I caught a glimpse of a duty roster saying otherwise. She hadn't assigned me to combat duty because this was to be my last mission. I'd have to pull something off exceptional if I expected to keep my wings by the next day.

While the other pilots made their morning preparations, Alexandra included, I ducked into my dugout and grabbed a small, leather-bound case I stored under my bed. Inside, I kept a picture of Mother and Father they had sent me along with a letter written a few months ago, as well as a simple silver necklace that had belonged to my grandmother and a handkerchief she swore brought good luck. I usually kept a bible wrapped in that handkerchief, but since joining the war, I'd left it at home for fear of it being discovered. Now, instead of Holy Scripture being wrapped in the cloth, I had two yellow containers, each holding five morphine syrettes. Perhaps they would be the keys to my salvation.

Each syrette had a red and white tube that reminded me of a miniature bottle of toothpaste with a needle on top. I took off the clear plastic head that protected the needle before using the wire loop at the end to puncture the syrette's seal.

I pulled up my shirt to expose my stomach as I'd heard it was a good place to inject the morphine. I didn't know how much I should use, and the instructions provided by the E. R. Squibb & Sons company were in English. I figured a quarter of the tube would do. The syrettes were often used for soldiers suffering from major trauma, and I didn't need a lot—only enough to take the edge off the pain.

I stuck the needle into my abdomen and gently squeezed the tube. There was a slight pinch and burning sensation as the medicine entered my body. I'd overheard the doctor a few weeks back say it could take a half hour for the morphine work, so I wouldn't know until I was getting ready for takeoff what the effects would be. Hopefully, I injected enough, and God forbid, not too much.

"Forgive me," I said, as thoughts of how the Almighty viewed me popped into mind. I didn't want to have to answer to Him on how I had obtained these syrettes and prayed He'd understand. I didn't sell my body to get the morphine, but I may as well have. When the doctor had stepped out for lunch the prior afternoon, I slipped into his office, picked the lock to his cabinet, and took the boxes. I wasn't a common whore, but I was a common thief.

I'd never stolen anything before, and I was ashamed that I did. But what choice did I have? If I didn't manage the pain, I'd never fly. I'd lose my identity and my hope at redemption. I'd likely be handed over to Petrov as well.

Thus, my decision was simple, and I prayed that the good I'd do would outweigh my sin. I promised God and myself that once winter was over or Rademacher was dead, I'd stop using. Stop stealing. With luck, those ten syrettes would be all I'd need.

I capped the needle and put the syrette in one of my coat pockets. I wanted to take it with me on the flight in case I needed another dose. I left the dugout after I tucked everything away and went searching for Alexandra. I found her near her plane, lying on the ground on her back, watching the clouds.

"Change of plans for this afternoon's flight," I said once I was certain we were alone.

Alexandra sat up. "We're not on patrol?"

"We are," I said. "We're going on a different route, one closer to the front lines."

"Do you know why Kazarinova changed her mind?"

I shook my head. "She doesn't know, but I don't want to patrol an area with no chance in hell of seeing action. We're going to find some on our own."

"What are you doing?" Alexandra whispered, taking to her feet. "You can't just abandon a mission. You could be charged with cowardice or treason, even if you do claim you went closer to the battle."

Despite the cold, my palms grew sweaty. I knew what she said was true, but this was the first time I'd considered the consequences. In the end it didn't matter much. I could be shot for being a Christian, for stealing the morphine, even for being a Cossack if the wrong person had a hunch or a bad day—and certainly for Father's ties to the White Army. It didn't seem to worsen my odds at being executed to stray from one mission. In a way, it was liberating to chuck caution to the wind.

"I need a kill," I said. "I'm hoping you'll understand. This is my last flight if I don't get one, and where Kazarinova is sending us on patrol, we won't see any Luftwaffe."

"Why would this be your last flight?"

I gnawed my lower lip for a few moments as I debated how much I wanted to tell her. I knew I had to tell her something, and I wished I'd thought all of this out more before bringing it up. I decided to give a short rundown of the last couple months. When I was done, I gave her an out. It was only fair. "I'll understand if you don't follow. There's no need for you to risk your life on my account. We've only known each other a short while."

Alexandra rested her forehead against mine. "I don't like deceptions, but I risk my life for you every time we're together. I know you'd do the same for me. If I have to fly your wing somewhere else to keep you safe, so be it. I won't let you go at it alone."

My heart soared over the heavens even though I could very well be dragging her down to hell. I crushed her in a bear hug. "Thanks. I owe you more than I can ever repay."

Alexandra gasped and laughed. "For love of everything, let me go before you squeeze me to death," she said as she wiggled out of my grasp. "How are you going to pull this off?"

"Ten minutes into the flight we'll still have radio contact with the ground. You and I will have a conversation about an unidentified aircraft headed southwest, low and fast."

Alexandra grinned. "And we're going to follow it."

"All the way to the Don, because that's where the Luftwaffe are."

* * *

"Little Boar, what is your status?" asked ground control. The transmission was weak and crackled as we were on the edge our radio's range, and before we left, I'd asked to ditch my Red Eight callsign for the nickname Klara had given me. I figured it would help rebuild my friendship with her, and I loved the smile it had put on her face when she'd heard the change.

"Unidentified aircraft last seen headed two-three-two. Lost visual contact approximately two minutes ago, still in pursuit," I replied, hoping they'd buy our ruse. Alexandra and I had called in the fake contact a few minutes ago and had been chasing it southwest ever since. Ideally, I wanted to head more toward Stalingrad, as that's where the majority of the fighting had been, but I didn't want to risk someone seeing we weren't chasing anyone, or worse, have them send us home and get fighters from the 437th to make the intercept.

"Copy, Little Boar," came the reply from our base. "Eyes on fuel and don't stray too far from your patrol."

"Understood."

We flew on, some four thousand meters over the earth, a grey cloud layer above skimming the tops of our canopies. We constantly checked our sixes, and periodically rolled our planes left and right to get a better view of what was underneath us, but saw only steppes below.

By the time we could see the Don, I was frustrated at the lack of Luftwaffe. We peeled west, away from Stalingrad, as I didn't want to fly into multiple Schwarms of 109s known to be in the area. What I wanted were easy pickings: a recon flight, stray bombers, or if we were lucky, a transport.

"What do you think?" Alexandra asked. "Fuel's about half."

I glanced at the fuel gauge on my wing. "I've got the same. We can probably land elsewhere if we have to, yes?"

"Where you go, I go."

Warmth ran through my soul, and I was grateful to have such a girl flying at my side. The effectiveness of the morphine added to my uplifted mood. My hands hadn't felt this good since before they were burned. The drug did give me a slight headache, and I occasionally felt distant, but neither were an issue if I concentrated on my tasks. Sadly, none of that would matter if I had nothing to show.

"Pushing two-fifths left," Alexandra said.

"I'm aware," I snapped. I knew she was doing her job, but the announcement rubbed me the wrong way. I grunted and hit the side of my cockpit. How was it possible we'd not seen a single other plane? Stalingrad was a short flight away and the fascists were knocking on its door. There should've been plenty of targets for us to engage. But there weren't! It was as if God was determined to see me handed to Petrov.

"Let's head back toward the city," I said, making a slow left turn. "We've got a better chance there. Hopefully we won't run into a bunch of Schwarms."

We stuck to flying near the river, as I knew we still had ground forces in the area that pairs of Stukas might want to soften up. Larger flights would be headed for Stalingrad. After a few minutes, I saw the faint outline of the city in the distance. It looked peaceful from where we were, but I knew it was anything but. Down on the ground, the Soviet 62nd Army fought for its life inside the city along with the 64th, while the German 6th Army supported by portions of the 4th Panzer threatened to take it all any day. The carnage, I was told, was nothing like I could imagine. I believed it and didn't want to try.

"Where the hell are the damn bombers? I thought we were in a war here," I said, hitting the side of the cockpit once more. Fuel was low, and we'd be running on fumes by the time we landed if we turned back right at that moment. But I wanted a kill. I needed one. I told myself we could always refuel at an auxiliary field if needed. Hell, I'd ditch the plane in a field if I had to, if it meant sticking around long enough to find a target.

"I think I see something, two o'clock low," Alexandra said.

It took only a fraction of a second to see what she did, and I nearly jumped through my canopy with delight. A flight of four Germans was speeding across the landscape toward Stalingrad, and we were in perfect position to make the intercept with the sun at our backs. They'd never see us coming.

"Orders?" Alexandra said, her voice as eager as I felt.

"We're going in."

I put the plane into a dive, and Alexandra followed suit. "One pass and we're out," I told her. "Make it count."

"Always."

I knew I'd have to do something special for Alexandra when we got back, but in that moment, I told myself to worry about that later and pick a target. It wasn't an easy choice. There were two Stukas and two 109 escorts. The foremost were slow and easier shots, but they were armored like a tank. The Messerschmitt fighters, on the other hand, couldn't take as much of a beating, but were nimble. They'd easily dodge my aim if we were spotted.

I decided we should hit one of each. "I'm taking the lead Stuka," I said. "Hit the 109 on the left."

"Will do."

My hands picked up a tremor as my plane picked up speed. I couldn't help thinking about how similar this encounter was to the one I had with Martyona. Would it end in a similar fashion with Alexandra going down in a flaming wreck? Or myself? I didn't see any other Luftwaffe around, so I set my jaw and focused on the gun sight.

The Stuka jinked as I pushed both triggers, but the plane was too slow. Machine gun and cannon fire raked the length of the bomber. To my utter frustration, it neither exploded nor came apart. I pulled up into a steep climb, cursing and telling myself all the reasons why making a second pass would be foolish.

"Burn in hell!" Alexandra screamed.

I rolled my plane so it was inverted while climbing and saw one of the 109s lose a wing and spiral out of control. My heart soared for her, but at the same time I was frustrated and jealous my target still plodded along. I'd been patient to not fire early and land all my shots, but a victory still eluded me. I was going to have to make another pass.

As I started renew my attack, black smoke belched out of the Stuka's nose, and the bomber listed to the side. Then I saw the pilot jump from his plane, his parachute blossoming round a few seconds later. My face beamed, and I was so proud of myself I felt I could take on the world.

"That's one for each of us," Alexandra said.

"Did you catch the numbers on their tails?" I asked.

"Five and three, I think," she said. "But they were red. Not sure if they were even Udet. Definitely not your man. Regardless, I suggest we leave. I'm going to have to get out and push my plane home if we stick around much longer."

"Agreed," I said, pulling on the stick to end in a shallow dive. "I'll race you back."

Alexandra followed, and we returned to Anisovka. I checked our six a few times, but the remaining 109 never gave pursuit. On the way, I grew frustrated that we hadn't killed Rademacher. I detested that he was still in the air, and the more I thought about that, the more my hate grew like a dark, hungry creature feeding off my anger. God, how I wanted the man dead and the rest of the Germans driven from our land. The only consolation I found was that while we hadn't killed him, I felt this mission had helped refine my shooting skills so that when I did meet Rademacher again, he'd be the one to die.

On the way back, I also wondered if he'd been as excited as I was for his first victory. Did it fill him with elation? Or was the death of another something he was amoral over? I guessed the foremost. He probably celebrated with the others in his unit, drinking beer and maybe even posing for pictures. He probably wrote his family home, too, as I planned to do. No. He didn't have a family, I corrected. He was born from a factory of death. I didn't want to think we had anything in common, even if it was something as ordinary as a father and mother.

When we were about eight minutes out, I made contact with ground control. "Den, this is Little Boar. We're coming home with two confirmed kills."

How I longed to say those words! They felt every bit of amazing coming out of my mouth as I had thought they would. I couldn't wait to see the new look in people's eyes when they saw me, a look of respect. Admiration. Best of all, I'd see it in the mirror.

"Repeat, Little Boar. You are claiming two kills?"

"Affirmative, Den. One Stuka. One 109. We saw them both go down."

"Congratulations, Little Boar. Celebrations are in order. Stay sharp, and we'll see you soon."

I checked over both shoulders once more and saw only Alexandra's plane sharing the bright blue sky with me. I was so thrilled to get down, I didn't even glance at my fuel until I was on final approach and the engine sputtered once before quitting.

"Oh damn," I said, laughing and feathering the prop for minimum drag. "Den, Little Boar is declaring no fuel and a dead-stick landing."

"Understood. We have visual on you. Will you reach the runway?"

I readjusted my grip on the stick and rolled my shoulders to try and relax. "I think so," I said, trying to sound more confident than I was. While a dead-stick landing was something every pilot had trained for numerous times, it still could turn messy. A sudden wind or a misjudged angle could force an off landing that might not end well. Uneven terrain had the tendency to ruin planes, and I didn't want this flight to be marred in any way. If I crashed, Tamara would likely strip my wings, regardless of the kill. Besides, dying for something so silly wasn't appealing either.

A tense half minute later, all of which I held my breath for, I made a perfect three-point landing a good hundred meters into the runway. I coasted as far as I could before pulling off to the side so Alexandra—who had to be running on fumes—could land behind me. God, I couldn't wait to see the look on Petrov's face when he learned what I'd done.

Once my fighter was parked, I opened the canopy, unbuckled everything, and stood on my seat, arms stretched high, and screamed with joy till my lungs gave out. I jumped out of the cockpit and slid off the wing as Klara bolted to me.

She grabbed me by my hands and spun me around. "You did it? Tell me you shot down a fascist!"

"Stop! You're making me dizzy!" I said, laughing.

"Oh, the big, bad pilot is losing her balance, is she?" Klara said, tightening her grip and spinning me harder.

Someone slammed into me a moment later, knocking me to the ground and the air out of my lungs.

"You're the greatest wing leader in the world, Nadya!" Alexandra said. "That was the most amazing, mind-blowing thing I've ever done!"

"That . . . really . . . hurt," I said, gasping for air.

Before I could find my own feet, my wingman pulled me up and into a waltzing position. A heartbeat later, we were dancing down the runway. "We're going to make the best team in the world, Nadya," she said with boundless energy. "Wait and see."

In that moment, I didn't disagree with her, but Klara's blank stare chilled me to the core.

Chapter Fourteen

A HAND GRIPPED my shoulder, pulling me from a blissful dream of sipping wine with Mother and Grandmother while stargazing, something all three of us loved to do. I fought returning to the land of the conscious with every fiber of my worn-out body, but whoever was at my bed shook me hard enough to make slumber elusive and give me a motive for murder.

"Nadya! Wake up!"

I cracked open an eye to see who was my victim-to-be. "For all that is holy, Klara, it's my day off," I said, rolling over to give her my back. "I want to sleep in for once."

"I've let you sleep, lazy," she said, forcefully tugging at my shoulder. "You said you wanted to be there when Valeriia came back. I swear you're worse than trying to wake my sister."

My eyes popped open and I sat up, clutching my heavy blanket around me. "She's back?" I asked. "What time is it?"

"Half past one. She'll be here within the hour."

I tossed the blanket to the side but grabbed it again when the frosty air bit my skin. "Did the sun forget to rise? How is it still this cold?"

"It's warmed since this morning, you big baby, and it's the warmest it's been since the start of October," Klara said. She tossed me a wool sweater and leather jacket, which were near the foot of my bed. "Put these on. I've got something to show you."

I smacked my mouth and ran my fingers through my grimy hair. The latter had become the norm for all of us at this point. The frigid weather kept dips in the river non-existent, though at times we used some hot water from our planes' radiators to clean up with. My last such washing was three days prior. "Can I wash first? I must look as terrible as I feel."

"After," she said. "Now dress."

I did as I was told, though I did it under the covers as much as possible. Neither the sweater nor jacket was warm, and I hated their icy touch against my skin. "Where's Alexandra?" I asked, noting her empty bunk.

Klara's face soured. "Does it matter?"

"Settle down. It was a passing comment," I said, perturbed at her attitude. Over the last week, I couldn't help but feel as if she wanted Alexandra out of my life. There wasn't anything specific I could point to, only a general sense I got from how Klara reacted when Alexandra was around. I didn't like it, but felt foolish bringing it up because I knew Klara would deny such things.

"I don't know where she is," Klara said as she handed me my boots and gloves. When I had both on, she pulled me out of bed. She spun me around, and despite my protests, used a long strip of linen to blind fold me.

"Where are we going?" I asked.

"It's a surprise."

"If you push me into the river, it'll be the last thing you do."

Klara laughed. "You'll have to catch me first. And no, it's not the river. Not yet at least. You need to get your bounty on that Stuka first so I can steal it."

I stuck my tongue out. "I'll curse that money if you do, and it will haunt you for the rest of your days."

"You should give me at least half since I'm the one taking care of your plane all the time," she said, ushering me out with her hand on my shoulder. "If it weren't for me, you'd be stuck on the ground."

She sounded playful for the most part, but there was envy under the surface. "Don't worry. I'll get you something," I said. "But I still think you should tell me where we're going."

"I don't care what you think."

I tried counting paces to get a feel for where we might stop. I gave up when I realized she was turning me in several different directions as we walked, twice even backtracking. Outwardly, I smiled at her deception. She'd put a lot of thought into whatever it was. Inwardly, however, concerns grew in my mind that I might not take to her surprise as she hoped and I'd end up making her feel ashamed or even rejected.

About five minutes and twice as many stumbles later, we came to a stop. "Want to take a guess?" she said, spinning me around one last time.

I shrugged. "A pair of Russian Dons?"

"Horses?" she replied. "Must be nice to have that kind of money you can buy whatever you like."

"You said guess. I did." I said, taken aback at the bite in her tone.

She must have felt awkward, for she gave a nervous chuckle. "And what on earth would you do with horses out here? Where would I even get them?"

"I don't know. But I give up. What is it?"

Klara untied my blindfold. "Well, it's not a smelly horse, but I hope you like it all the same."

My plane, once shades of olive, had been given a fresh winter paint job of whites and greys. On the lower cowl, Klara had painted an open maw full of jagged teeth with bloody tusks pointed upward. Fierce eyes were set above, near the start of the engine's exhaust pipes. Though the design was far from intricate, the lines were clean, and the artwork was shaded so well the design seemed three-dimensional. It wasn't as personal as my Hospitaller cross I still wanted, but it was close.

I realized I needed to say something, but what came out was barely adequate. "This is amazing."

"You really like it?" she replied, her eyes bright and her voice full of pride.

"I do," I said. "Those tusks look painful. Exactly what I wanted."

"Thanks. They're for show only. Don't go ramming anyone with them."

I chuckled. "I'll try not to."

Klara squeezed me tight from behind. "I'm so glad. I still want to do something with the tail, but I hadn't figured that part out yet. All I managed to do so far was put your kill marker on it."

I looked to the rear of the plane, and sure enough, underneath the bright red star of the Soviet Union there was a smaller red one representing the Stuka I'd brought down, a symbol to all that this plane was deadly and its pilot should be feared. "Don't worry about the tail," I said, the feeling of accomplishment swelling inside. "You'll have plenty more stars to paint."

"I hope so," she said. "I didn't have time to put the 'Fighting for country and Stalin' back on, but it might be best if I didn't."

"Why?"

Klara shrugged. "You might make me get rid of it," she said. "And then I'd have to report you for being unpatriotic."

"Even your mechanic questions your loyalty," I heard Petrov say from behind. "How grand."

I spun around to find the Commissar a few paces away, amused, slowly puffing away on his pipe. I could feel my face drain of color, but I still managed a reply. "She was joking."

"Behind every joke there's a little bit of truth. Isn't that right, comrade Rudneva?"

"No, comrade commissar. I mean, yes, sometimes," she said, stammering. "But I was joking and didn't mean anything by it."

Petrov raised an eyebrow. "So you don't believe she'd make you strike a slogan dedicated to our leader?"

"No, comrade commissar."

"Did you know she's one of the few that still cling to religion?" he said. I went to say something, but he quickly held up his hand and cut me off. "Come now, Nadya. Don't deny it."

"I wasn't going to," I said. The air surrounding me seemed to drop thirty degrees. My fingers went numb, and no matter what I did, they wouldn't stop trembling, so I stuffed them in my pockets.

"I didn't know," Klara said with a hint of disappointment in her eyes. "But I don't care."

Petrov laughed. "What did you tell me religious people were the other day? Gullible or swindlers? Maybe you think Nadya is the former, but I'd say she's the latter."

A surge of anger ran through me, not for what he was doing to me, but for putting Klara in such an awkward position. "I've done nothing wrong," I said. "Leave her alone."

"You keep saying that, but why should I trust someone who clings to fairytales that are childish and dangerous? The answer, of course, is I shouldn't. But do you know what I should do, Nadya?"

I wanted to say he should jump off a cliff, but I was far from being suicidal, so I shook my head. "I haven't a clue."

"I should see what else I can find out about you," he said, pointing his pipe at me. "I have a feeling your belief in a god is one of many things you never wanted me to find out. So I must say, I'm curious what I'll learn when I dig deeper into your past and family."

I don't think any set of words had caused me so much fear in my entire life at that point. I felt my mouth hang open, and I knew I should say something, but my mind was stuck replaying his words over and over again. If he learned about Father's history, every last one of us in my family would be tossed in a shallow grave.

"That's what I thought," Petrov said. "I'll talk to you later. Have a pleasant rest of the day."

He turned his back to me and walked away. As he did, my imagination ran wild with what they'd do to my family. The beatings. The burnings. Electrocutions. My fear turned to anger and then hate. I glared at the back of his head, intent on protecting everyone I loved from this mad man. I could take him down if I had to. I would take him down. Before I knew it, Klara had a death grip on my forearm.

"What are you doing?" she hissed.

I looked down to see my sidearm in hand. Shocked, I shoved it back in its holster. "I don't know."

"Don't you dare even pretend you are what he says," she scolded. She ran her fingers through her hair and bit her lip. "Nadya, about what I said about religious people. I had no idea you believed such things when he asked."

Now that Petrov was gone, my anger at him was replaced by a deep hurt. "You really think I'm gullible? Or a swindler?"

"Mother died when I was four," she said with a sharp edge to her voice. "If there was a caring god out there, he would've stopped that. Maybe-"

She was cut off by a PS-84 flying over, flanked by a pair of Yaks. "That'll be Valeriia," Klara said, exhaling sharply and visibly relaxing. "Look, I don't want what you believe to come between us. Please, forget all of this and catch Valeriia before Tamara scoops her up for briefings. I think she's slated for duty tonight."

"She is? No rest for the famous, I guess," I said, deciding it was in both our interests to let the previous matter drop. As much as it pained me to hear what she thought of my beliefs, I didn't want to exacerbate things and lose her again. Besides, with Petrov closing in on me, I wanted friends, not more enemies.

"No rest for any of us," Klara replied. "I should get back to work."

After we parted ways, I trotted down the airfield as Valeriia's transport landed and taxied off the runway, grateful for the distraction from Petrov. By the time it had parked, I wasn't the only one waiting for her to make an appearance. A crowd of girls waited for her, excited—some giddy even. I pushed my way through them, but everyone was trying to be upfront. Everyone wanted to see the girl who had made the 586th famous and had told her story to every newspaper and magazine in the country.

The passenger door at the rear of the plane opened, and Valeriia appeared, wearing a dress uniform tailored by a god, a stylish new haircut only the powerful and famous dared to have, and makeup second to none. I screamed along with the others, clapping and jumping like a schoolgirl who had lost her mind over something silly. But this wasn't silly. Our heroine had returned, and I couldn't wait to tell her she wasn't the only one with a kill to her name.

"Thank you, thank you all," Valeriia said, hopping off the plane. She had a spring in her step, and waved to everyone, but her energy felt muted, and her bright eyes held hints of fatigue. "I've missed everybody."

Tamara stepped out in front and saluted Valeriia, despite the fact she was the superior officer. Then, even though she bore a smile and was trying her best to keep things joyous, Tamara killed the mood. "All right ladies," she said. "I know everyone's excited, but I'm going to cut this short right now. Get back to work. I need to speak to my pilot, alone. I promise you all can catch up with her soon enough."

There was a collective groan from the crowd, and we slowly dispersed once Valeriia followed Tamara back to the command post. She yawned and stretched along the way, and I suspected the trip had been even more draining than she was letting on to. In all the time I'd known Valeriia, she'd never been one to show weariness, always carrying on no matter what without complaint.

That being said, she probably would've traded entertaining us for a bed if given the option.

Zhenia appeared next to me. Her brow knitted, and her arms were folded over her chest. "This isn't right," she growled. "Valeriia shouldn't be flying the day she comes back. It's dangerous if she's exhausted."

"I don't disagree," I said, "but shouldn't you be telling the Major that?"

"I have. And I'm about to march in there and tell her again."

My eyebrows rose at the harshness to her tone. "Good luck, then? I'm not sure what I can to do help or why you're telling me."

Zhenia laughed, which eased the tension in the air for a brief moment. "I'm telling you, Nadya, because I think there's a good chance I'll be in the box before the night is out," she said. "If that happens, I want you to look after Valeriia for me."

I nodded. I still didn't know what I could do, but I'd try my best regardless. If Valeriia was that wiped out from her trip, maybe I could switch nights with her and she could go up tomorrow instead. "I'll keep an eye on her, but you don't want to go to the box. It's about as fun as watching lint grow."

Zhenia smiled. "I'll keep that in mind. Now go do something else before I drag you down with me."

I said a quick goodbye, and with not much else to do, I went in search of Alexandra. I found her near the mess hall, propped up against a birch tree. She held a mammoth-sized book in hand and didn't look up from its pages when I stood at her feet.

"Valeriia's back," I said, feeling awkward standing there, smothered in silence.

"I saw the transport land," she said. "I guessed it was her when I heard all the cheering."

"She's not as important as your novel?" I teased. "How rude."

Alexandra looked up and threw me a wry grin. "Why? Should she be? She's not as famous."

"As your book?"

"Of course. It's *War and Peace*. Have you read it before?"

I shook my head. I'd certainly heard of it. I couldn't imagine any Soviet alive that hadn't at least heard of Tolstoy's famous work. "One day, I'd like to," I said, but it was a half-truth at best. "Is it good?"

"It's good. Lengthy, but good. Did you know Tolstoy's wife copied it by hand seven times? Talk about dedication. I hope my fiancé is as dedicated to me as she was to him."

"What do you like about it, other than his wife?"

"Everything," she said. "The characters. The story. I love how it makes one think."

"About?"

"Life. Everything," she said. "Take for instance the part where the prince is trying to find God in an amoral world—that's a topic everyone should think on at some point, you as well."

Looking back, I think I jumped the gun, but at the time, I thought she was aiming that comment at me. "What makes you think I haven't?"

Alexandra straightened like I'd splashed her with a bucket of ice water. She closed the book, though was careful to keep her place with a finger. "I didn't mean to say you hadn't," she said. "You've always struck me as a smart girl. I'm sure you realize how silly the idea of gods is."

My skin warmed, and with my brewing anger came feelings of hurt. Though she was my friend, I wanted to knock her down a couple of pegs. I had to be careful, however, with how I framed my beliefs. As much as I tried to be true to them, I didn't want to be a martyr. "Old gods, yes," I said, "but if I had to bet on some sort of creator of everything, I'd put my money on that rather than not. The universe doesn't make sense otherwise."

Alexandra laughed but quickly looked mortified and covered her mouth. "I'm sorry," she said. "I shouldn't be disrespectful, but I'm being honest when I say you're the first person I've met who thinks such things—well, who isn't seventy years old."

"What's wrong with being seventy? My grandparents turned seventy last year."

"Nothing," she said, holding her hands up. "But they're probably clinging to such things out of habit, not proper education."

"So we're stupid now, is that it? If I was as smart as you, I'd believe what you do?"

"Likely," Alexandra said with a shrug. "And I wouldn't say you'd have to be smart—because you are—just better read. Look, I don't want to fight about it. But haven't you ever thought why believing some sort of god exists is only held by the minority at this point?"

"Maybe there would be more of us if Stalin hadn't executed them all," I spat.

The color drained from Alexandra's face and her eyes frantically scanned the area. "Are you trying to join them?" she whispered. She stood and tried to gently take me by my shoulders, but I stepped away.

"I have no love for anyone who's slaughtered and exiled us by the countless thousands merely because of our religion," I said with a sharp tone and spiteful eyes. "And that's not even considering the millions of Cossacks he starved to death in the thirties. So forgive me, dear, if my voice sounds a little harsh."

"I'm sorry. I can't even imagine," she said. "But Petrov will shoot you dead if he hears even a whisper of that."

"Not if I shoot first." I started to leave, but she called my name and I stopped.

"I hope I'm not out of line," she said, slowly picking her words. "But I want to ask you to do something, sometime, and I'm only asking you because I'm your friend and I want to help."

I snorted. "Help me what?"

"Be free of superstition."

I shook my head, annoyed at her for keeping this conversation going and at myself for continuing to subject myself to it. I should have left. "Say what you will. I guess I should know what my wingman thinks of me."

"I want you to pray for something tonight," she said. "Anything, but make it something miraculous. And if it happens, tell me, and I'll admit I'm the one wrong about all things divine. Otherwise, I hope you'll realize your prayers don't fall on deaf ears. They fall on no ears because there is no god out there. Maybe then you'll stop torturing yourself."

"A miracle, huh?" I said. I wanted to retort with something along the lines of even Christ said to not test God, but I figured it was pointless. I was also curious at her answer to my next question. "So what would count as a miracle? The dead rising from the grave?"

Alexandra smiled. "Maybe not as dramatic, but if you could turn water into chocolate, that would do it. I'd prefer a sweet treat to walking corpses any day of the week."

"Fine."

"And when it doesn't-"

"Yes, I know what you said," I snapped as I left. I knew if I stayed much longer I'd say or do something I'd regret. Or worse, I'd do something I didn't regret and would never be able to fix.

I went back to my dugout and stewed over her words. It irritated me to no end for her to dismiss my beliefs in such a fashion. I was by no means the world's greatest theologian, but to insinuate I hadn't ever wondered why some prayers were answered and some were not was insulting, even if she wasn't trying to be. I think deep down I was also mad because I didn't have an answer, and that birthed insecurities as to whether or not my worldview was the correct one.

I flopped on my bed and stared at the ceiling. My arm cramped, and the chronic pain in it grew from both cold and stress. I thought about dipping into my morphine supply, but there were only a handful of syrettes left, and I didn't want to have to use them unless I had to. Not to mention the fact I didn't want to steal any more, since at some point the missing supplies would be noticed. I already had had two nightmares that the doctor had gone to Petrov about the matter.

Those dreams paled in comparison to the one I had when my father confronted me. In that dream, he didn't come at me with anger, only disappointment. Having always been his little girl that could do no wrong, it broke me to see him like that. When I woke from that dream, I stayed awake for two hours with nothing but my conscience for company.

I ended up napping as a way to cope with both pain and frustrations. I'd planned on getting up for dinner, but when I woke again, it was dark outside, and Valeriia was messing with the lantern near the entrance.

"Sorry," she said with a yawn. "I'll turn it off in a moment. I was trying to find another pillow."

I sat up and rubbed my eyes. "Zhenia got you out of flying tonight?"

"No. The doctor told Kazarinova I was fit to fly," she said, making her way to a bunk. "So I'm on duty. The plane is ready on the runway. Kazarinova is letting me sleep in here until I'm called."

"Is there still food in the mess hall?" I asked when my stomach rumbled.

"There's stuff there they say is edible, but I wouldn't call it food. If you're going, can you get the light?"

"Of course."

I slipped on my boots, grabbed my jacket, and left after turning off the lantern. I nearly tripped on the way out as my eyes hadn't adjusted to the darkness yet. Funny how the body was like that. I got about dozen meters before someone ran by, yelling for Valeriia.

I was about to fetch her from the dugout when I saw the light from the lantern come on. Valeriia came dashing out a few moments later. She stumbled as she did, likely hitting the same spot that had tripped me moments ago.

"There's a step there!" I yelled, having a bit of light-hearted fun at her expense. "You'll never get your second kill if you can't keep from kissing the ground."

"I'll get mine before you get yours!"

The corners of my mouth drew back. So she had heard about what Alexandra and I had done. I wondered if she was as proud of me as I was of her. I reminded myself to ask her when she got back. In a friendly rivalry way, I prayed she wouldn't get to shoot anyone down that night.

I didn't see her climb in to her fighter, but I did hear the engine start, and I did hear her plane race down the runway. Then I saw the fireball, and her plane disintegrated.

Chapter Fifteen

THE THUD OF my feet echoed in my ears. Behind me I could hear alarms. The fire truck would be coming soon, but it would be too late to save Valeriia.

With every stride I took, my lungs gulped massive amounts of air. My legs burned. Half way to the crash site, I tripped on some unseen object in the shadows, but it barely slowed me. With years of gymnastics under my belt, I tucked, rolled, and was sprinting again across the airfield. My eyes fixed on the flames surrounding Valeriia's wreck. My mouth whispered prayers for her salvation.

"You can save her," I prayed, searching the scattered fires for any sign of life. "I know you can. I know you will."

The last bit slipped from my mouth without any thought, and a calmness settled over me. This, I decided, was the miracle Alexandra would see—a miracle I needed.

I stopped and scanned the area. She had to be close. If she couldn't get to me, perhaps, I thought, she could answer me. "Valeriia! Where are you?"

I found her dark form, lying about twenty meters away, at the edge of light from a burning patch of ground. She was still for the most part, but I could see her trying to raise her arm to beckon me over. My jaw dropped, and I was both shocked and thankful for the answered prayer. I decided right then and there I'd never doubt the Almighty again.

I sprinted toward her, calling to the others I'd found her and she'd survived. In a few days, maybe a week at the most, all this would be a painful memory we'd laugh at. We'd all tell our grandchildren about the day Valeriia danced with Death in an inferno, and the older ones would roll their eyes and complain about how many times they heard it before.

When I got to her, everything changed. She hadn't been waving me over. It was just the sleeve of her leather jacket, torn and flapping in the wind. Her left arm was missing, and in the flickering light, I could see her skull had been caved in on one side and had a jagged piece of metal sticking out the other.

"Oh God, no! You're going to be okay," I said. The world seemed to close in darkness. All I could see were her lifeless eyes staring back at me, and all I could do was utter my denial and rock back and forth.

A spotlight hit her, brightening the patch of charred ground she was on. My eyes snapped right to see a couple of girls from the ground crew race off the truck. One of them knelt beside Valeriia's body and shook her head. The other draped a heavy fire blanket over the body.

"Stop, you idiots! She won't be able to breathe!" I started for the two of them, but someone grabbed me from behind.

"Don't look, Nadya," Alexandra said, spinning me around. "You don't need to see this."

I fought with my wingman, trying to get away, but she kept me in place. "Let me go!"

"She's gone!"

"No, she's not!"

Alexandra tightened her grip. "There's nothing you can do. Don't let this be how you remember her."

"You're wrong," I said, jerking free. "I prayed. I prayed with all of my heart she'd live, and if she doesn't . . ."

Alexandra's face paled. Her eyes were wide, and despite the gloom surrounding us both, I could see her trembling. "It doesn't mean anything, Nadya."

"Yes, it does," I said. My throat tightened, and I couldn't get the words out.

"I'm a stupid girl," she said. "I like to pretend I know things, that I've got it all figured out, but I don't. So don't you dare listen to what I said earlier. Don't you dare lose it on my account."

Losing it would be nice, I thought, to be anywhere but here, to be anyone else or nothing at all. The hairs on my body stood on end, and I felt as if I were being pulled out of my body. I didn't know what to say, or do, or think.

"I want to sleep and wake from this nightmare," I whispered. "And if I can't do that, I don't ever want to wake up."

Alexandra slipped her arm around mine and led me away. My feet shuffled as we went, moving more out of reflex rather than conscious desires. I hadn't the slightest clue as to where we were going until I found myself at the side of my bed.

"Lie down," she said, easing me off my feet.

She started talking about something else, God or gods or something, but her voice faded to the background. It was nothing more than a gentle murmur, like a barely audible brook on the other side of a rise.

I stared at the empty bunk across from me. It was the same bunk Valeriia had slept in. I wondered if she knew what had happened to her, if it hurt, if she was in a better place or had just ceased to be. I wondered if Martyona had died in pain or fear. Had she been as terrified for herself as I had been for her? Or somehow in her last seconds did she know she was going to an eternal home and everything would be okay?

I didn't know, and I feared that last thought was more foolishness than anything. All I was certain of was that for both girls, I'd flooded God's ears with prayers to save them and those prayers went unanswered. Tears formed in the corners of my eyes, and I held them in check until Alexandra put a hand on my shoulder. That one act pushed me off the cliff of detachment and into the sea of grief.

My body shook as I sobbed. My stomach knotted so tightly I was sure my insides were splitting apart. I don't know how long I cried, but when I was done, I was exhausted with tear-stained cheeks, Alexandra was kneeling at the side of my bed, holding my hand, murdering a lullaby.

"You're terrible," I said.

Alexandra stopped. Her mouth twisted. "What?"

"You can't hold a pitch to save your life," I explained. I wiped my nose with the back of my sleeve and cleared my eyes.

"I thought I was helping," she said. "I know I'll never be an opera star, but am I truly awful?"

I nodded. I tried to keep a straight face, but thinking about how clueless she was as to the sound of her own voice resulted in me laughing harder and longer than I ever should have. "Sorry, but I'd rather chew glass."

"I wouldn't want you to do that," she said. "Do you feel any better?"

"No," I said, shaking my head. "I know you were hoping otherwise, but I'm too tired to cry anymore, too tired to sleep, and-" I stopped midsentence and winced. I held my right arm up in the air and flexed the hand a few times. "And my arm is killing me."

She took my arm as she had so many times before and massaged the burns. "It's probably stress. Your wounds have been so much better the last few days."

"The burns aren't the worst of it." My voice trailed off. I knew what I wanted to say, but I could barely think it, let alone put those thoughts to words. No matter how painful something was inside my head, it always seemed as if once it was given breath, it would take on life and grow into some hideous monster that would never stop trying to devour me.

Alexandra, however, was undoubted by my demons. "What's the worst of it?"

I paused, trying to find a way to sum up what this evening had done to me. Before I answered, Klara came running into the dugout, panting.

"Are you okay?" she asked. "I was searching for you everywhere. The Major said you looked like death."

"She's fine," Alexandra said without even a glance in her direction. "You can tell the Major I'm with her." When Klara didn't leave, Alexandra turned to her and put a bite to her tone. "That was an order, comrade Rudneva, not a suggestion. Leave us."

Klara shook her head and stepped toward me. "She's my pilot," she said. "I want to hear it from her."

I was touched at her concern and stubbornness, but keeping Alexandra entertained was exhausting enough. I didn't need more company. "I'm okay, Klara. Catch up with me in the morning, yes?"

"Okay," she replied. "If you need anything, anything at all, let me know. I'll look in on you later."

Klara left, but not before giving a silent snarl to the back of Alexandra's head. I sighed, wishing I could understand whatever rivalry they had going on enough to put an end to it. "I wish you two wouldn't fight."

"I wish she'd remember her place," she said. "But enough of that. You were saying?"

"About what?"

"The worst of it."

I rolled over and pulled the blanket up to my chin. Up close, I studied the weave in the fabric, found some odd pleasure in watching the fibers twist around each other. It was all I needed to focus on to answer her question, to spit out the words and be detached from it all. "You were right," I said. "My prayers do fall on deaf ears, but it's not because God doesn't exist. It's because He hates me. I don't care if you think I'm stupid or crazy for believing such things. It's true."

"No, it's not. You are far too wonderful of a person to be hated."

"You barely know me."

"And yet I've already seen how amazing you are."

I sighed. "Then tell me why my prayers go unanswered. Why am I ignored by someone who's supposed to love everyone?"

"Growing up, my parents ignored me," she said, her voice quieting. Her touch became as distant as the new look in her eyes. "I don't think there's anything worse than not feeling loved by those who are supposed to care for you. Maybe that's why I cling to you so. I wish I could change that for both of us, but I can't. All I can do is promise to never ignore you."

I squeezed her hand, grateful that she could be vulnerable with me, but if she discovered I was a thief, I was certain she'd tell me what I'd been telling myself: God doesn't listen to the wicked. He probably doesn't listen to those drowning in self-pity either.

"For what it's worth and if I remember my studies," she added, "even Christ felt abandoned at one point."

"I don't want to think about it anymore," I said. She was trying her best, but it wasn't helping. All she gave me in terms of an alternative to being ignored was to equate myself with Christ. I wasn't delusional. There was no grand scheme at play, no salvation of the world at stake. I was a silly girl who thought she could get the attention of the divine. Not only that, but I was a girl who also lied and stole.

Worst of all, I hated my enemies—I dreamed of killing them, even boasted about my first kill. Hardly the teachings of Christ, the man who forgave those who executed Him. When I thought about all of that, part of me felt lucky God was only ignoring me. Maybe that was His mercy toward me.

Or maybe I was fooling myself. Maybe I did believe things rooted in tradition and superstition. If there were no God, today didn't need explaining. It simply was.

Chapter Sixteen

THERE WAS A small service for Valeriia the following day at the end of the runway. I couldn't pay attention to any of it. I simply stood there thinking life was cruel and hoping she was in a better place. When we were dismissed, I somehow got back to my bunk and lost consciousness.

Sometime late that afternoon a pair of soldiers carrying PPSh-41s pulled me out of the dugout and brought me to the command post, barely giving me enough time to put my boots on. I didn't know what was going on. I only had the vague idea that Tamara was sending me up on a flight and was ordering me in for briefing. When I stepped inside, however, and saw Petrov leaning back in her chair with his feet kicked up on the desk and his pipe in his mouth, my heart raced faster than any dogfight I'd been in.

"I'm so glad you could make it, Junior Lieutenant," he said. "This doesn't have to take long."

I sat in the chair across from him. No one else was in the room save the two armed soldiers who had brought me in. As I felt my tongue stick to the roof of my mouth, I could think to ask only one question. "Is something the matter?"

Petrov snorted. "Many things are, Junior Lieutenant. First, the food here is terrible. Second, sleep has not come easily to me as of late, and third, while not a problem for me but you, the previous two points have left me in the mood to shoot first and ask questions later. But as I don't want to leave a mess in Major Kazarinova's office, I thought I'd at least give civility a try."

My throat tightened, and though I prayed that Tamara would return quickly, I asked my next question as casually as possible to hide my fear. "Where's the Major, anyway?"

Petrov took out a silver pocket watch from his coat and gave it a quick glance. "She'll be gone for at least another hour," he said. "So don't concern yourself with her. Instead, concern yourself with me and answering my questions truthfully."

"What sort of questions did you have?" I asked.

"Familial ones." He reached under the desk and pulled out a small candle in a squat iron holder, like the one my grandmother would use late at night while penning letters. He put it on the desk, and from his jacket pocket he took out a box of matches and lit the wick. "I know you think I'm an evil person," he said. "But I like to think we have the same goal."

"My only goal right now is shooting down Germans."

He smiled and tipped his head. "See? We are similar. We both want them dead. The difference is, I'm more passionate about the Motherland than you."

"What does that have to do with my family?"

"Everything," he replied, drawing deeply on his pipe. When he exhaled, he blew a perfect smoke ring and watched it rise to the ceiling before continuing. "I realize that not all Cossacks are treacherous, and not all of them fought with the White Army, but a great number did. They fought against progress and killed many of their Soviet brothers because they clung to a dying past. While I suspect your family was part of that, I'll give you a chance to show otherwise—or at the very least, prove your own loyalty."

"They've done nothing wrong."

"Good," he said. "Then you won't mind giving me names of those who have. I know we didn't punish everyone who fought against us in the Revolution. There are some that escaped. I want to know who and where they are."

My brow furrowed. "But I wasn't even alive when that took place."

"Come now, Nadya," he said, putting a sickening emphasis on my first name. "You Cossacks are a close-knit group. People would have talked. Help me, my dear comrade, and I'll see you are well praised—perhaps even receive a commendation from Stalin himself."

I smiled as best I could, despite my inner revulsion at the man's name. While he was wrong about us talking, Petrov was right overall. I did know names. Or more specifically, I knew a name: Father's. Worse, I abhorred how a small part of me admired how on target he was. Such accurate intuition was rare and something I'd wished I'd had on more than one occasion. "I'd help if I could, but we're from Tula and had nothing to do with any of that. We were vetted long ago."

The last part was true. We had been vetted, or at least our new identities had been. After the Revolution, Father had used what resources he had left to erase our past and give us a new one just before moving us to Tula. Bribery wasn't cheap, but the quality of papers we each got were so good that when investigators looked into me and the family just prior to my acceptance to flight school, I passed without question. That said, none of the investigators at the time had had a personal vendetta against me either.

Petrov set down his pipe and opened a drawer. From it he brought out an icepick with a wooden handle. He slowly rotated its tip in the candle flame. "Who helped you sabotage Valeriia's plane?"

"The hell I did!" I tried to jump out of my chair, but one of the soldiers kept me in place with an iron grip while the other kept his weapon trained on me. Petrov came around with the icepick, and I stared him down. "You can't do this."

"I can if I must," he said, studying me. "Let me ask you something, Nadya, do you believe Valeriia's death was an accident?"

"I hope so," I replied. "Only because the alternative is far worse."

Petrov nodded. "As do I. What if I told you it wasn't an accident? What then would you do?"

I'd never considered that to be the case, but for the moment, I entertained the possibility. "Valeriia was a wonderful pilot and twice that of a woman. I'd do anything to catch those responsible, and when I did, I'd take my time ripping them apart."

My answer, spoken without filter or hesitation, surprised me, but apparently it didn't surprise Petrov. "So you can imagine what it's like to lose friends and family to traitors."

"I can." I didn't like how much I was agreeing with the man, but there I was, and there was nothing I could do about it.

"This can still be a friendly encounter, Nadya," he said. "Help me find the turncoats. As much as I've gone after you, in my heart of hearts, I'd truly like to be wrong and find you an ally instead of an enemy."

I kept my eyes on him as I tried to judge his sincerity. I loathed that I thought he was telling the truth. That didn't make him insanely evil, simply misguided, albeit greatly. "As much as I believe you, you have a funny way of showing it."

"So you're saying you know nothing of Valeriia's death or others?"

I shook my head. "No. She ran out to her plane, tired, and crashed."

Petrov sighed. His face turned downcast, remorseful even. "Our country has been infected by conspirators for two decades now. A number of fine people I've personally known have been lost to them, and like any infection, the wound must be made sterile.

Sometimes that results in burning good tissue—and I admit, you are a skilled pilot—but a good doctor knows that sometimes the body must endure harsh treatments to ward off gangrene. So if you are loyal, consider this ordeal a sacrifice for the greater good."

Before I could reply, he grabbed my wrist and pressed the icepick into my forearm. I gritted my teeth as it seared my skin. My eyes watered, but I didn't scream, though I wanted to. I wasn't going to give him that satisfaction. A hate for the man grew in my soul, one worse than I had for any German, Rademacher included. Part of me grew jealous at the Luftwaffe pilot. Surely he didn't have to endure such scrutiny by his own officers. Then again, I'd heard Hitler and his upper echelon were as brutal as Stalin and his company. Maybe we were both suffering on opposite sides of the same coin.

My minor parallels with Rademacher were a fleeting distraction. Petrov was my real enemy, a coward that hid behind guns and position to terrorize his own people. As he burned my skin twice more, I knew one day I'd be his end, literally or figuratively. I hoped it would be the foremost, as the evil side of me delighted at the thought of putting him into the grave.

"Anything to say now?" he asked.

I shook my head and locked my jaw. Anything I said at this point would be so vile I was certain he'd kill me without a second thought. Still, if he was going to kill me, it would be nice to unload on him.

"I know you think you're being clever by not crying," he said, reheating the pick. "But only saboteurs and spies train to be so resilient. Do you think you could still fly if I put this in your eye?"

He brought the tip close to my face, and I tried to squirm out of the chair and break free. I even kicked at the man—pitifully, for he easily dodged it—and one of the guards hit me in the side with the butt of his gun.

Everything came to a crashing end as Tamara stormed in. The shock on her face was replaced with a mother bear's fury as she drew her sidearm. "What the hell are you doing?"

"My duty," Petrov replied, straightening. Though the two men guarding me appeared rattled, he was calm as ever. "All aspects of Valeriia's death need to be looked at, Major. It's only natural to question one of the last people who saw her alive."

Tamara kept her pistol raised. "You touch her again and I'll shoot you myself. From here on out, you stay away from my girls."

"Are you openly threatening me?" he said, visibly appalled at the idea. "I should have you brought up on charges."

"Try it and General Osipenko will exile you to a labor camp to die in disgrace."

"You would run to your lover for protection," he said with a snort. He motioned for the guards to follow him out, but before leaving, he stabbed the icepick into the desk.

Once he was gone, Tamara hurried over to me. I was still in shock at it all, but at least I could function again. Sadly, that also meant I could feel the burns he had inflicted as well.

"I really despise that man," she said, gently holding my arm and inspecting the damage. "I'll make sure he leaves you alone from here on out. I suppose the good news is he's good at his trade. These burns look painful, but I don't think they're serious."

"On my life, I had nothing to do with Valeriia's death. You have to believe me," I said, my voice cracking and my body shaking. It was then that it dawned on me how close to dying I'd gotten.

Tamara sighed heavily. "I believe you," she said. "But I don't know how the brass will take her loss, or worse, how Stalin will. She was a heroine of the Soviet Union. I'm afraid her death will have dire repercussions for us all."

Chapter Seventeen

THE NEXT TWO days were filled with interviews into Valeriia's crash. People who were both internal and external to our regiment came to poke their noses around. I told what I saw to Tamara three times, and to the investigators command sent four more after that. I wanted to fly, hoping even a mundane escort would give me some respite, but since I was one of the last to see Valeriia alive, I was temporarily grounded and forced to relive the ordeal over and over and over again.

No matter how many times I told my story with excruciating details that ranged from her bright smile to inspiring attitude, no one was ever satisfied with what I had to say, most of all me. Part of me felt recounting it time and again was more painful than Petrov's interrogation the other day. He only wounded my skin. These stories wounded my heart. Thankfully, the Commissar was nowhere to be seen during that time. I wish I had thanked Tamara for that, but once the interviews were done, I barely saw or spoke to her.

In the end, the official report was that Valeriia died in battle in order to preserve her fame and the honor of the 586th, but we all knew the truth. She'd climbed into the plane and taken off before her eyes had adjusted to the dark and crashed. That said, I wanted the world to believe the lie. She didn't deserve to be killed in such a stupid manner.

Over the next week, I flew a half-dozen times. Alexandra and I went on four quiet escorts and a pair of uneventful patrols to the northeast. I'd hoped being back in the air would help me cope, but each time we went up, all I could think about was how there were now three girls who would never fly with us again. I did think about Rademacher a few times, but the zeal I once had at the thought of shooting him down was never a part of those thoughts. In fact, I even wondered what good shooting him down would do since it wouldn't change anything. I laughed at myself when that thought occurred, seeing how up until now I had wanted nothing more than to blow him apart.

We also got our bounty pay. I wasn't sure what Alexandra did with hers. I didn't think she cared about it as I came to find out she came from a well-connected family. I stuffed my earnings in my sack under my bed. I didn't have the energy to go into town and find something for Klara, though it was on my to-do list. I also wanted to send a portion back to my parents since they could probably have used it more than me.

I woke one cold morning to a right arm that felt as if it had been caught in the rusty jaws of an old bear trap. I whimpered and tucked the arm across my side, but it didn't help. I tried flexing the hand a few times under the covers. The pain almost became manageable, but when haunting memories of both Valeriia and Martyona came back to me, I injected another shot of morphine into my side.

I put the leather case with my last syrette under my bed. I thought it might be empty, but I hoped I could squeeze out another drop or two if needed. I knew it would take time for the morphine to work its magic, so I decided to get dressed and drag myself outside. My stiff legs protested every movement, but I needed to keep my mind occupied on something—*anything*—else for the time being.

A faint glow crested the horizon, and I stopped to appreciate the sunrise. I hadn't seen it for four days and had partly forgotten what it looked like, a side effect of ramping up my morphine dose. I should have cared about losing some of my short-term memory, but I figured it was a small price to pay to be free of physical and emotional torment.

"Nadya?"

I turned to find Klara fast approaching with a heavy coat pulled tight around her and a bag of tools in hand. Both her face and voice were filled with equal parts shock and concern. "What's wrong?"

"Are you flying today?" she asked.

"I can't remember," I said, scouring my brain for the answer. The morphine must have kicked in sooner and stronger than I'd anticipated, and I grew fearful for what that meant for the rest of the day. "Did Kazarinova say something?"

"No, but then again, she hasn't said much to anyone," she replied. "Doesn't matter though. She's not going to be around much longer."

"Why?"

"Zhenia has been calling for Kazarinova's head," Klara said. "If she doesn't get it in the figurative sense, I dare say she'll take it on her own literally. How could you not know this?"

I shrugged. "The last few days have been a blur."

Klara closed the distance between us. She dropped her bag and brushed back my hair as she studied my face. "You've lost weight. I can't believe I didn't notice before."

I touched my cheeks. They'd thinned. "Probably. I haven't gone to the mess hall lately."

Her brow furrowed. Her tone became sharp, almost scolding. "No one made you go?"

"Alexandra brought me some bread a few times. I took some nibbles to appease her, but I haven't been hungry."

"Of course she did." Klara snorted. "Have you met any of the boys yet?"

I cocked my head and raised an eyebrow. "What boys?"

"Wow. You have been out of it. We've added a third squadron. This one is full of men."

Now that I thought about it, I had seen a number of boys around the base but hadn't put much to it. There'd been talk before about them coming, but I'd always assumed it was gossip. Why would they mix the regiment? Most of the boys didn't want to be flying with us girls anyway, and we didn't need to have them around to show us how to do things.

I wanted our unit to be only us, sisters who'd proven themselves as capable as any other. I hated the idea that some would think we needed the men for whatever stupid reason they'd dream up. Besides, they'd be a distraction, and I assumed my mechanic had already fallen for one by the nervousness in her voice. "You found one you like?"

"I'm not looking at them. Besides, love is so cruel you could even fall in love with a goat," she said. "Anyway, taking care of you is enough for me, but I guess I haven't been doing a good job of that. You look like hell."

It was so tiring to keep up the façade, and I almost told her about my pains, the morphine, and how I was barely functioning, but I feared I'd lose her too if I did. "Valeriia's loss did me in," I said, opting for a semi-confession. "I'm not sure how to snap out of it."

Klara took my arm, and we walked in silence for a few minutes. Eventually, we found our way to my plane. She rested her head against my shoulder and said, "Do you know the history behind your fighter?"

"No, other than it's mine."

"Not quite what I meant," she replied. "When it first entered the war, it was an unproven design. We had no idea how well it would match up against the German Messerschmitts. Brass and the politicians boasted it would dominate the skies, and the pilots ate it up, but deep down, we all knew that until it saw combat, there was always a measure of uncertainty."

"And now it's proven and has a new paintjob."

"It's more than proven. It's been shot up, banged up, and overworked. Despite all of that, it still flies and even made a kill. Do you know why that is?"

"Because I have the best mechanic in the world."

She squeezed me with a wishful sigh. "I hope you always will," she said. "But listen, Nadya, no matter the damage, it can always be put back together. It takes time, and sweat, and others helping sometimes, but it can be done. Whatever the war throws at it, it can be made to fly again."

Her analogy wasn't lost on me. "I'm not a plane. You can't stick a wrench to me and fix everything. If you could, I'd have begged you to do it long ago."

"I can help when you stop going at whatever is bothering you alone," she said. "Or you can decide to tell the Major you'd rather stay on the ground. If you do, you'll be like any other plane that sits neglected. Winter's chill will freeze you in place, burst your hoses, crack your block, and then you'll be ruined. And the worst of it is you're the one who will do that to yourself."

I chewed on her words while admiring her artwork on my fighter. There was extra detail in the tusks I hadn't noticed before, hints of shading and texture that rivaled any other. "You love this plane," I said. "It shows with the paint job alone."

"I care more about its pilot," she said. "I'm afraid if you don't pull together soon, that's going to be it. No one will give you another chance, not with so many other girls out there wanting to be pilots."

"I know. I know," I said, hanging my head in shame. "But-"

"Enough!" I jumped at the ferocity of her words, and she didn't ease off one bit as she went on. "Do you think Martyona or Valeriia would want you to wallow forever in misery? Both of them would tell you to act like the pilot you are, to be proud of who you are. Don't dishonor their memory by making excuses. Do whatever you have to do so you can get back in that damn cockpit and fly like you used to."

Her rebuke stirred my heart. My posture straightened. Determination rooted in my soul. God might not exist, might not care one bit for me or help me when I needed it the most, but Klara did on all accounts, and that was enough for me.

"Thank you," I said, hugging her tight. "For everything. You're right."

"Anytime. What do you plan on doing?"

"First, I'm going to get some food and then get cleaned up. Once I'm done, I'm going to find Gerhard Rademacher and blow him out of the sky."

"I'm glad to see you again, Little Boar."

As was I. Funny how a few simple words could make or break a person. We made chitchat for a while. Klara talked about how she wanted a bakery when the war was over but didn't think she had the money to start one. It was too bad that a person's passion could be limited by practical considerations like monies. When I got the bounty from Rademacher's kill, maybe I'd keep some tucked away and invest in her dream.

The conversation halted when Zhenia came over, looking as if she bore the weight of the world's troubles on her shoulders.

"What's wrong?" I asked, dreading the next words out of my squadron commander's mouth would be news of another death.

"As of ten minutes ago, the 586th has a new commanding officer," Zhenia said. "Kazarinova is gone, and Major Aleksandr Gridnev is taking charge. They aren't saying where she went, only that she's never returning."

Unease grew in my stomach. I'd never heard of Major Gridnev before, and though he was male, I was certain that fact wasn't what was troubling Zhenia. "You look as if that is bad news," I said. "I thought you wanted the Major gone."

"I'm furious she's not being brought up on charges for gross incompetence, but General Osipenko is keeping his lover safe," she replied, popping her knuckles one at a time. "But that's not why I'm here. Gridnev is calling a general formation at the top of the hour to address all the squadrons. After that, Nadya, he wants to talk to you."

Sweat gripped my palms, and my arms ached. "What for?"

"I wanted you to hear it from me first, but you're being pulled from the roster. I'm sorry."

* * *

For about fifteen minutes, the entire 586th regiment stood in formation outside the command post and listened to Major Aleksandr Gridnev introduce himself. I stood in the back, so I didn't get a good look at him, which was just as well. After what Zhenia had said, I was so irate I think my tongue would've come loose the moment he and I made eye contact.

Gridnev explained that he'd been transferred from the 82nd Fighter Aviation Regiment, and though he'd commanded them for some time, he looked forward to working with all of us. All of the girls except for myself were both attentive and pleasant. I, on the other hand, was plotting all the nasty things I'd say—and do—when he finally told me my wings were clipped. I also was trying to figure out how long I'd be in the box afterward. My best guess was four weeks. Five tops.

Though I missed most of his speech, I did catch his answers to two direct questions. The first of his answers was the 586th would be moving to the front lines when he felt satisfied we were all ready. He indicated he'd like this to be sooner rather than later since the

Luftwaffe continued their relentless pounding of Stalingrad. The tractor factory in the city, a mini-stronghold for our forces, had recently weathered seven hundred attacks by dive bombers alone. His eagerness to see us in action energized the crowd, as most of the girls wanted to prove themselves in combat and had yet to do so. The second thing he told us was he was here to stay forever as Tamara had been transferred to the Air Defense Headquarters.

The girls were split on Tamara's reassignment. Some, like Zhenia, wished she'd be stripped of her rank and sent to a penal brigade. Others were much more forgiving. I think I was more in the latter group. While I did feel Tamara shouldn't have sent Valeriia up that night, I knew she was under immense pressure from brass and tried her best. Unfortunately, her best wasn't good enough. Maybe she should have quietly retired. I did wish I could've said goodbye to her. Not being able to felt as if she'd died since she'd vanished.

When it was over, Gridnev dismissed us all, and then had me follow him to the command post. To my surprise, he also had Alexandra join us as well. I figured that was probably a good thing. I might kill the man if we were alone when he said I was no longer a pilot.

"Sit, sit," he said, taking his seat behind Tamara's old desk.

I eased into one of two chairs across from him and studied my new adversary. He was taller than I was by a half-dozen centimeters. He looked solid under his olive jacket, which was as immaculate as I'd come to expect from any upper officer. His face was round with a jaw as strong as a Soviet winter. He wore a clean shave and short hair that had a touch of grey. He tried to look serious, but his brown eyes smiled like a newborn's.

He kept the desk neater than Tamara had, for there were only two things on it, the officer's hat he'd tossed there a moment ago and the picture of an intense-looking man with large eyes that stared into the distance with a face that hinted at being Flemish. He wore the uniform of a marshal. The dark coat with two rows of gilt buttons and large stars on the collar made his rank obvious. I felt like I should know the man, but I drew a blank. "Good morning, Major," I said, remembering to be polite. "Was he a friend of yours?"

Gridnev glanced at the picture. "Tukhachevsky? No, but he was of my father's."

I straightened in surprise. While I didn't know what he'd looked like, I knew the name. Everyone did. Mikhail Tukhachevsky was one of several high-ranking officers killed by Stalin's purging of the Red Army five years prior. "Why do you have his picture?" I asked, unable to come up with any guess of my own. "I'd think displaying such a . . . person would bring unwanted attention."

"I've already had unwanted attention, Junior Lieutenant," he said. "Twice, in fact. I keep his picture as a reminder of what this world can be like."

"Comrade major?"

"A place where friends can be enemies and enemies can be friends, and being a hero makes no difference in the end." He stopped, and I was certain he was going to say more on the matter, but didn't. "Enough of that. I'd like to discuss your flying."

"What about it, comrade major?" I asked, exchanging a brief glance with Alexandra.

"I've been going over your file," Gridnev said, pulling two folders from the drawer in his desk. "Hers as well."

Concern washed over Alexandra's face. Though she had her hands folded in her lap to appear professional, I could see her fidgeting with them. "Have we done something wrong?"

"Commissar Petrov seems to think so."

I swore. Gridnev arched an eyebrow and Alexandra gasped. "Apologies, comrade major," I said, even though I wasn't at all sorry. "Permission to speak freely on the matter?"

"For the moment."

"Commissar Petrov has had it out for me for months and is looking for any excuse to do me in. He's a liar and a loose cannon, doing far more harm than good. I'd also like to mention Major Kazarinova nearly shot him herself for his behavior."

"Those are serious remarks, Junior Lieutenant."

"It's all the truth," I said. "I don't know what he's told you, but I'm sure they're lies."

"Honestly, I don't care," he said. "About a week ago, all of the political commissars lost their command functions, which means all military decisions are back in the hands of military officers. Since I don't know Petrov from the ass end of a badger and I'm not fond of the NKVD, I don't care what he has to say, and I told him that. I also told him I intended to keep Major Kazarinova's order in place that he's not to bother any of you, or I'd send him away as well."

I could have kissed him right then and there. I almost did. "Thank you, comrade major. You won't regret it."

"None of that, however, addresses my original concerns regarding your flying," he replied. "Tell me what happened on your patrol on 30 September."

Alexandra and I exchanged confused looks. I was the first to speak. "Was the after-action report lacking?"

Gridnev pulled our statements out of the file and lined them up next to each other. "The two accounts were thorough, especially near the beginning where you both describe spotting and subsequently following an unidentified aircraft. Curious, don't you think, that you two say the exact same thing?"

"I'm not sure I follow," I replied.

"Don't insult my intelligence, Junior Lieutenant," he said, leaning forward with a grunt. "This never happened."

I mentally kicked myself for such a dumb mistake. We were too specific in the same details for the story to hold up under scrutiny. Tamara was likely as excited as we were that we brought down two Luftwaffe to have noticed. Despite being nailed to the wall, I refused to give up. Maybe I could salvage something. I didn't want to lie anymore, but I hoped I could redirect. "We brought down those planes. I wouldn't lie about that."

"I know. The recon flight that spotted the wreckage is in the final report. But you did lie about the aircraft you spotted prior to the fight."

"It was my idea," Alexandra said. "I wanted to head south. Our patrols were boring, and my little brother Viktor keeps writing, wanting to know how many Germans we shot down. I wanted to be able to write him back with exciting news."

Gridnev eyed us. The shine in his eyes disappeared, and his stare chilled me to the bone. "Is this accurate, Junior Lieutenant Buzina? That's a severe breach of responsibilities."

For a brief moment, I thought about letting Alexandra fall on the sword for me. I'm not sure why she volunteered to. Perhaps she thought she would only be reprimanded while I was facing much worse, but I couldn't let her do that. "It's not true," I replied. I put a hand on Alexandra as she started forward, I presume to argue. "She's trying to protect me. The truth is, I'm the one who had to prove myself. I gave the order to fly south as the patrols we were being sent on amounted to nothing during the day. I needed the kill."

"Still your wingman even while on the ground, eh?" he said. He leaned back in his chair, looking impressed. "What did you need the kill for? Pride?"

"To make a difference in the war," I said. That part was true, but it wasn't the entire truth. I sensed he might suspect such a thing, so I filled him in on the rest. "I was also afraid Kazarinova was looking to have me replaced once we returned. I didn't want my service to end in disgrace, and I figured if I had a kill under my belt, she'd reconsider."

"Why would she replace you?"

"On account of my burns," I said, showing him my palms. "She was afraid they'd interfere with my ability to function in the air."

Gridnev stuffed the reports back into the folder. "That's close to what I suspected," he said. "Major Kazarinova had mentioned them in your file, but I wanted to hear all of this from your mouth before I committed to any decision."

"So I'm losing my wings then?"

Before he could answer, Alexandra scooted forward and weighed in. "Comrade major, she's one of the best pilots here, even if she's not the easiest to manage. She'll be an ace before this war is over."

"Thank you, Junior Lieutenant. I've got a good enough picture of what she's like," he replied. "I've already decided-"

"No!" I said, jumping to my feet. My heart skipped a beat, and the room seemed to shrink all around us. "I'm sorry for the outburst, comrade major, but please reconsider."

"Sit down, Junior Lieutenant," he said. As soon as my butt hit the seat, he continued. "I'm not stripping you of your wings, but I'm not going to tolerate you losing your bearing either. I am your superior officer, and if you value your freedom and ability to fly, you will remember that."

My mouth hung open. My world had flipped so many times in the last hour I couldn't make sense of it all. "But Zhenia . . ."

"Would do well not to make assumptions based on a few scribbles to the roster sheet," he said.

I shrank back in the seat. "Oh thank goodness."

"Or me," he said.

"You too."

"Now then, I am moving you from the standard rotation," he said as Alexandra nudged me with her shoulder. "What I want is something special, top secret. Something I only feel comfortable enough giving to girls who do what you two did a couple of weeks ago."

"What is it?" I asked.

"We're going to make some deep strikes behind German lines," he said. "Command will have a fit if they find out what I'm proposing, as they'd say it's far too risky and this is a defensive regiment. But I'm of the opinion we need to do more than babysit bridges if Stalingrad is going to hold."

"Are we going to fly there then?" I asked.

"No. Luftwaffe have that area in their grasp, and I don't want to send you to your deaths," he said. He pointed to a few areas on the map west of us. "There are supply lines the Germans consider relatively safe. If we hit those a few times, they'll have no choice but to divert some of their airpower away from the city."

"Thereby helping our soldiers," I finished.

"Exactly. It also means you can't speak of this to anyone for now. You also have to volunteer. I will say this, however: if we're successful, there's a good chance we can bait Gerhard Rademacher out of Stalingrad. Kazarinova mentioned you wanted to avenge Martyona's loss, and I'd be happy to help make that happen."

Pride rose in my chest, and at the same time, I was astounded he thought I was skilled enough to be put on such daring missions. However, I didn't need any convincing. I didn't care where he wanted us to fly, how heavily defended the target was, or if we would even be expected to come back. If agreeing to his plans meant shooting down the man who killed Martyona, I was ready. "Tell us where to go, Major."

Chapter Eighteen

THE FOLLOWING DAY, Alexandra and I took off from Anisovka before sunrise and headed west toward Voronezh, a city built near the site where the Voronezh River dumped into the Don. It was also a city the Germans had taken three months prior on their march to Stalingrad. Reports of what enemy forces now occupied the area varied since the bulk had moved southwest, but Gridnev felt it was a prime location for our first hunt. Given all the uncertainty, I prayed it would be a fruitful one—a safe one—and then prayed again begging for an answer when I felt as if those prayers fell yet again on deaf ears.

We landed sixty kilometers east of the city on an old field serving as a secondary landing strip. All we had to guide us in were two small fires, one lit at each end of the field. Once we were on the ground, a truck pulled in between us and began refilling our fuel tanks. Two men worked the line between the truck and our planes while another stood guard. He wouldn't be able to do much with his rifle, but I suppose it was better than nothing.

Alexandra and I had been ordered to stay in our aircraft during the refueling before we left, and we were also on radio silence to help conceal our location. I didn't like not knowing how she was, so I popped the latches to the canopy, slid it back, and made the excuse I needed to see her for the sake of the mission.

It was a short trot to her plane, and I hopped up on the wing and knocked on her canopy. She jumped in fright, and I nearly fell off the plane laughing. Once she opened her cockpit, I tried to recompose myself as best I could. "Did you think I was the Baba Yaga come to steal you away?"

"Not funny," she said, soured. "I hate being this close to the front and not in the air. You should have at least warned me you were coming over."

"Wanted to make sure no fascists snuck up on you. Still up for this?"

Alexandra nodded. "Where you go, I go."

"Shouldn't be much longer. Glad you're okay."

"Are you okay? That's the real question," she said. "Your arm bothering you?"

I looked down and realized I had it tucked hard against my midsection. She knew me far too well for me to outright lie, but I didn't want her to worry. "It hurts, and it's so cold I feel like I'm only wearing a nightgown," I said. "It should be better once dawn comes and things warm up."

"We're almost done, comrade pilot," one of the soldiers called out. "I must insist you return to your plane."

Alexandra nodded toward my fighter. "Better go. If you say you can fly, I'm with you, but if not, let's scrub the mission. We can always go out again."

"I can fly. I promise." I hopped off her wing and returned to my plane. Climbing into the cockpit and strapping in, I wished my words had been true, but while the cold made my wounds worse, I'd noticed lately even when I was bundled and warm, the pain threatened to get the better of me. Only one thing helped.

I pulled a morphine syrette out of my pocket and turned it over a few times in my hand. I'd managed to snag another box the prior night, knowing I'd need more. Relief was but one tiny stick away. I didn't use the morphine prior to leaving Anisovka as the higher doses I was now taking ruined my night vision and muddled my thoughts. The former spelled a recipe for disaster when flying in the dark, and the latter could be dangerous as well, even more so when it came to navigation.

Now, however, I wondered how well I could fly if I couldn't use my arm whatsoever, which felt like a real possibility. I'd be leading Alexandra to her death. But returning without accomplishing our objective was not an option either. I could lose my wings and be branded a coward. I cursed and muttered to myself as I weighed the two options. The loathing I had for the position I was in was second only to my shame. How I wished I was stronger, and how I resented all the other girls who could fly without pain.

"So be it," I said, pulling the cap off the syrette. I checked to ensure the ground crews were still busy, pushed back my sleeve, and stuck myself in the arm. It wasn't an ideal spot, but it worked well enough. Better to be relaxed and have to concentrate more than paralyzed with pain.

Five minutes later, we were up in the air again, a couple hundred meters above the ground.

Alexandra sighed over the radio. "I'm glad that's over with. I hate being down there in the dark."

"I'll second that," I replied. "Turn to two-six-eight and maintain speed at four-fifty."

"Where you go, I go."

We flew on, and in the dark, I could barely see the Voronezh River pass beneath us. I wondered how many Germans heard us go by and prayed they couldn't spot us or radio others about us. It was silly to think we'd never be spotted, I knew, but I hoped it wouldn't be for some time, or better yet, well after we reached our target: lines of transport deep within German-held territory.

The sun crested the horizon. I welcomed the golden light and smiled. Now that we could see the snowy terrain, it was time to hunt. I hoped we'd stumble on a transport plane, as Gridnev had said they had reliable intel on recent lines of flight we might intercept this morning, but I would settle for a ground convoy as well. Either target would stir up the Luftwaffe. And if we kept hitting them deep in their lines, as Gridnev pointed out, they would be forced to pull some pilots from Stalingrad for defense, and with luck that would mean Gerhard Rademacher.

"Drop to five meters, maintain heading," I said, easing the plane down.

"Repeat. Five meters?"

I shook my head. "I meant fifty meters."

Alexandra obeyed, and I cursed under my breath. It hadn't been a slip of the tongue. For a moment, I thought it was not only flyable, but a good idea. I checked the clock, and tried to figure out where we were based on the maps I'd studied the night before. We were past Voronezh and well on our way to Kursk. It was almost a half-hour flight from one to the other at our speed, which meant we had five minutes left. No, fifteen, I corrected.

Fifteen?

My mind strained to bring back the exact time we took off from the airfield, but it came up blank. It had to be well before dawn. I didn't think there was any light. Or was it first breaking? A crushing headache took hold of me. I kept my right hand on the stick and used my left to massage my temples. I never should have upped my dose.

"Nadya," Alexandra said. "Did you see that convoy?"

I twisted in my seat. A two-lane road was a kilometer or so off to the right, flanked on either side by trees. I didn't see any trucks and assumed we passed them. "Negative. How many?"

"A dozen?" Alexandra said. "A couple of kilometers behind us by now."

Twelve trucks. A good score by any measure, but I wanted more. I wanted something flying, something noteworthy. Shooting up supplies paled to dropping a plane. Still, it was better than nothing, and we might not catch anything else before fuel levels forced us back.

"Okay, follow me in. We'll reassess after we tear them apart on the first pass."

"Let's do it."

I eagerly pulled the plane into a gentle climb and banked right. I spotted the convoy as I swung around and counted eight Opel trucks. They were the backbone of Germany's motor vehicles, four-wheeled speedy machines that weighed a couple thousand kilos. Most of the ones we spotted carried crates and equipment in the backs of their open flatbeds, while two others were covered—possibly carrying troops inside. Whatever they held didn't matter. They were all about to share the same grisly fate.

My zeal faded as I leveled the plane at three hundred meters, which was low enough to get a good angle on the trucks but high enough to avoid small arms. The hairs on my body raised when the last vehicle in the convoy entered my sights about a half kilometer away. My soul shrieked in horror when I mashed both triggers.

My twin machine guns pumped a steady stream of bullets into the convoy, while the 20mm ShVAK took large chunks out of everything it hit. The trucks swerved off both sides of the road, and one of them even caught fire. Soldiers jumped from one of the covered ones, and I adjusted my aim to shoot into their ranks. Bodies fell. As I zoomed by a moment later, I caught sight of the carnage in full detail. My stomach churned at the slaughter. They hadn't a chance. Though I was defending my homeland, I detested being a butcher.

I put my moral arguments to the side and banked left while dipping low so the trees shielded my movements from the surviving Germans. I checked the skies as well for enemy fighters, and thankfully, there were none. "Status?" I asked.

"South of their position, swinging around," Alexandra said. "We tore them apart. Good thing we caught them with their pants down."

My brow furrowed as I tried to understand what she was referring to. "Why?"

"Second Opel from the front had a 20mm anti-air in its bed," she said. "Not something I want pointed back at me."

"Or me," I said. "Or anyone else."

The last words slipped out of my mouth without much thought, but once they hung in the air, I chewed on them. I pictured it being placed at Stalingrad and shooting down countless numbers of our planes. I couldn't let that happen, even if it meant a dangerous gamble to our own life and limb. "Set up for another pass," I said. "We're not letting that thing stay intact."

"It's one 20mm," Alexandra protested. "It's not going to tip the war."

In the back of my mind, I knew she was right. Regardless, we had to take it out. There was a reason we had to. Briefing, was it? God, that headache was back, and it was too hard to think. I traded my thoughts for action. "Where I go, you go, right?"

Alexandra sighed. "Always. If it starts shooting at us, it's not going to be pretty."

"I know," I said. "Come from the south. I'll hit them from the north. Whoever they target, takes evasive action while the other blows it apart. They can't possibly hit us both, right?"

"Copy," she said, still sounding less than pleased. "Starting my run now."

I popped my plane up to five hundred meters and brought it around for another strafing run. At first, it was hard to pick out which truck had the AA gun. My eyes had trouble focusing on everything that far away. I rubbed them with my left hand, and as soon as I did, tracers zipped in my direction. It took me a moment to realize what that meant and half as long to respond.

"Taking fire," I said, turning sharply. I cut across the road and then rolled back in the direction I'd been traveling. I didn't want them to lose sight on me, only their aim.

Time crawled. Streaks of fire stretched through the air and missed my plane by a dozen meters. Half dozen. Hit.

My ears rang, and I felt a concussive blast across my body. The air smelled of gunpowder. The wind howled in my cockpit. I dove the plane to the ground, ducking it out of sight of the Germans.

"Nailed him!" Alexandra screamed over the radio, her voice giddy. "It won't even be fit for scrap!"

"Some of my gauges are toast," I said, staring at the several large pieces of shrapnel sticking out of the console. At least I could still read the oil pressure and temp. They looked right, and the blood covering them was barely noticeable.

My vision dimmed, and I felt woozy. "Oh God," I said. "I'm bleeding."

"Where?" Alexandra said, sliding her fighter next to mine. A cubit wouldn't have fit between our wingtips. "Damn it, Nadya, answer me."

"I don't know," I said, trying to keep it together. I prayed I'd remain composed enough not to crash, but I could feel myself coming unglued. Everything I touched had blood on it. My pants. The stick. The throttle. I breathed deeply, but it didn't help. "Blood is everywhere."

"Okay, okay," she replied. I knew she was trying to sound calm. She was anything but. "Where does it hurt?"

Such a simple way of finding an injury, but I couldn't feel anything other than my heart pounding against my chest. Endorphins must have kicked in, preventing me from feeling the wound. Maybe the morphine had something to do with it as well. Regardless, it had to be severe. "My arm hurts," I said. "But that's normal."

Alexandra banked left when I accidentally drifted toward her. She swung back when I stabilized my flight, though kept more distance. "You're going to make it. We're what, an hour away? I can tell you about my barn incident on the way."

"I don't think I want to know," I said with a nervous chuckle. "What happened?"

"First boyfriend—well, serious one—and the first time we really ravished one another. We snuck in to a barn late at night, and in the midst of flying clothes and fumbling kisses, I tipped the lantern and started a fire. Barely got my clothes before the whole thing went up in flames."

"Could we not talk about a raging inferno?" I said, cringing.

Alexandra cursed. "Sorry. Forget I said that. We'll be back home nibbling chocolate and sipping wine before you know it."

"Except you don't have either."

"Stop spoiling my fantasy, you dullard," she said with a laugh. "I'm trying to help. Think of something pleasant instead of being so argumentative."

So I did. I thought about riding horses back home, singing for my grandmother, and being read to by Father when I was five. Sadly, those thoughts all led to the same thing. I'd never see my family again.

My eyes locked on the clock that sat to the bottom left of the console. I found the second hand's ticking hypnotic. Klara's words about finding beauty in moments of angst came back, and so I tried to look at everything in a new light. The sky was a gorgeous blue and reminded me of pure water from mountain lakes. The howling coming from the hole in my cockpit sounded like how Grandfather would blow across a jug when I was young.

The blood still rattled me. I ran my hand over my head, and cringed at the stickiness it left behind. Frustrated, I looked at my palm, and that's when I noticed the gash in my glove. Blood seeped from the hole, and I peeled back the leather to get a better view.

"God, I'm such a fool," I said, laughing so hard Alexandra had to pull her plane away when I knocked the controls.

"What?"

"Shrapnel cut my hand. Nothing bad, but it's messy."

"You're kidding."

"Not one bit. Half dozen stitches at the most."

Despite the minor injury, I hit the side of my canopy, disgusted at what it represented. I'd been incredibly lucky, and had I been flying better, clearer, I could've avoided the hit altogether. God, this morphine road was not one I wanted to walk down any further, but the pain from my wounds wouldn't simply go away either. Though I didn't have an answer for the latter, I hastily pulled out the syrette and threw it out the hole the AA gun had made in my cockpit. I even spit after it for good measure. I'd find a way to cope, I prayed, for my wingman's life if not my own.

We flew the rest of the flight without incident, sticking low and fast to the ground. I was certain when we landed Major Gridnev would be glad with our efforts. It turned out glad was an understatement. Once we were debriefed, he was thrilled. He did, however, make me promise two things before leaving. First, to get my hand looked at, and second, to never get shot up again. A 20mm shell through the cockpit was too close of a call for him, especially as it was his first official day as the commanding officer, and we were flying missions brass hadn't a clue about.

At Doctor Burak's office, my hand needed nine stitches. He tried to make small talk with me, even tried a couple of not-so-subtle passes. I paid half attention to him as he worked. My mind was thinking about the hit I took.

How was I still alive? Had the shot been a little lower, it would have taken off my leg. A little higher and rearward and it would have ripped through my chest. And why did the shell explode mostly on the outside of the plane? They had fuses that were designed to penetrate an aircraft a certain amount before detonating. Had the shell exploded inside, I might as well have had a grenade in my lap.

I left the doctor's office and wondered if God was looking out for me after all. Grandmother would have said so, always did. If He was, why hadn't He looked after Martyona or Valeriia? Were they worse than me? On the other hand, maybe He was toying with me, flaunting His power and showing He could save me or end me on a whim. Or maybe it was a wakeup call about my drug use. Who the hell knew?

I rubbed my temples, worried at how little sense my train of thought had. The morphine was still in my system and felt stronger than before. I had to be peaking. I couldn't feel any pain from my burns, and if I could think better, maybe I could work all this out.

My head cleared by lunch, and I realized how unfit to fly I was on the drug. I came to this conclusion when it dawned on me Alexandra had given most of the debriefing—thankfully—and I was barely able to remember the general order of events, let alone specific details.

Anger at endangering my wingman's life in such a careless fashion reignited in my soul. Preserving my self-worth as a pilot wasn't worth losing anyone over, especially such a dear friend. I could tough it out. I could fly. I had to. I'd find a way to manage my burns and bring down Rademacher.

That anger turned into self-loathing when I thought about the German and how I was sure he'd never stoop to using drugs as a way to cope. He had me there, sadly, a far more strong-willed individual than I proved to be, yet another trait of his I was envious of. But at least I was determined to quit. I had that going. And at least my family would never know. God, that would send both parents to an early grave out of shame if they ever found out.

My determination to stop the morphine did lift my mood, and I napped through the afternoon. I skipped supper when I briefly rose, deciding I was so tired I could easily sleep until morning. Sometime around midnight, I was torn from sleep by thunder in the skies and lighting coursing through my hand. It felt like I was being stabbed over and over, and for five minutes I lay in bed, gritting my teeth, sweating profusely as I promised myself I'd endure at all costs. I even prayed for strength.

At some point, I had a syrette in hand and wanted to use it more than ever. Alexandra stirred, giving me a jolt and a panicked escape from my desires. I was too afraid to get out of bed and rummage for my box for fear of getting caught, so I cautiously slipped the syrette into a hole in the mattress. I promised myself I'd destroy it and the rest later. As I finally fell back asleep, I prayed I'd have the resolve to do so when the time came.

Chapter Nineteen

THE NEXT MORNING I woke, unsure what the day would bring. I wasn't scheduled for patrols since my fighter was so torn up that Klara would need a day or so to patch the damage and clean out the cockpit. Or so I assumed. I hadn't seen her since I'd returned. All that changed when I left the mess hall after a hearty breakfast of stale bread, bland cheese, and frigid water, and bumped into her on the airfield.

"What the hell is the matter with you?" she said. Her eyes held a fire I'd never seen before, and she toyed with the wrench in her hand as if she wanted to brain someone with it.

"What are you talking about?"

"You come back with a hole blown through the cockpit, your blood everywhere, and you can't even bother to tell me you're all right?"

A pit of guilt took home in my stomach. God, how had I forgotten? The Divine didn't have to respond for me to know the answer: morphine. "I'm so sorry," I said. I stepped closer in an effort to diffuse her anger, and she shied away. "I don't know what to say. We came back, and I wasn't thinking-"

"That's just it, Nadya, you weren't thinking. Damn it, I already had to clean one body up. You could've at least checked in with me when you returned instead of giving me a damn heart attack when I got to your plane."

"One body?" I barely got the words out, and I wondered if forgetting most of yesterday was a blessing or a curse. "Who?"

Klara grunted, and she looked at me with equal parts incredulity and concern. "The mail plane crashed yesterday," she said. "I helped pick up pieces of the pilot. After that, when I got done washing, I found the inside of your fighter."

Her face paled, and her eyes looked distant. The memory, fresh as ever, tormented her. My words, however, were anything but understanding and the moment I spoke them, I wished I could've taken them back. "You should've asked Alexandra."

"I talked to her only as long as I could stomach her," she said. "She told me you were in the dugout, and I went there to find you sleeping. That's how little you think of me, is it? You'd rather take a nap than let me know you didn't get your leg blown off."

As bad as I felt about giving Klara the shock of her life, her ill words toward my wingman took me off the defensive. "I wouldn't let her talk about you like that, and I won't let you do the same. Mind your place and remember she's an officer, and you are not. And for that matter, so am I."

"Of course," she said, giving a half-hearted curtsy. She tried to sound tough, but the waver in her voice and tears in her eyes shattered her façade. "You're just like her, aren't you? Looking down at us lowly folk, only bothering to speak when it suits your fancy."

I groaned in frustration. What I had hoped was going to be a simple day had turned into anything but. I felt like wrapping my fingers around her thin neck and throttling her. My hand ached, and I could tell it wouldn't be long before it became bothersome. "Go away, Klara, before I say something I'll regret."

"Gladly. I'm tired of you playing games with my head," she said. She turned her back on me and walked off, and as she did, I heard her mutter one last thing. "Stupid, stingy Cossack."

I grabbed her by the shoulder and spun her around. The momentum generated whipped her wrench through the air, and it connected with the side of my head. I crumpled to the ground, my world a mess of shapeless colors and a high-pitched ringing.

Slowly, everything took form. Klara was kneeling over me, eyes wide with terror, patting my face. "It was an accident I swear," she said. She looked up for a second and the color drained from her face. "You have to believe me."

In a quiet pond, devils dwell. I gave that proverb life when I grabbed her by the back of the head, pulled her in, and kissed her.

Chapter Twenty

KLARA'S LIPS WERE exactly what I expected the winter goddess Morena's would be like, soft as down and as cold as a Siberian winter. Klara put a tentative hand on my shoulder. While we were pressed together, I could feel her hold her breath for a few heart beats before pushing away.

"Why did you do that?" she said, her face pale and voice weak. She traced the edge of her mouth with her finger, and her eyes glazed. "It's not what I wanted."

I took to my feet, probing my head where she clobbered me. I winced, and my hand came back covered in blood. "I don't know," I said. "Seemed funny at the time. Better than hitting you back, don't you think?"

She stepped away. "Are you crazy? It wasn't funny, and I don't want attention."

"Klara, to the box! Nadya, with me right now!"

I spun around, which caused me to stumble on account of dizziness. Gridnev marched toward us with a couple of armed soldiers. He moved like a dark storm carrying the fury of the sea. I put myself between them and Klara. "I'm fine, Major," I said. "It was an accident."

"Step aside and come with me now, Junior Lieutenant," he said. "This isn't a polite suggestion."

I hesitated. I didn't want to leave Klara to the wolves. Gridnev opened his mouth to say something else, something I guessed would make things a thousand times worse, and I capitulated. "Yes, comrade major," I said. My shoulders slumped and I moved to the side. "Where are we going?"

"Command post."

I fell in step behind him when he spun around and left. The two guards rushed by and took Klara into custody. As they led her away, she silently pleaded with me to save her. I prayed I could. Striking an officer was serious, and kissing one—of the same sex no less—was probably as much so. The 20s were friendly to such relationships, relatively speaking, but under Stalin, persecution had been common up until the war. Now the consequence of such behavior was a gamble, largely depending on who saw it and what their attitudes were. I had no idea where the Major stood on the matter.

We entered the command post and from a corner drawer, Gridnev grabbed and threw a cotton rag at me. "Keep pressure on it."

"Should I see the doctor about it, comrade major?" I asked while doing as told.

"You tell me," he said. "You said you were fine."

The side of my head warmed, and I wondered how much it was going to affect a chance at a good night's rest. However, I wanted the injury to be seen as lightly as possible for Klara's sake. "It can wait, I think," I replied. "But maybe if I have some time after we're done here I'll still have him take a look."

"Fine," he said, plopping down behind his desk. He didn't ask me to sit, which I took to be a bad omen. "What the hell was that about?"

"She was upset I didn't let her know I was okay after coming back yesterday," I explained, trying my best to find a way to put the entire encounter in a positive light. I was navigating tricky waters here, I knew. "She left and I grabbed her to finish the conversation. When I spun her around, the wrench went flying and found my face."

Gridnev crossed his arms over his chest and frowned. "So she was insubordinate."

I shook my head, even though I'm certain we both knew he was right. "She was hurt."

"And she lost her bearing, Junior Lieutenant," he said. "We have rules and order for a reason. Or do you disagree?"

"No, comrade major," I said. "I don't disagree. People do things when they are scared and worried that they wouldn't normally do."

"Box, nonetheless."

I shook my head and cursed under my breath. Though I knew he was aware of both, thankfully, he said nothing. "If I may ask, for how long?"

Gridnev chuckled. "A day. I'll tell her a week, and you'll not say otherwise. But the truth is, I can't lock up a mechanic for long and expect the regiment to be combat ready."

I relaxed. Hopefully that meant his anger was for show and this would blow over soon. "Is there anything else, comrade major?"

"You also need to address that kiss."

My hopes for a quick and easy dismissal were shattered. "I don't know what to say," I replied. "It was unplanned. I was a little dazed, and it seemed funny."

"Was it?"

Deep down, it wasn't funny. It was hysterical. I could barely hold a straight face thinking about the shock I gave her pulling her from violence to tenderness. But I couldn't say that and expect things to go well, so I lied. "No, comrade major."

"Are you two having any sort of relationship other than professional?"

I could feel my face contort in shock. "Of course not, comrade major," I said. "I've never even considered it."

"That's not an 'of course not' question," he said, leveling a finger at me. "I'm giving you a chance to come clean. If you are, I'll sweep it under the rug and transfer one of you to a different regiment since I'm more interested in killing Germans than I am anything else. If I find out you're lying later on, I'll have no choice other than to call in a commissar for an investigation. If you're engaged in immoral and deceitful behavior, who knows what else you're involved with. Do I make myself clear?"

I swallowed the lump in my throat. "Yes, comrade major. It was bad judgment on my end. Nothing more."

"You're damn right it was," he said. "From here on out, the two of you will not engage in anything that could be construed as fraternizing between an officer and an enlisted member. Understood?"

I nodded. What else could I do? "Of course, comrade major."

"You girls will be the death of me, I swear," he said, sighing. The tension left his voice, and he eased back in his chair. "Now then, on to strategic matters. I'm pleased with the results of your first deep strike. A few more of those and the Germans will have to pull fighters from Stalingrad to cover their rear. That'll give much needed relief to our fighters and bombers in the area, not to mention some hope for everyone on the ground."

"I'm eager to do my part."

"I want to put more pressure on the fascists," he said. "The 8th Army Air is down to two hundred planes. They've all but given the skies over Stalingrad to the Luftwaffe. While we still can't contest them, I'm not going to sit here and do nothing."

"Alexandra and I are up for more," I said. "But we're a pair of fighters. Our guns only do so much. Send some bombers with us, and you'll get the German's attention."

Gridnev's eyes lit up and his cheeks dimpled. "Precisely what I plan on doing, Nadya. I'm going to try and get some of the ground-attack regiments to assist us from here on out. So expect escort duty for the next few weeks."

"Looking forward to it, comrade major." I said. Though I replied in an even manner, internally I was thrilled at being assigned more strikes and scared at the dangerous nature of it all. Protecting bombers was a different beast than hunting on our own. If things went bad during the latter, our Yak-1s had a good chance to run. Bombers didn't have that luxury, and we had to stick with them no matter what. Of course, the added responsibility also meant Gridnev was confident in my abilities as a pilot. My soul beamed at that thought.

Gridnev dismissed me after a bit of small talk, and I decided to head to the infirmary to have my newest wound looked at. A dull ache radiated across a large part of my head, and I wanted to be sure Klara hadn't cracked my skull or chipped a cheek bone. Judging from the bloody rag in my hand, I knew I also needed stitches.

"Still getting yourself torn up, I see," Doctor Burak said as I entered the room. He had a stethoscope in hand and was listening to a freckled boy breathe—a pilot from Third Squadron I presumed. He gave me a passing glance before returning to his work. "Take a seat. I'll be with you shortly."

When his patient left and he finally got to me, it was apparent that his idea of shortly was not at all what mine was. I suspected it was his passive-aggressive attitude due to my previous rebuffs. "Is it broken?" I asked, sitting on a wooden stool and pointing to the side of my head.

Burak's fingers probed the wound. "No," he said, "but it does look like quite the lover's quarrel."

I sighed and shook my head. News had spread across the base faster than the blitzkrieg, and already I was irritated at the jabs. If they thought we were a real couple, those jabs would have turned vicious. "It was nothing like that."

"If you say," he replied. "I have no ill-will to those desiring uncommon relationships. I was, however, going to suggest you seek a tenderer companionship with someone else before something like this does you in."

My skin crawled, and I pulled away. "The only thing I'm looking for right now is a set of stitches so I'm not bleeding all over the place."

"We got off on the wrong foot earlier," he said. He was trying to sound friendly, but there was an underlying edge to his voice that showed he was more annoyed than anything else. "Why don't we start over tonight, Nadya? I'll have some decent food brought in. Maybe a bottle of wine, yes? We can relax and get to know each other."

I smirked at his absurd persistence. "I don't drink. Just stitch me up."

Burak grunted and went over to a row of new, green crates lined up on a nearby table. They had English words across them, in white, which I couldn't read, but the black caduceus on each one's front told me all I needed. The short staff with wings and intertwined serpents clearly labeled the crates as medical supplies. From one he pulled a dark bottle of iodine, some gauze, and a folded cloth pouch.

"We're low on anesthetics," he said, putting the iodine on the gauze. "This might hurt a little."

He cleaned the wound like he was scrubbing pots caked with grease. It hurt, but the pain was nothing compared to what I'd endured with my burns. In a way, I was glad they'd tormented me because they gave me the resolve not to flinch as he tended to my head. Still, I wasn't going to let his lie go unchallenged. "Looks like you have quite the supply right there from the Americans."

From the folded pouch he took a suturing needle, thread, and forceps. "I haven't catalogued it all," he said. "No telling how much or little we have. They sent some better rations, too. Not that it's for you, but I thought you should know."

A fire ignited in my soul. A trickle of perspiration ran down my back, and all I wanted to do was to drive him into the ground. I knew I couldn't do that, but I was through being treated like a dog. "What do you think Major Gridnev will say when I tell him you're neglecting your duties as a physician?"

"I don't think he'll respond kindly once I inform him the accusations come from a girl unfit to fly and who tried to change my mind about my recommendations with physical advances."

"Stitch me up and get it over with."

The needle burned as it pierced my skin time and again. With hard pulls, he drew the wound closed with the sutures. More than once my head jerked to the side with the tugs he made, but I didn't make a noise. I didn't even let my eyes water. I took all that pain and let it fuel my disgust for the man.

When he was done, I stood, looked him square in the eyes, and spoke with an even tone. "Next time you threaten me or decide to get cute, remember this: I've been shot at, blown apart, and set on fire by my enemies, and every day I still get in my plane and hunt them down. I'm not someone you can intimidate, and I'm not someone who won't fight back."

Doctor Burak's face reminded me of a child who had discovered what an angry bull looked like when its tail was pulled. The look was fleeting, and he turned stoic in a couple of heartbeats. "Are you threatening me?"

I narrowed my eyes. "I'm telling you who I am. Take it as you will."

I left feeling his glare on the back of my head. Outside, despite the icy October air biting my face and paining my burns, I smiled. I was proud I'd stood tall and was certain Father would've been too had he seen what had transpired. Actually, he would have broken the poor doctor in half had he been there. The thought of seeing

Father wrap his large hands around Burak's neck and wring the life out of him drew out a dark chuckle from deep inside me.

Chapter Twenty-One

THREE DAYS LATER and two hours before sunrise, I tossed in bed. I'd spent the majority of the night unable to sleep, replaying our mission briefing from the evening before over and over to distract myself from my ailments. Sweat covered my body. A phantom blade dug and twisted in my palm, and I wondered if amputation might be the only thing to ever bring me permanent relief. My stomach cramped, and my eyes lost focus for a moment. Had it been any worse, I'd have sworn my insides were ripping themselves apart. I'd never born a child before, but if it was anything close to what I was feeling, I wanted nothing to do with motherhood.

I could taste bile rising in my throat. Half-blind, I rolled out of bed and stumbled out of the dugout. Snow soaked my socks and numbed my toes. I pressed on, trying to get as far away from our sleeping quarters as possible before I wretched. I made it a few dozen meters before falling over. I caught myself on my hands and knees and then emptied my stomach. It didn't have much in it, as I hadn't had an appetite for the past two days.

For several tense moments, I stayed on all fours, panting and watching my breath crystalize in the air until the pain eased. The taste in my mouth was wretched. Off in the distance I heard Bri and that stupid mutt getting into another fight somewhere nearby, but didn't bother to look. At the sound of crunching footsteps in the snow fast approaching, I pushed myself up to my feet.

"Nadya, are you okay?"

I wiped my mouth on the back of my sleeve and turned to find Klara nearby, holding a bag of tools. This was the first real interaction we'd had since she'd clobbered me and was sent to the box. I wasn't sure how to act, so I looked at her in an awkward manner until I realized I should say something. "Upset stomach," I said. "I'll be fine."

"You'll catch your death out here, dressed in nothing," she said. She pulled off her leather coat and put it around my shoulders. "Are you sick? You look terrible."

I drew the coat around me, relishing the warmth it brought. I couldn't help but crack a smile at her last remark. I must have looked like a corpse for her to say such a thing, for the moon above was barely past the first quarter and didn't offer much light. I suspected had she been able to see me well, I'd have given her a heart attack. "I think it was something I ate," I lied. "Awful way to spend a birthday, huh?"

"It's your birthday?"

I feigned a deep hurt and clutched my chest. "How could you forget? I'm an old maid of twenty-one now."

"Because you never told me," she said. "Even if it was something you ate, you should let your weary bones rest, you hag. There's plenty of time to find a new pilot."

"I can fly. Honest, I feel better already." I hoped my performance was enough to get her moving. Though I knew I was having withdrawals from the morphine, I couldn't tell her. She'd have too many questions, too many concerns. She might even report me for stealing once she found out where I got the supply from. I'd go straight to the gallows if that happened.

"I still need to finish the prep on your plane," she said, taking me by the arm and leading me back toward the dugout. "Bundle up and I'll check on you in an hour when it's time to rise."

"How was the box?"

"Cold. Dark."

"That all?"

Klara stopped a few meters away from the dugout. Her gaze drifted off into the darkness, and she rubbed her arms for warmth. "About as comfy as my foxhole during night watch," she said. "But it was lonely, not that this is much better. I'm sorry for what I did, what I said. It was a bad day for me, and I snapped."

"No, I should apologize," I said. "I should've found you when I landed and let you know I was okay, but . . ."

She waited a moment after my voice trailed to prompt me. "But what?"

"But . . ." I sighed heavily, wishing I could tell her exactly why my thoughts were so muddled that day. "I was struggling with other things—not that you aren't dear to me—but they hit me more than I expected."

"What other things?"

"I can't tell you." When pain flashed in her eyes, I quickly added, "Not now at least. One day, I'd love to. Honest. Right now I'm asking—begging—for you to let this go."

Klara bit her lip and toyed with her hair for far longer than I would've ever liked. "Think you could at least tell me before the war is over?"

I laughed. "Yes. I'm sure I could by then." My shoulders fell with relief. "You have no idea how glad I am we could work this out without any more wrenches to the noggin."

"Me too," she replied. "But Gridnev said I'm not allowed to talk to you outside of duties anymore. I should be thankful, I guess. He should have stretched my neck or sent me to a penal brigade."

"He'll forget it all soon enough," I said. "His real concern was me smooching you. I told him I'd never to it again, and I want you to know I meant it. I didn't mean to put you off as I did."

Klara shifted her weight from one foot to the other and fidgeted with her hands. "Oh, I see," she said. "That's okay, I guess, but why did you?"

"Kiss you?" I shrugged and gave back her coat. "I told you. I thought it funny, but after a crack in the head I guess I wasn't thinking straight. Was it that awful?"

"No, it wasn't," she said, stumbling for words and then shaking her head with a huff. "Never mind. I don't even know how to get it out."

"Try," I said. I was trying my best to ignore the stabbing in my ice-cold feet, but God, how I wanted to get back inside and find some warmth. That said, I figured I should give Klara at least a chance to spit out what was gnawing on her mind.

"Not now," she replied. "Not here."

My curiosity died. "Okay, then I'm going to bed. I'm freezing."

Klara headed toward the airfield, and the moment I turned around, Petrov made an appearance. He was bundled in a quilted jacket with matching trousers. Despite the early hour, he didn't appear tired, making me wonder if the man ever slept, or needed it for that matter.

"Good morning, Junior Lieutenant," he said, stopping a few paces away. "You're up early."

"So are you," I replied. I didn't want to sound as if I was hiding behind Gridnev's and Tamara's orders, but I had to know why he was here. I didn't think his presence was a chance encounter. "What do you want with me? We both know you've been told to stay away."

"I like watching the night sky. Gorgeous, isn't it?" he said, sounding sincere. He pulled his pipe from one pocket and a yellow tin of Dunhill Royal Yacht tobacco from the other. As he went on, he packed the bowl and started to smoke. "I often wonder how many stars there are. Ever tried counting them?"

"No," I said. "I'm sure there are more up there than I can imagine."

Petrov chuckled. "Lots of things have to be left to the imagination, I suppose. But one thing doesn't."

"What's that?"

"What you're doing here. It's obvious you're sick as a dog. You ought to see the doctor before it gets worse."

I cringed as my stomach revolted once more. Though it was painful, I was glad I had enough self-control to keep from throwing up again. "I don't need to. I'll be fine."

"I suppose you will," he said. "All the same. It's probably good that you aren't bothering him as he's busy taking inventory. It seems he's misplaced a few items."

I was glad that the dark covered my reaction. "Perhaps he'll look after his stethoscope better."

Petrov motioned to the doctor's office with his pipe. "Oh he didn't lose that. He can't account for some medication."

Damn. Damn. Damn. My chest and the back of my neck warmed, and I stopped fidgeting with my hands the moment I noticed I was. "I'm sorry to hear that."

"I'm sure you are," he replied, amusement twinkling in his eyes. "If you happen to see anyone with morphine syrettes, be sure to bring them in."

"Of course, but I'd like to go back to bed. So if you'll excuse me, Commissar."

Petrov sidestepped and made a sweeping gesture with his hand. "As you were, Junior Lieutenant."

I hurried inside the dugout and darted into bed and under my blanket. The squeaks of mice let me know I was now sharing the space with the little fur balls. Over the last few weeks, I'd gotten used to having the extra company. They were still everywhere, despite the cold, and despite Zhenia's mouser (who was good at being one, but one cat a rodent genocide does not make). I lay there, staring at the dark above, tired, pained, shivering, and thinking about this morning's encounters with Klara and Petrov.

I was in no shape to fly, yet I had to. Not only because I didn't want to lose my wings, but I wanted to fight. I wanted to bring Gerhard Rademacher's plane down, and the only way that would happen is if I was well enough to get out of bed.

As I reached under the bed for a syrette, my hand went numb as if it were reaching into the deepest parts of the abyss. I was at a crossroad, and though the morphine beneath my bed promised the sweet allure of a pain-free life, it carried with it a price of isolation and fear. I'd already pulled far away from my friends, my God, my family, and I shuddered to think how much further I could go. Still, I couldn't rid myself of those awful syrettes. I needed help.

Before I could change my mind, I dressed as fast as I could, stuffed the box in my coat, and hurried out into the dark. I stumbled over the terrain as I ran to the airfield. My eyes watered, partly from the frigid air biting at them, but mostly because of the anxiety of wondering what Klara would say when I came clean and pleaded for help. I didn't have to wait long. I found her at my plane, loading ammunition belts into the machine guns.

"Something the matter?" she asked.

"Everything," I said. I fumbled inside my coat for the yellow box and shoved it into her hands. My eyes fixated on the ground, and my skin deadened as I forced myself to talk. "Take it. Destroy it. Just don't ask questions. And please don't tell anyone."

A deafening silence settled between us, and I thought I was about to go mad when she finally spoke. "Morphine? But . . . why?"

"For the pain," I said, my throat tightening. "I couldn't fly without it, and now I can't fly with it. Worse, I can't get rid of it."

"You're a common thief," she whispered. "Why would you steal from us?"

"I'm not." I wiped my nose and cleared my eyes. "No, I am. But the doctor demanded . . . favors for help, so I stole it instead."

"Damn jackass. I wish someone would bump him into a prop," she said with a snarl. "So is this what you were talking about struggling with before?"

I nodded.

"Is this all of it?"

I nodded again. When she didn't say anything, I dared to look up at her. Her eyes held a righteous fury to them, like the angels who've been given the authority to judge this fallen world. Her hand grabbed mine, and she pulled me around to the other side of the plane where the moonlight couldn't find us.

"I'm so mad at you I can barely think. I don't know if I should punch you for being dumb or kiss you for trusting me so," she whispered, stuffing the box inside her coat. "I'll get rid of it. But I swear, Nadya, you use or steal again, and that's it. I'll hand you over myself, so don't make me choose between you or the Motherland. There are no second chances."

My body relaxed, and I blew out a sigh. "Thank you. From the bottom-"

Before I could finish, Klara grabbed me by the back of the head and rested her forehead against mine. She hesitated before kissing me awkwardly on the cheek and letting me go. "I should get back to work," she whispered. "Get some sleep."

I didn't leave, but instead kept a grip on the small of her back. I wanted to melt into her embrace, find her lips with mine, and watch her eyes adore it all—I hoped. I almost did all of that, but these new desires were alien to me, at least toward Klara. I wasn't sure if I was simply elated at her continued acceptance of me or if my heart was longing for something more with her. I hoped the latter, but fear of the foremost drove me to leave. I told myself I'd sort all this out later. "If you insist. Wake me up in time for the sortie?"

"Of course."

She squeezed me tight before disengaging. I made my way back to the dugout with a stupid, happy smile on my face. The encounter had gone exceedingly better than I had ever anticipated, and I playfully scolded myself for not going to her for help sooner. Moreover, I wanted more with her, time, company . . . affection. Sadly the stupidity of both the war and my own country would interfere with most of it. My arm hurt, and my stomach cramped, but with my thoughts flowing around Klara, I drifted off to a sleep that rivaled any mother's embrace.

"Nadya! Wake up!"

I groaned, and batted away the hand shaking me.

"Nadya! We're flying in thirty minutes!"

I opened my eyes enough to make out Alexandra's blurred form looming over me. "I can get dressed in five," I said. I tried to pull the covers over my head, but she held them fast. "Please, let me rest a bit longer."

"Why? Are you dreaming of your lover girl?" she teased while jabbing my ribs with her fingers. "I bet if I kissed you the way you kissed her you'd get out of bed."

I sat up and hoped she could see my scowl in the dark. "It stopped being funny two days ago."

"I'd rather find it funny than sad, Nadya," she replied. "Has it been that long since a boy touched you that you have to run after girls? Did you forget what a boy is like?"

"No, and no." Resigned to the fact I would not be getting any more rest, I tossed on the rest of my clothes. "Keep it up and I'm dousing you with water next time you're asleep."

"Will you hold me close and warm me up?" she said, laughing. "I wonder if you kiss better than my fiancé. If so, maybe I'd become as depraved as you."

I groaned. "Shut it," I said. "I mean it. I'm tired of you teasing me about the biggest mistake of my life."

Somehow Alexandra found my boots and handed them over. "Okay, okay. Don't be so testy. But if you're lonely-"

"I mean it-"

"I'm being serious." She paused, I assumed so she could show she was no longer kidding, and then continued. "If you're lonely, my fiancé's brother is single. Good man, too. A professor. I bet we could arrange an introduction at my parents' home when the war is over. We can all play cards and drink wine, and you can see if you like him."

With stiff movements, I put my boots and jacket on, and grabbed my gloves from underneath the foot of my bed. "No thanks," I said. "All I want is to fly."

"Think about it," she said, following me out. "Then we could be family forever."

I stopped in my tracks and smiled at the thought. "We'll always be family."

We headed across the airfield and split to get in our fighters. I was amazed at the vigor in my steps. Apparently, a little solid rest and a numbing of the nerves did wonders for my spirits. I saw Klara near the tail of my plane, leaning against the fuselage, with a mournful look upon her moonlit face.

"It's ready," she said. "Are you feeling better?"

I stopped a couple of paces away. She sounded as if she was asking out of formality rather than genuine concern. "Much. I thought you were going to wake me up?"

"You don't need me. Alexandra had that covered."

"How-" I stopped myself from finishing that question, and after my stomach tightened, I forced myself to ask the next. "You heard us talking?"

Klara looked away. Her silence was all I needed.

"You're taking it wrong," I said.

"I'm not sure how to take being the biggest mistake of your life in a nice way."

I took her by the shoulders. "I only regret getting us in trouble. That kiss was supposed to be funny, and now it's become anything but. You were my first real friend here and still are. No one looks after me the same way you do. Not even Alexandra."

She eyed me suspiciously. "Would you kiss me again?"

"Only if it wouldn't land us both in the box or worse," I said. I gave a playful laugh. "I can't believe you even have to ask."

Klara's head dropped. She sighed with equal parts heartache and relief. "I'm sorry," she said. "I've been so paranoid about losing you. All the blood. The dying. The orders to leave you alone, and then I hear you make comments like that and don't know what to think."

"I'm not going anywhere," I said. "I have to come back to you safe, yes?"

That brightened her face. "Yes. Always."

"Then that's what I plan on doing." I stifled a yawn, and smacked myself a few times to wake up. "Tell you what, when I get back and the day is done, we can spend the night at the river, just you and me. If it goes well enough, we could make it a standing date."

"That's not right. It'll be considered fraternizing."

I shrugged. "I don't care what it will be considered. Besides, if we pull off this attack, Gridnev will be so elated he won't care one bit what we do. Trust me."

Klara pushed off the plane. Her eyes looked hopeful and scared to be so at the same time. "If you promise he won't care."

"I promise."

"Then come back to me safe, Nadya."

* * *

Seven of us zipped through the overcast sky, a dozen meters beneath the cloud layer. Gridnev flew lead and a girl named Tania from First Squadron flew on his wing. Alexandra and I cruised next to them about thirty meters away. I pictured myself as a modern version of my ancestors who rode into battle on horseback, courageous and strong. If only they could see me now, sailing through the air to drive off the invaders. I wondered if they'd be proud or jealous. Maybe both.

The four of us escorted a flight of three Pe-2s from the 150th High-Speed Bomber Regiment across the snowy landscape. That unit was led by Lieutenant Colonel Ivan Polbin who I'd heard was quite the commander. I'd also heard he enjoyed music and sang well, like me, which made me think we'd get along—even if he was a die-hard communist and loyal to Stalin.

The twin-engine Peshkas flew nearly as fast as our fighters, something I was grateful for. I'm certain the three crew members inside each bomber were thankful as well, since unlike the German Heinkels and Stukas, these planes were tough to catch for any aircraft. That being said, I was glad I was in my Yak-1. I wouldn't have wanted to fly one of those bombers at all, no matter how prestigious they were. They were still big targets, and far less nimble than the fighter I had. I prayed we'd keep them safe.

All the Pe-2s, however, did have fresh, winter paint jobs. Their off-white and tan colors hid them well in the surroundings, and if I wasn't paying close attention, I'd even lose sight of them from time to time. Their target was a rail depot the Germans were using to bring in supplies and troops headed to Stalingrad. Obliterating it would disrupt logistics and force the Luftwaffe to keep it safe once rebuilt.

With luck, the Germans wouldn't spot the Peshkas until the bombs were already dropping and they were headed home. I fantasized about how easy of a mission this could be as we went deeper into enemy lines. Those thoughts almost turned into dreams as the drone from my fighter's engine combined with the dreary sky nearly put me to sleep, despite the digging pain in my arm.

"Tighten up, Little Boar," Gridnev called out over the radio.

My eyes snapped to the formation. I'd drifted away from the bombers by a good fifty meters sideways and at least that in altitude. I glanced over my shoulder to see Alexandra off to my right. She'd stayed with me even as I wandered. "Reforming now. Thought I saw something below and wanted a better view."

It was a lie, but no one challenged me on it. I didn't want to admit I was overtired because my body was craving morphine. I checked the clock. It was about a quarter till seven. I tapped the glass face, trying to remember how much longer we had until we reached the target. I grunted with frustration when I couldn't figure it out and decided to make a routine check with the Major. "Confirm time to target?"

"Four minutes, thirty seconds."

I eased back in my seat. That seemed right. I slapped my cheek a few times to wake up. God, I needed more rest. My response on the controls was sluggish, and I probably couldn't navigate my way home to save my life. I feared I was going to be more of a danger to myself landing than any dogfight would be. I reminded myself that once I was clear of the withdrawals, sleep would come easier.

I scanned the sky and kept a constant vigil on the clock. Two minutes to target, I spied four dots in the sky, closing fast in a finger-four formation. Identifying the group was easy, even in my groggy state. "Luftwaffe Schwarm, three o'clock, six or seven kilometers out." I said.

"Attack on my order," Gridnev said. "Stay with our bombers."

We held our formation for the next half minute in tense silence. Then the lead bomber's pilot spoke on the radio. "We're starting our run. Doors open. One pass and we're gone."

"Nadya, Alexandra, engage the enemy fighters," Gridnev said. "Tania and I will be right behind."

"Going in," I said, peeling my fighter off to the right. Tension mounted in my chest and arms, not from nervousness, but eagerness. The pain in my burns even dulled under a sea of adrenaline. I wanted to prove myself again and be known as the girl with two kills now on her plane. Funny how such a boost to confidence and self-esteem came from what was a barbaric act—the death of another.

Our planes raced toward the Luftwaffe, and images of our two groups clashing violently with each other made me readjust my grip on the controls twice over. Since I was the lead plane, I should have been proud to lead the charge, but since I was out in front, what I really felt was exposed.

I changed the line of our attack by giving some rudder and angling my plane so it flew to the right of the German formation. This way, they'd have to make a choice to engage us or continue to chase our bombers. I didn't know which I'd prefer and never had the time to figure it out. One moment the 109s were still two kilometers away, and seemingly the next, I was shooting by, nearly scraping my wing tip against one of the Messers.

I pulled hard on the stick, rocketing my plane up through the sky. I shot through a cloud layer a couple hundred meters thick. When I broke through the top, I caught a glimpse of heaven. The sun shone like an angel and the cloud tops were as pure as any saint. Up there, there was no fighting, no war, no struggle for life and death. Paradise disappeared when my fighter plunged back toward Earth, and a frozen hell took its place.

Gridnev and Tania were each engaged in rolling scissors with two of the German fighters. A third Luftwaffe came at me from my right, guns blazing. I barely had enough time to snap roll out of his line of fire. I pulled hard on the stick, trying to force him to overshoot, but he went into a high-G yo-yo and barreled toward me again.

"Nadya, bank left," Alexandra called out. "I can clear him soon as you do."

I followed her order though I couldn't see where she was. As I entered the turn, I kept my eyes on the Messer above me and smiled when I saw Alexandra's tracers rip through his tail. The Messer rolled away, and I breathed a sigh of relief. "I owe you one, Alexandra."

"Just one? If I'd known you were worth so little, I wouldn't have bothered."

Her jab brought a smile to my face as I assessed the situation. The Pe-2s were nearly at the railway station, but Gridnev and Tania were still locked in a fur ball. "Alexandra, stick with that other Messer and protect our Peshkas," I said, angling my plane to enter the dogfight. "I'm going to clear tails."

"Understood," she replied.

Tania appeared to be holding her own, something I was grateful for. She was easy to pick out as her plane was the only one lacking a winter color scheme at this point. Gridnev, on the other hand, was losing both speed and position against his adversary. He'd be in the enemy's sights soon, and I feared there was nothing he could do about it. My gut grew queasy, knowing how helpless he must feel.

"Major, reverse roll, come right," I said, lining up the shot in my mind. If I could get Gridnev to extend the fur ball where I wanted, I'd have the fascist dead in my sights.

Gridnev obeyed, and at the same time, the German opened fire. Pieces of metal flew from Gridnev's wing. "I'm hit!"

His plane entered a dive. The Messer and I followed as he pulled out and banked hard. Again the German fired. I exhaled as his shots flew behind Gridnev.

"I can end this if you level, Major. I only need a half second," I said.

"Take the bastard out," he replied, leveling his nose with the horizon.

I chopped the throttle and squealed as the German followed the Major as I'd hoped, presenting me with a perfect target. I mashed the triggers, and large chunks blew off the 109's tail. A piece of his rudder even bounced off the root of my right wing.

The Messer fired at Gridnev, but with half its vertical stabilizer gone, its aim was sloppy. I pumped another burst into the fighter, and it tumbled toward the earth like a drunk trying a cartwheel.

"You're clear!" I shouted. My elation grew tenfold when I saw the 109's canopy open and its pilot bail. "And he's down!"

Gridnev sighed with relief. "There's a bottle of vodka with your name on it when we get back."

Fiery streaks zipped by my canopy, and I instinctively snap rolled to the right to get out of the way. The shots weren't for me. They hit Gridnev and drove through his left wing and rear fuselage.

"Damn it," he said as his plane dropped a good five hundred meters in the sky. "This thing's almost had it."

My head spun left and right, trying to find where his attacker had gone. Pain raced through my arm, further distracting me. "I can't find him anywhere," I said. "Coming down to you now, Major."

"Negative!" he barked. "I'll get home. Regroup with Tania and Alexandra and make them pay."

"Yes, comrade major," I said, cutting left.

A 109 appeared, corkscrewing around my plane and banking away. The plane's bright red Jagdgeschwader Udet emblem and yellow eight on its side burned in my eyes. Rademacher was here, and he had at least a dozen more victory tallies painted on his tail since last we met.

"God, this can't be happening," I said, horrified he'd been on me again and I hadn't known it. He must have been using Gridnev's fur ball for bait as much as I had.

Rademacher flew off, and I wasn't able to bring my plane around in time to shoot. I wanted to pursue, but Tania was still fighting about a kilometer away. I turned toward her, hoping we could bring her Messer down before Rademacher could reengage. It would be two versus one if we did, and I was confident Rademacher would lose against those odds.

Tania had the upper hand, and the German pilot tried to get her to follow him into a hard turn. She pulled a high-G yo-yo and peppered the 109's fuselage with her machine guns. To my dismay, there was no noticeable effect.

"This is a tough one," she growled over the radio.

The German flipped his plane and dove. Tania followed, shooting the entire way. Instead of giving chase, I brought my plane in a high arc and searched for Rademacher. It was a good excuse to give my throbbing arm a rest. Besides, he'd be using our fixation on this Messer against us and I had to account for him. Sadly, he was nowhere to be seen. How that was possible was beyond me.

The lead Peshka pilot radioed in. "Bombs dropping. Egressing."

I looked left and caught sight of the bombers a few kilometers out, racing away from the rail station. German anti-aircraft fire sent a relentless barrage at all of them. Eighteen bombs hit a split second later, their blasts mesmerizing and horrifying. I could practically feel the concussive wave in my chest.

"I need help!" Tania said. "They're both on me!"

Her panicked call stopped my heart. I couldn't see where she was, so I inverted my plane and looked out the top of my canopy. I found Tania skirting the treetops, headed south. She weaved back and forth as two German fighters were locked on her tail and alternated shooting at her. God, how did Rademacher get on her without me knowing?

"Alexandra, we need you," I said, pushing the throttle all the way forward and going into a dive. "Where's that German you were on?"

"Put him in the ground," she replied, matter-of-factly. "I'm with the bombers, but coming to you now."

It would be three on two at this point. I tried to stay positive, but my mouth ran dry and my hands shook. The pain in them increased tenfold and I wondered if I'd even be able to press the triggers. I distracted myself from those thoughts by talking to Tania. "Keep moving, girl. You'll be fine."

She was over a kilometer from my position, but at least I was gaining. All I could do was pray I'd reach her in time. I prayed harder than I had ever before. With each beat of my heart, with each desperate sharp turn she made, I begged for her to live. I didn't care about shooting down Rademacher, though I'd gladly have smashed my plane into his if that's what it took. I only wanted Tania to get home. I even offered myself in her place.

Both 109s opened up on her at the same time, and her plane burst into flames. Before it hit the ground, I was already headed to Anisovka, calling Alexandra off and choking back the tears.

Chapter Twenty-Two

I SAT NEAR the bank of the Volga River with Zhenia's cat Bri in my lap. I stroked the top of her head while I stared at the water. The glass-like surface was seductively dangerous, for as inviting as the scene looked, the combination of strong undercurrents and freezing temperatures would prove fatal in short order. As I replayed the loss of Tania over and over in my head, I entertained the idea of swimming out as far as I could and letting Fate do the rest.

Those dark seeds, however, never blossomed in to action. Suicide would result in eternal damnation, and while I felt God had little care for me and my plight, I didn't want to do anything to seal my fate forever. I'd also dishonor my lineage of ancestors who'd lost family and friends time and again, yet still fought on with heads held high. The pain of Tania's loss would pass, I told myself, and I refocused my thoughts on the gentle sound and vibration of Bri's purrs.

Stupid cat. As much as I tried to find my strength, I knew I was pretending to be the huntress. Clearly I was not. The huntress didn't sit at home, worried to death, and question everything she did. The huntress, like the mouser, lounged, purred, and knew who the mice were. A mouse could never change that.

"There's nothing you could have done, you know."

Klara approached with a thick blanket wrapped around her. I shrugged at her comment and went back to my staring. "You weren't there," I said. "I anticipated the fight with Gridnev's Messer. A good pilot would've done the same with Rademacher and brought Tania home. So what does that make me to everyone else?"

"It shouldn't matter," she said. "You should be proud of yourself no matter what anyone else thinks of you."

"It shouldn't, but it does," I said. "Funny thing is, I get the feeling that even if I had shot Rademacher down, I'd still feel the same way."

"I think if you shot him down you'd explode with excitement," she said.

Two months ago, I would've agreed without question. Now, I couldn't even force myself to. "In the moment, maybe," I said. "But I don't care about my victory today, and I'm not sure why. I honestly don't think having Rademacher's name attached to it would change anything."

"You're crazy," Klara said with a stifled laugh. "But for what it's worth, Gridnev thinks you did well. So does Alexandra."

I perked. "Since when do you talk to her?"

"Since you came back looking like Vladimir Sukhomlinov and told Alexandra to leave you alone."

I snorted. Vladimir Sukhomlinov was the Minister of War during the Great War, disgraced and exiled for near-traitorous performance. "Perhaps I should be punished like he was. I couldn't save another girl, and I turned tail and ran the moment I could. Hardly the daring warrior I should be."

God, I was a wreck. Part of me wanted to defend and fight as I should, both of which required me killing the enemy, and I was starting to realize that the other part hated every bit of it. This idea was new, small, but clearly there, like a lighthouse barely cresting over the horizon, calling in the dark. This put me at odds with myself, and I was certain the war wouldn't ever let it be resolved.

Klara sat next to me and put half the blanket across my shoulders so we could share it. I'd been out here so long, I'd grown numb to the cold—palm aside. A rat gnawing on my bones would've been more pleasant than what raced up my arms. For the love of all, I wanted a syrette more than I wanted life itself at that point.

"I'm sorry I'm such poor company," I said, nestling into her. "I know this was supposed to be our special time I'd promised, but I'm stuck on that sortie."

"It's okay. I'm glad to be with you through thick or thin." Klara leaned her head on mine. "You know, if you hadn't been there, no one might have come back."

"What do you mean?"

"Despite the fact Rademacher was there, you still shot down one of his own," she replied. "Alexandra sent another into the ground, and the Major came home alive. Not to mention, all the bombers made successful drops and got back alive. There are a lot of girls here who wouldn't have fared as well."

Her words sank into my mind. She had me there. Many others in our regiment would have ended up as a tally on Rademacher's tail, but I also knew if I hadn't been in pain, I might have reacted fast enough clear Tania's six. "I wish I could've done more is all."

"I know," she said. "I'm sure the Major and Alexandra think the same about themselves. But you've got to stop beating yourself up. You're destined for greatness."

"No. Greatness isn't reserved for a-"

I cut myself off, and Klara picked it right up. "A what?"

I wanted to say it wasn't reserved for a drugged-addicted thief, but I couldn't get the words out.

She rubbed my shoulder and gently wiped my cheeks. "Why are you crying?"

I sniffed and cleared my eyes. "I really want some morphine."

"We'll get through it."

"No, you don't understand." I paused for a good three breaths to work up my courage. "I almost took some today."

"But you didn't." Her words were quiet now, barely audible over my heart pounding in my chest.

"Not by choice. After the debrief, I tried to slip into the doctor's office, but he came back early from lunch." I felt my soul retreat far away out of shame, and I sat there for God knew how long, waiting for Klara to disown me.

Instead, she turned my chin and planted a kiss square on my lips. She brushed my cheek, and my hand pressed into her chest with a slight quiver. All I could do was hold my breath while my mind ran wild with delight and shock.

She sucked in a breath before kissing me again. Passion flowed from her into me, and my body warmed in response. The tip of her tongue found the inside of my mouth, and her hands went under my coat. I ran my fingers through her hair before running them down her neck.

The engagement lasted for eternity yet ended in a flash—such is the way of love. When I finally pulled back, it was only because fear gripped me as to what destiny we were both barreling out of control toward. She wanted it all, but I couldn't spare the energy for secrets, and female couples were not looked highly upon. "Klara-"

She put a finger on my mouth and silenced me. "I need to say something," she said with her voice trembling as much as my body. "I love you, Nadya. I've loved you ever since we first met. I've wanted to tell you so many times but was afraid. All I could do was pen a thousand love letters in my head and imagine you lighting up each time you read them."

"Why are you telling me now?"

"Because I want you to know there's nothing on Earth you could say or do to drive me away," she said. "I'll be here for you through anything and everything. I know I said I didn't want attention, but I meant from others, not you. I want your attention more than anything else in this world."

Goosebumps rose on my skin. My mouth opened, but no words came out. Somehow, the gravity of my addiction paled to the seriousness of her confession.

"Please say something," she said, looking as vulnerable as a lamb lost in the wild.

"I love you, too," I said. "But . . ."

My hesitation filled in the rest. Klara's brow furrowed, and there was pain in her eyes that could have only come from a twisted knife to the heart. "I thought-" She scooted away, and she stared at the ground while fidgeting with her hands. "We've always been so close. I don't understand. You kissed me. You let me kiss me."

"I did. God, I was about to kiss you again long before this."

"Then why the 'but'?"

I loved the intimacy of our souls uniting to where the world around meant nothing. Tania's loss, however, hammered a lesson I loathed to learn. The war did not cooperate with one's plans for the future. "I don't want you to get hurt," I said. "Not with all the fighting and paranoid officers everywhere. One of these days I might not come back. Worse, they could drag us out of our bunks while we slept if certain people caught wind."

"Stop it," she said, her eyes scolding me as much as her words. "Don't you dare tell me who I can't love. I know what the risks are. We can keep things quiet until the war is done."

My fingers traced the sides of her face. I dared to believe. "Can we?"

"For you, I can be as patient as need be, especially if it means you're mine once the Germans are gone."

The hope shining in her eyes made me want to grab her by the hand, steal a car, and run off right there. But I still had responsibilities, to my lineage, my God, my sisters in arms. "About the post war . . ."

"Yes?"

"Where would we go? What would we do?"

She laughed. "I don't know. If this place doesn't kill us, I'm sure we'll be strong enough to figure that out."

She had me there. "If you really want to stay together, instead of finding you something with my bounty, we should save it for that bakery of yours."

Klara beamed, more joyful than any angel singing hymns. "And here I thought you forgot."

"Never," I said, shaking my head. "Nothing I could think of seemed special enough. Not even chocolate."

Before I knew it, her lips pressed against mine, tighter and more passionate than before. "Is that a yes?" I asked once we parted.

"Yes." She cleared her eyes. "We'll need more than one bounty to get it going, though. I hope you know that."

I shrugged. "Guess we better start saving." I grimaced and flexed my hand. "Of course, all this assumes my arm doesn't do me in first."

"You could try valerian. Doctor Burak has given it to some of the other girls to help them sleep," Klara said, taking my hand and rubbing it. She didn't do as good of a job as Alexandra did, but there was a thousand times more love put into it.

"What's that? A drug?"

"An herb the ancient Greeks discovered," she said. "Could help. All you would have to say is you're having trouble sleeping. Some of the girls in the other squadron are already using it."

"I'll try anything at this point."

"And you'll have to tell Alexandra about the morphine," she said. "I can't be the only one to keep you honest."

She was right on that, though I was terrified of doing so. I'd have to work up the courage to bring my wingman in on the problem. Before our conversation went on, I heard someone whistling draw near. I looked over my shoulder to see Petrov a dozen paces away with a delighted face. "Hope I'm not interrupting, but I wanted to let you know your dugout is being searched."

My heart felt as if it jumped into my throat. "What for?"

"I'm looking for missing medication," he replied. "Well, some men along with Doctor Burak and Major Gridnev are, I should say. The Major insisted I stay away when I brought my case to him."

"You're chasing a dream," I said. I prayed he truly knew nothing, but understood the possibility he might actually have me. "It's not my fault the doctor can't keep track of his own supplies."

Petrov shrugged and smiled knowingly. "I don't need your confession. You've got the strongest motive around here to be stealing it with your chronic pain, and you look sick often enough to point to withdrawals. He'll find what you stole, and when he does, I'm going to stretch your neck for the entire regiment to see."

"You're wrong," Klara said, leveling a zealous gaze at him. "I know her better than anyone. She'd never steal."

"You're a fine mechanic, Klara—if I may call you that—and you're a shining example to all of what a Soviet should be. Strong. Dedicated. Selfless. But your good friend here has been manipulating you since you first met," Petrov said. He popped out his silver pocket watch, gave it a glance, and said, "So, Junior Lieutenant, if you want to keep our game interesting, I suggest you start running. I'd say you've ten minutes at the most."

"I don't need to," I said, knowing there was nothing to be found.

Petrov left with a brief goodbye. Klara and I watched him go. When he'd disappeared, I turned Klara's face toward me and whispered, "Do you think he saw us?"

I saw her swallow, and before she answered, I knew she feared the same thing I had. There was no telling how long he'd been watching before we noticed him.

Chapter Twenty-Three

THE FOLLOWING DAY, Gridnev apologized for the search, stating he wanted the matter closed with Petrov and had had full confidence in me and nothing would be found. I ran into Petrov shortly thereafter on the airfield, asked if he'd heard about my second, confirmed kill, and said I looked forward to being not only the first female ace, but the first Cossack one too.

I made the conversation polite enough that I couldn't get into trouble with Gridnev, but I'm sure Petrov knew my intent: to dig under his skin with my success and stir the proverbial hornet nest. Risky, yes, but I wanted to flaunt my victories in the face of my enemies and show them I was far from beaten, even if he had burned my arm and combed my dugout. Despite my barely concealed taunts and the fruitless search he had ordered, Petrov remained cheery throughout our conversation. That could only mean he had something in the works. I loathed to find out what it was and was terrified that he'd been witness to Klara kissing me.

If there was one good thing that came of it all, Gridnev was so embarrassed—though he never openly said so—that he practically gave the okay for Klara and I to be social with one another.

Truthfully, he never verbally expressed consent, but simply turned a blind eye to our nightly escapes. I wasn't complaining. Despite my fears on what Petrov might have seen, over the course of the next few nights, Klara and I spent countless hours watching the stars and fantasizing about the future. When bold (or careless) enough, we slipped further away from the airfield to further heat up the chemistry between us.

Near the end of the week, I sat bundled on my bunk. The oil drum in the corner glowed from the burning coals inside. Water pooled around it, but the warmth it offered lasted a half pace at most. Snow crept in from the outside, and the dugout floor was frozen solid. The makeshift heater had needed more wood for hours now, but no one wanted to go cut some in the frigid dark, least of all me.

Alexandra was at my side. She held my right hand in her lap and massaged my palm and forearm. "Is this still helping?"

"Thankfully, yes," I said. Though now each press of her thumb was like glass twisting in my arm, I knew once she finished, the rest of the day would be better, but I still wanted a syrette, even if most of my physical withdrawals were gone. I sucked in a breath, shut my eyes, and jumped off the cliff of uncertainty. "I need to tell you something," I began. "Something only Klara knows and no one else, and something I should've brought up a long time ago."

"You two fancy each other," she said, not missing a beat. "I realize others might not like it, and it's nothing I'd do, but I don't care as long as you're happy."

The corners of my lips drew back. As good as it was to hear those words, she'd missed the mark and I forced myself not to take the easy out. "No, I'm talking about me using morphine."

Alexandra stopped her massage. She cursed several times under her breath and dug her nail into my forearm. She did it to the side of the burns, so it wasn't excruciating, but she made her point before she spoke. "You're better than that, Nadya."

"I was," I said. "I want to be. That's why I'm telling you now. I've stopped for over a week, I think, but God the cravings are driving me insane. Worse, the colder it gets, the harder it gets."

"So, you're asking me to keep an eye on you?"

I shook my head. "No. I'm telling you not to let me out of your sight. At least not until winter is over or I can ignore the pain."

Alexandra tousled my hair and squeezed me tight. "Where you go, I go," she said. "You know, if you'd told me sooner, I could've helped more. Papa taught me some other non-drug ways to help pain on top of massages. We could have been doing those too, you know, but I thought this was enough."

Alexandra returned to working on my arm. "We should cut extra wood for the barrel today. That will help, especially at night."

"You're busy enough as it is."

"If it means keeping you off that stuff, I'll find the time."

Her words warmed my soul, and I wondered what I'd done to deserve such a friend. "You're too good to me."

She looked at me playfully. "I am. Don't forget that."

"Have you thought about what you wanted?" I asked.

"For?"

"Keeping me alive that last dogfight."

Alexandra gave a wishful sigh. "Ah. A Stradivarius would be nice."

I arched an eyebrow. "You play the violin?"

"I'm no Mischa Elman, but I'm quite good, thank you. Is there something wrong with that?"

"On account of your singing, yes," I said with a laugh. "How can you not hear how out of tune you are?"

"Maybe I don't care," she said, sticking her tongue out at me. "Anyway, what's in that new sack of yours?"

She was in reference to the large, worn burlap sack I had placed at the foot of my bunk last evening. No one else had said anything about it, and I doubted the other girls even noticed. "Might be something for you."

Alexandra grabbed the sack. The contents clanked as she dove into the bag like a child at Christmas. "Milk," she said, pulling free a couple of bottles. She stuck her hand back in and pulled out two smaller bottles. "Wine? Wine!"

Her face was radiant, and I was thrilled such simple pleasures were not lost on her. The fresh milk wasn't easy to come by, let alone good wine. I was proud of myself for piecing it all together so fast.

"There's one more thing," I said. I leaned over and rummaged under the bunk until I found a small box I had wrapped in butcher paper and tied off with twine and a fancy bow.

Alexandra's eyes went wide. "Now this looks special. Did you chop a pig for me? Because nothing says special to a girl like hunks of bloody pork."

I laughed. "No. It's much sweeter than that."

Carefully, Alexandra undid the knot and unwrapped the paper. Underneath were bars of chocolate, two kilos worth in all. "Chocolate?" she said as if I'd parted the Red Sea before her very eyes. "Nadya, you didn't."

"I did."

"You shouldn't have," she said. "How?"

"A lot of barter over the past couple days," I said. "And a lot of persistence."

"This must have cost a fortune."

I shrugged my shoulders. "Maybe a small one."

"Seriously, what did you give up?"

I laughed. "Manners not your forte anymore? Who told you it was all right to ask what gifts cost."

"I can't take all this," she said, setting it all aside. "You've spent far too much. I mean, the wine alone must have been half your bonus pay."

"Pretty much all that was left," I said. When I saw the breath leave her, I added, "I'd already set some aside for after the war, so don't act like you got it all. Besides, you're more important to me than some stupid bundle of money. Now stop being insulting."

"If you insist." Alexandra delicately peeled back the paper to one of the chocolate bars and broke off a small piece and offered it to me. "You should have some."

"I can't. It's yours."

"Then it's mine to give. I insist."

When I balked, Alexandra gave an impish grin and held the chocolate over the oil drum.

"What are you doing?"

She didn't answer. Instead, she mashed the now warm and soft hunk of chocolate into my hand, leaving my palms and fingers covered in sticky sweetness. "Too late now."

"You're such a child," I said, planning my retaliation. "I can't believe you did that."

"Believe it," she said, biting into the bar. "What are you going to do about it?"

"Not stoop to your level."

I popped the piece in my mouth and bided my time. My taste buds delighted in the sweet explosion of flavor. My mouth watered, and I breathed deep. God, this tiny morsel was a slice of heaven. After all of the bread, water, and salted mush we'd been eating day in and day out, I'd forgotten what good food was like. Then, like a snake striking its prey, I planted my left hand on Alexandra's face and smeared chocolate over half of it.

Her jaw dropped, and she stared at me. I could see the little gears turning in her head trying to comprehend what had taken place. "Oh . . . you are so dead!"

I bolted out of the dugout before she could make good on her promise. I shielded my eyes from the morning sun. Snow-covered ground crunched under my feet. The sounds of her laughter as she gave chase struck a chord in my soul I'd never heard. This is who I was, who I wanted to be. Someone who gave laughter and fun, not death and misery.

I ran down the length of the airstrip. I could hear her gaining. Several onlookers watched the spectacle with mixes of amusement and confusion. "Don't let her get me!" I yelled, but none came to my rescue.

"Nadya, look out!"

I rooted myself to the ground, nearly falling over as I did. I spun around at Alexandra's sharp warning and caught a snowball in the face. The hit sent me stumbling backward, and I lost my footing. I fell on my rump, bracing myself with my right hand. A stab of pain shot up my arm, but I dug deep, pushed it aside, and vowed to defend my honor.

"That was dirty!" I said, brushing the frozen debris from my eyes.

"No, it was clean. I took it off the top," she said. "This one is dirty."

I rolled sideways, and a grey ball of slush impacted where I'd been a split second before. I tried to scoop up enough snow to return fire, but Alexandra was faster and more merciless than I could match.

"Do you yield?" she said, driving snowball after snowball into my side and head. Another one popped me in the mouth, and I ended up coughing and spitting. I hadn't planned it, but Alexandra let up for a moment, clearly concerned she'd gone too far. "Oh no. Are you okay?"

"I . . . I don't know," I said, crouching and breathing loudly. Predictably, she dropped her guard even more, and I packed a handful of icy slush and nailed her right between the eyes.

"You girls can play when your duties are done," said a voice to the side.

I turned to find Zhenia walking by, dressed in her full flight suit and heading for her plane. "Yes, Mother," I said, rolling my eyes.

"Don't you start, Nadya," she said, holding up a finger. "I've got enough to do already for tonight's exercises."

"You're such a killjoy," I said, dropping the half-formed snowball I had as Zhenia left.

Alexandra came to my side and leaned her shoulder against mine. "I really, really don't want to chop wood."

"Or re-write all the post-op reports from last week," I said with a heavy sigh. "Did you have to be such a klutz and spill Gridnev's tea on them?"

"Fate seemed to think so."

"Do you want to go to the bathhouse after?" I asked, thinking a trip to the banya sounded divine. "We haven't used our time this month."

"I'd like that," she said. "There's one other thing I have to do first, though."

"What's that?"

"This," she said, smashing a handful of snow into my face.

* * *

We still had a couple of hours of daylight left by the time we finished everything needing to be done. We would've had more had the second round of our snowball fight not lasted so long. Rounds three and four didn't help either, especially when we were supposed to be chopping wood. Pounding slush was exponentially more fun than hacking away at the trees, and my cramping hand made me take breaks from work, and those breaks turned to good excuses to pelt Alexandra in the face with a ball of ice. Despite the cheery nature of our fights, in the back of my mind, melancholy thoughts of all the fallen girls who could no longer enjoy such things lingered.

With all our mundane tasks behind us, we made for town, frigid, exhausted, and thoroughly looking forward to a good steam. I hummed along the way to keep my mind from my aching palm, and it wasn't long before we passed through the banya's imposing wood door and into its sitting room.

Alexandra and I put our clothes and towels on one of the high-back chairs and left our boots on the stone floor before entering the steam room. As we did, we passed by a local woman, with twenty years and at least as many kilos on us both who left without a word.

Birch panels lined the steam room's walls, and moisture clung to all of them. At the far end was a small window looking out over the Volga River. I only knew because of my sense of direction. The glass pane was fogged and only let in a blur of hazy light.

"It was kind of her to have it ready for us, don't you think?" Alexandra said. She sat on one of the benches and began using a nearby cloth and bucket to wash off. "When I'm rich and famous, I think I'll like getting use to that. I wonder what it costs to have a maid tend to me all day."

"What are you going to make your fortune from? Cheating at snow fights?" I said, laughing. "Besides, I thought your family was already rich."

"Just because our bread isn't moldy doesn't mean we've got hoards of gold," she replied.

I took to another bench and started cleaning. At first, I shut my eyes and enjoyed the hot cloth gliding across my skin, taking with it equal amounts of grime and stress. I ran it time and again over my face and down my neck, shoulders, and arms.

"Can't believe you're ahead of me in kills," Alexandra said. "Well, I can, but I'm jealous you're going to make ace before I do."

"What makes you say that? We both have two."

"Kazarinova robbed you of your first," she replied. "You should be at three, not counting the one you gave to Valeriia, which would be four. Face it Nadya, you'll score three more before I do and become famous."

"I don't want to be famous."

Alexandra straightened and raised her eyebrows. "Surely you jest. Who wouldn't want to be an ace?"

"I'm not kidding," I said. "I've been thinking since we lost Tania. I don't want my life to be measured by how many people I've butchered."

"They're the enemy," Alexandra said. "They deserve to be shot. They invaded us, remember?"

"I know," I said. "I'm not saying they aren't or they haven't. What I'm saying is at this point I do what I do because that's my job, because it's necessary. I don't want it applauded, no matter how boring that makes me."

Alexandra laughed. "You're crazy and hardly boring. You're a damn fighter pilot, Nadya. It doesn't get any more exciting than that. Besides, how long did you dream of your first kill?"

"A long time, but that's changed now," I said.

"Well, I'll be wing leader then, and you can watch my tail so I can make ace first," she said. "Seems like a win-win to me. Yes?"

"Sure, why not?" I paused the conversation as I worked the washcloth between my fingers. The dirt there was stubborn, and it took some effort to clean under my nails as well. When I was finished, I looked at the scars on my palms. It had been a while since I'd studied them. The spots on my hands and arms were dark and shiny, and looked as if I had some old plaster stuck to my skin that would never come off. There were still faint traces of burns on my leg and neck I could feel, and though they were not as visible, they were as much of a testament to what I'd gone through as the more severe ones.

"Silly, isn't it?" I said with a snort as I continued inspecting my skin.

"Me wanting to be wing leader?"

"No. These scars. I let them have so much power over me, and they hardly cover any of my skin."

Alexandra laughed. "I suppose it's a good thing you weren't totally covered then. Think how much under their spell you'd be then."

"I'm being serious," I said, feeling put off. "Why do we let such small portions of our lives define us?"

"A lot can happen in a moment. A birth. A death. A first kiss or a broken heart. It makes sense those things would shape us."

"I think I've been shaped more when nothing happens."

I wondered if Alexandra would know what I was in reference to, but like the good wingman she was, she followed me close, not missing a beat. "Unanswered prayers."

"I don't even want things to be my way anymore," I said, feeling my gut tighten. "All I want is to understand why the world is so broken, why He's not fixing it when He's supposed to be able."

"Maybe He can't tell you."

I tilted my head sideways. "What do you mean? You're telling me He can't open His mouth and speak? He supposedly spoke with other people."

"I'm saying maybe you wouldn't understand," she replied. Before I could argue, she went on. "A few years before the war, my baby brother had his first teeth come in. Naturally, we brushed them, and he screamed bloody murder the entire time. He looked at us in terror as we held him down as best as we could and brushed his teeth. As much as we wanted to tell him why we were 'torturing' him, we couldn't, because he'd never understand. But we weren't going to stop because he hated it."

Her unexpected insight struck a chord in me I'd never heard before, and the idea of not having answers, not knowing why, became far less scary. "It's weird to hear you talk about such things, being atheist."

Alexandra shrugged. "I've been trying to come up with an answer for your not-so-silent midnight prayers for a while now. I figured if this life isn't the only life, if there's eternity to consider, who can say what's good or bad when we've got such a small view of things? Hell, if anything, dying is going home. That can't be all bad."

"I never thought about it like that," I admitted. "Still, I worry. I lied. I stole. What if He's silent because I've done such things?"

Alexandra didn't say anything for a while, and for that, I was glad. The last thing I wanted was an off-the-cuff answer, one born from unease and not deep thought. "In the end, I think, if God is God, He'd understand the pain you were in and why you did what you thought you had to. If He doesn't understand it, well, He's not God, is He?"

Her words warmed my heart far more than the steam room ever could. I reclined on the bench and stared at the ceiling. "Keep it up and you'll be an abbess before you're thirty," I said with a laugh.

"Don't get ahead of yourself, Nadya," she said. "I'm not pious, nor do I intend to be. The first chance I get, I'm ravishing my fiancé so hard it would take a week for them to hear the entire confession."

Chapter Twenty-Four

ON THE MORNING of November fifth, I lay on my mattress, staring at the frozen bunk ceiling, trapped in the land of exhaustion. Winter had been cruel all night, despite the wood burnt in the oil drum, and my wounds had kept sleep at bay for nine hours now. I could barely think. Worse, I was slated for an escort soon, and I was certain it would take a tiny miracle for me not to fall asleep and crash on takeoff.

For the third time in the last hour, I wondered if I and the rest of the squadron would be better off if I handed in my wings, but I still feared Petrov would pounce on me the moment I did. He was still around and asking questions, even talking sweet to Klara, and each day I wondered if that would be the day he would strike.

I massaged my arm as best I could, trying to remember what Alexandra had taught me as I shut my eyes. I slowed my breathing, imagined a warm summer day filled with laughter and friends, imagined my body letting the pain go. It worked, slowly, but not as well as the morphine did. Probably a good thing, I thought, that Klara had taken the box and I hadn't any.

My eyes snapped opened. In a panic, I rolled to my left and slipped my hand between the mattress and the earthen wall, feeling around for the tear. It didn't take long to find it, and even less to probe the hay and pull out the syrette I'd stashed there long ago. I had one left. God . . . I had one left.

I turned it over several times, studying its small body and pointed tip. I could fly, if I wanted, free of misery, but also free of friends and self-respect. My gut tightened. I hurried over to the oil drum and tossed it in. "Burn in hell."

"Scramble, Nadya! We're flying early!"

I jumped at Alexandra's call. "God, please tell me we're not."

"Nadya! Get out here!"

I heard her coming and fumbled putting on my boots.

Alexandra ran in. Her cheeks were rosy from the weather, and her smile was as bright as the gleam in her eyes. All that faded when she held my gaze. "What's the matter?"

"I'm exhausted," I said. "I was hoping to catch a quick nap. Why the sudden rush?"

"I don't know," she said. "I guess they wanted Rakhinka resupplied sooner rather than later."

Before I could protest, Alexandra grabbed my hand and pulled me out. We raced across the airfield, passing pilots and crews, and soon I was hopping onto the wing of my fighter and climbing into the open cockpit.

Klara appeared at my side and yanked my belt tight. "Be careful," she said with a flutter in her voice. "I'm looking forward to picking up where we left off last night, so you better come home in one piece."

Oh, how I wanted to return to the other night as well, where my kisses found a way down her neck and her nails found their way down my back. And God how I hated how secret it all had to be. I took her hand and pressed it against my chest. "As long as it beats, I'll always come back to you. Don't worry."

"I mean it," she said. "Something's felt off since I woke, and I know the cold has to be affecting you more than usual. So don't take any chances, yes?"

"I won't. I promise."

Klara leaned in and kissed my cheek. She wanted more, I knew, but there were too many eyes on the airfield. "Come back to me safe, Nadya."

"I always do."

She jumped down, and I went through my pre-flight checklist. Focusing on everything I needed to do to get off the ground helped ease my worries as it built my confidence I could still function despite lack of sleep and a gnawing arm. Once I was done, Klara cleared the prop, and I started up the engine. It roared to life, and Klara pulled the chocks free. My plane rolled forward, taxiing toward the runway. A couple of minutes later, Alexandra and I were southbound with our escort.

"Little Boar, this is Raven," said the pilot of the Li-2 transport. "Nice to have a pair of budding aces along with us for the trip."

I smiled at the praise, but anxieties persisted. This was one flight where I didn't want any Luftwaffe around, most of all Rademacher. "If it's all the same to you, Raven, I'd be more than happy with this being a boring run."

"Negative, Little Boar. Stay alert," the pilot replied. "Fascists are fighting tooth and nail at Stalingrad. There's a decent chance of us being intercepted."

"Wonderful," I muttered, making sure the radio didn't pick up the comment.

Alexandra and I took staggered positions high and on opposite sides of the transport plane. The three of us flew over the landscape, less than a kilometer above the earth in order to keep our chances of being spotted to a minimum. However, so close to the ground, if we were caught, we wouldn't have a lot of options to escape or fight back. Altitude, after all, could become speed. And speed was life. The only thing I could do was keep a sharp watch on the skies and pray they remained empty.

"We should dance more," Alexandra said over the radio. "I miss it, and I need the practice."

I giggled at the thought. Here we were, escorting supplies and ammunition to an airfield near the front, likely about to be pounced by Messers, and my dear, sweet wingman could only think about her waltz. Maybe once we landed, we could pass the time doing that.

"You do need the practice," I said.

"At what?"

"Dancing," I teased. "I'd be embarrassed to be your fiancé. You'll probably topple you both dancing at the wedding."

Alexandra laughed. It was nervous and unsettling. "Finally decided to reply to me? Or could you not wait another ten minutes till we landed?"

I bit my lower lip, and I checked the clock. Nearly an hour had passed since we'd left Anisovka. Frantic, I looked left and right and over both shoulders, looking for something, anything, to show I hadn't lost track of that much time.

The snowy terrain beneath the three of us looked unfamiliar. I didn't recognize any of the roads or buildings I could pick out over the landscape. But the view of a large, round lake off my left wing made my heart skip a beat.

It was Lake Elton, no doubt about it. As much as I wished otherwise, it meant we were on the final leg of our journey, and I had indeed lost track of a half hour. God knows why I didn't crash or veer off course. I could only thank Him profusely that I'd managed to subconsciously fly where I was supposed to despite how tired I was. Maybe He still smiled on me from time to time.

"Welcome to Rakhinka, Little Boar," said a male voice I didn't recognize over the radio. "This is Badger. You are to circle the airfield until Raven has landed."

I slapped myself across the face as hard as I could. I cursed myself for becoming distracted again. I had to think. Had to concentrate. Had to wake up. Had to reply. "Understood, Badger. Holding."

I checked Alexandra's position off my wing and entered a slight bank. The Rakhinka airstrip had a similar layout to the one in Anisovka with one main runway and a few taxiways that led to parking, hangars, and refueling areas. There were a lot more gun emplacements because of the airfield's close proximity to Stalingrad. In fact, if I looked west, I could see plumes of smoke rising on the horizon—signs of the continued conflict in that great city. I wondered how the morale was for those on the ground. Did they fight with valiance or desperation? Possibly both. One thing I knew: the killing was far from over.

"Little Boar, correct your heading to zero-nine-zero! Acknowledge!"

"Correcting," I said, slapping myself one more time and turning on heading. "Got caught up looking at Stalingrad. Apologies."

"Understood, Little Boar." The man over the radio sounded calmer, which helped me relax. "You're cleared for landing, right-hand approach. Little Boar Two, you will remain in pattern until she's clear of the runway."

"As always," Alexandra replied.

I flexed my hands and rolled my shoulders. I craned my head to the right, and my eyes locked on to the runway over my shoulder. Even if my mind was an exhausted mess, this was a simple approach. The day was beautiful. My plane was in tip-top shape. I could do this.

"Nadya, when we land, can we talk?" she asked.

Her voice had a rare seriousness to it, and I wondered what it was she wanted. I pushed those thoughts away and banked hard to pull the plane around and put it on final approach. I cut back on the throttle and deployed the flaps.

"Looking good, Little Boar," the radio said. "Winds are light and variable."

"Light and variable. Copy."

I talked to myself the entire way down. *Piece of cake. Piece of cake. Piece of cake. Adjust throttle. Adjust pitch. Concentrate.* I checked the altimeter. *Hundred meters. Ninety-five. Ninety. Airspeed. Two-ten. Cake. Cake. Cake. I got this.*

I flipped the gear lever down to lower my wheels. The indicator lights on the right turned from red to green. I tensed in anticipation of touch down and continued my internal instructions. *Mind the flare. Mind the flare. Wheels down in ten. Nine. Eight.*

"Little Boar, Wave off! Wave off!"

I slammed the throttle forward and retraced my gears. The plane surged. I wasn't sure what I'd botched on the landing, and I dreaded to find out. Worse, I feared my second attempt would be disastrous.

"Little Boar, we have incoming bombers to Stalingrad, heading two-six-three, forty-two kilometers away, altitude two thousand meters. Intercept them at once."

"Oh God," I said, putting the fighter into a climb and raising the flaps. "Alexandra, you with me?"

"Where you go, I go."

Gravity pressed me into my seat as we rocketed upward. Soon we hit five hundred meters. A thousand. Two. I leveled off when we were over three thousand meters high, hoping combat would shock me fully awake.

"Badger, what's their escort look like?" I said.

"Unknown. Large flight. Be advised, the 437th is unable to assist."

That figured. I'd heard our fighter regiments had taken a beating and couldn't contest the skies. I'd even heard our bombers had ceased daylight operations altogether. I guessed it was our turn to be thrust into the meat grinder with only a prayer to see us home safe. As we flew toward Stalingrad, a large part of me didn't think we'd go home. Oddly, I was at peace. At least I'd have my wingman with me until the bitter end.

The city raced beneath us. Stalingrad was littered with burnt-out husks of buildings, each filled with rubble and many with rising smoke columns. All across the once majestic area I could see flashes of light and concussion blasts from tanks and artillery trading shots. The men and women in those streets knew a nightmare I never would.

"Enemy formation, eleven o'clock low," Alexandra said. "Damn that's a lot of them."

It took me a moment to find them. My eyes kept tearing and losing focus. Only after I cleared them twice did I see the speck of dots off in the distance. I gasped, hypnotized by their numbers. We were headed for a swarm, and I hadn't a clue what we were going to do about it.

"Orders?" Alexandra asked.

I didn't know. My mind was a blank. All I could do was stare with a cotton mouth as we raced toward them. How many were there? Eight He-111s? It looked like five were in front in a V-formation with three more in the rear formed in a similar fashion. Each of those bombers was bristling with machine guns I knew were eager to tear into any fighter that dared near them. They had at least that many escorts surrounding them. We were higher, and thus could keep our speed up when we dove to attack. We'd also have the sun at our backs, and they hopefully wouldn't see us coming. But was all that enough? God, this was suicide.

"Nadya! What do we do?"

"Where I go, you go."

It was the only thing I could think to reply. I pulled the plane higher, rolled, and made an inverted loop. I picked out the He-111 on the far right of the lead formation and dove toward it. It looked to be the easiest shot. My vision tunneled as I focused on my target through the gun sight. I could feel the plane increase speed. I lifted in my seat, and even the smallest twitch of the controls bounced my aim.

Tracers flew by my cockpit from all directions, but I stayed the course. I mashed both triggers until I flew under my target, missing it by a few dozen meters. I pulled back on the stick and was slammed into the seat. My vision darkened as the G's sent my blood rushing to my feet. Even in near blackout conditions and my arms feeling as if they were wrapped in lead, I held back on the stick until I guessed I was climbing away at a good angle. When I relaxed, the G's eased. My vision returned, and I blew out all the air I was holding.

"Still with me, Alexandra?"

"Right behind you," she replied. "We chewed that first one up, but he's still flying."

"We clear?"

"For the moment. They're probably worried there are more of us."

"I'm sure. Who in their right mind would send two against twenty?" I banked left and brought us around again. Pride swelled in my chest as I picked out the bomber we had attacked in the formation. Three trails of mist streaked behind it, two white and one brown. We must have hit some coolant and one of the fuel tanks. After watching him a few seconds, it was clear he was staying with the group and wasn't going to break for home. *Damn it to hell,* I thought. *Whatever they're going to bomb has to be important.*

"Little Boar, this is Badger. We think they're targeting the Red October factory. We've got a lot of troops there, and they've been trying to take it for a week now. Do not let them hit it."

I set my jaw. Those were the only words I needed to hear. I could make a difference. I would make a difference. I would bring honor to the Cossack name, remind all how fierce we were in combat, and that fierceness was not because we fought for Stalin and his filth or that we sought some barbaric glory, but because we fought for ourselves and for the Divine.

['\n']

Into the lion's den we went once more. Machinegun and cannon fire tried to tear us apart from all angles. After that second pass, I pulled around to make a third and kept my speed high to deny the enemy any chance at following me. I had a few scattered holes in my wings at this point, but as best I could tell, my fighter still flew without trouble.

I leaned forward and squinted, trying to pick out the bomber I'd hammered. I couldn't find it. The formation looked different than I'd remembered it—messier. No matter. I chose another bomber, rolled left and countered with right rudder to line up my shot. I blew past the fascist, ripping into the bomber with all of my guns.

"Did he go down?" I said, leveling off and extending away from the fight. I craned my head to both sides, but couldn't get a good visual. "He should be in pieces."

I found the He-111 a moment later. Fire poured from its wing as it fell from the sky. I watched it burn all the way to the ground. This marked my third aerial victory, but I wasn't excited for it, not even when I realized I was now over halfway to ace. The world would see me as an even more skilled pilot than before, but my soul said that wasn't going to make me proud of myself. I needed something that this war would never provide, and I still didn't know what that was.

"Nadya, I'm in trouble."

Her panic ripped through my heart. I whipped my plane on edge and looked out the top of my canopy, desperate to find her. The bombers, still a good minute from their target, had broken off the attack. Some trailed far behind the main body, while others were turning around and making a run for home. Far below I saw Alexandra's plane with a Messerschmitt 109 on her tail.

"I'm coming, hang in there," I said, diving to her aid.

Alexandra weaved left and right dodging constant fire from her adversary. There was a bright flash on her left wing, and a section came off. Her rolls slowed. "I lost an aileron," she said. "I've got to get out of here."

"Almost there," I said. With my plane still in a dive, I rapidly closed the distance. My exhaustion faded under a surge of adrenaline. I felt in control of my plane and myself, but Alexandra's constant maneuvers were throwing my aim off as much as her enemy's. "Alexandra, level off. I need the shot."

"Can you make it?"

"Absolutely," I promised, hoping it wasn't a lie.

"Waltzing," she said. "I'll straighten on the third."

The tremor in her voice drilled home how crucial the next few seconds would be. I chopped the throttle to maximize my firing time, and studied the rhythm of her moves. *One, two, three. One, two, three. One, two, three.*

She straightened out, and so did the German. I fired.

The Messer's engine exploded, and flames poured out of its nose. My heart sang like the heavenly host ushering in the Second Coming. I didn't stop shooting. My cannon pumped shell after shell into the 109. The German's canopy broke away, and I saw the pilot jump. He flew by my plane, narrowly missing my wing. For a frozen moment in time, I got a look at him. He looked around my age and every bit as terrified as I'd pictured Alexandra to be. It was then I realized we were skimming the ground, less than a hundred meters in the air. His chute would never open in time.

"He's . . . dead. You're clear." I told her. Though I saved her life, my words sickened my soul. I'd seen pilots bail before, but this was the first time I saw the face of a dead man—a man I'd sent to the grave.

Alexandra kept up her evasive maneuvers as she replied. "Are you sure?"

"Very." I scanned the sky. No other Luftwaffe had followed us. The chaos we'd sowed paid off in our favor. "Pull up. Let's get clear of ground fire."

Alexandra gained altitude and leveled. "Next time I go where you go, let's find someplace nicer."

Movement grabbed my eye, and I turned to see another 109 diving down on us. Cannon fire spewed from its nose with vengeful fury and slammed into Alexandra's plane. The Messer was gone as quickly as it had come, but before it flew off, I caught sight of the bright yellow eight painted on its tail.

My jaw dropped. Alexandra's battered and leaking plane limped through the sky as if any moment it would disintegrate. I tried to ask her if she was okay, but fear at the answer kept the question in my mouth.

"I'm all right," she said softly. "Make sure he doesn't come back around. I can barely keep this thing in the air."

"You'll make it. Leave him to me." I weaved back and forth to keep a watch on our six. Rademacher hung back, shadowing, waiting. My mind raced through the possibilities of what he was thinking. Surely he knew he could finish Alexandra off before she crossed the Volga. I wasn't that much of a threat either, given I'd be outnumbered in no time. Was he that confident in his kill or was he simply not interested in another victory tally on his tail?

I never came up with an answer to that as we limped home, but I was more than prepared to jump into his line of fire and shield Alexandra from another pass. I prayed he wouldn't reengage. When the Rakhinka airfield was in sight, I thanked God profusely for answering that prayer.

"Still okay?" I asked, eager to set foot on the ground.

"Little shaken, but fine."

Alexandra got emergency clearance to land so she didn't have to circle around. She'd said she was okay. And I believed her. Then her plane hit the runway. Her landing gear shattered, and the fighter tore its wings off as it slid.

Chapter Twenty-Five

"WAVE OFF, LITTLE Boar," the control tower said over the radio. "There's a crash on the field. Circle around to runway zero-two-zero."

"The hell I will," I muttered, flipping off the radio.

I eased off the throttle and pulled the nose up. Off to the side I saw a fire truck and one of the squad cars racing down the airstrip toward the crash site. My plane flared and the wheels touched the ground. The moment they did, I hit the brakes, hard. The tail picked up, and I had to let off them a touch as well as pull on the stick to keep the fighter from tipping over forward and giving the base a second wrecked plane to pick up.

I didn't speak a single word to God, terrified of His constant silence. Instead, I decided I would be the one to determine what would and would not happen. I opened the cockpit and leaned out the window to steer better. I managed to dodge the larger chunks of debris on the runway, though I did feel a distinct jolt in the seat when I hit some that couldn't be avoided. Thankfully, the wheels took the abuse.

I killed the engine and let the plane roll. With a little rudder, I steered it next to Alexandra's wreck, unbuckling my belt in the process. My fighter had yet to come to a stop before I was out of the cockpit, sliding off the wing, and rolling on the ground with a thump.

I bolted to Alexandra's mangled plane. Each and every bullet hole in the fuselage bored into my mind. At least the plane hadn't exploded, I told myself. At least there was no fire.

"Alexandra!" I yelled once I reached the side of the cockpit, banging hard against the glass. "Wake up!"

She lifted her head. Her gaze, full of bliss and confusion, held mine, and she smiled. She fumbled for the canopy latches. Together we opened the cockpit.

"You're alive," I said, tears rolling, breath leaving. "I feared the worst."

"I can be stubborn like that," she replied.

I reached in to help her out, but my hands retracted when I saw her blood-soaked jacket and the splatter covering the gauges. "Don't move," I said. "They'll be here in a moment."

I tore off my jacket and pressed it against the wound in her right side. It was a little lower than her ribcage. She whimpered when I touched her, and I kept the pressure up when she tried to bat my hand away.

Emergency crews were on us within a few breaths. They pushed by and had to pry me away from the cockpit, shouting as they did. Two of the men pulled her from the plane while a third waited nearby to help put her in the back of the car. I jumped in with her, despite more shouts and yells for me to do otherwise.

The car took off. I stroked Alexandra's head as she laid it in my lap. I wanted to say something, anything, but words failed me. Two things raced through my mind. First, all of this was my fault. Second, she wasn't going to see tomorrow.

Alexandra opened her eyes. "Nadya? You're here?"

"Where you go, I go," I whispered.

We came to a stop at a two-story building. Men came and took her from me, men with a stretcher, men who kept me from following her into the operating room. Despite both verbal and physical protests, all I was allowed to do was sit in a large hall, filled with beds and the wounded, and wait for the news that she'd earned the highest glory: dying in defense of the Motherland against the fascist horde.

An hour later, I looked up from my seat with weary, bloodshot eyes as Alexandra was brought into the room on a stretcher and placed in the empty bed next to me. The men who came said nothing and moved with a purpose that said they had far too much to do to entertain any sort of pleasantries. Still, my spirits were so low, I would have lapped up any kindness like a stray dog dying of thirst at a newly found puddle.

Another hour passed, maybe two or three, before she came to. The entire time I sat there, holding her hand, my eyes watched her chest rise and fall and stared at the fresh, bloodied bandage on her side.

"Hi," she said, giving a feeble squeeze of my hand. "You're still here."

"Where you go, I go," I said with a sniffle.

She laughed stiffly. "I feel . . . different."

"You should. There's a new hole in your side. Or was, at least. They said they stitched it."

Alexandra shook her head. "No, not like that. You know how normally you walk around this world and in the back of your mind, it's how everything should be, like this is your home? I don't feel that anymore."

"It's because you're tired," I said, knowing full well it was a lie. "Besides, you're not allowed to go. Who will massage my arms and keep me out of trouble?"

"Maybe. But you're strong enough on your own Nadya. Always have been." She sighed, and right then I knew I'd done her a great disservice. As much as I feared everything she might say, in the end, I'm glad she didn't retreat from the conversation as I had. "When tomorrow rolls in, promise me something Nadya."

"Anything."

"Promise me you won't hate yourself."

I turned my head, reliving every moment from the last few hours in vivid detail. How could I ever meet such a request after failing to look out for her? "I don't think I can."

"It's not your fault," she said.

I leaned over and rested my head on her shoulder. "I'm a terrible wing leader. I never should have gotten us separated."

"No, you're a human one."

Her kind words kept me from entering an awful spiral of self-hate. Though she didn't say it, her forgiveness couldn't have been any clearer. I started to wonder when I'd cross paths with Rademacher again and who would win the encounter. History said I wouldn't. Even if I did become the victor, what would that change? Avenging Alexandra, Tania, and Martyona wouldn't bring them back, and it wouldn't make me a good pilot. Skilled, yes, but not good. There was nothing good about war. It simply was.

"When I was three, I got lost once when I wandered out in the woods. I'd never been more frightened in my life, and it turned out I was only a few hundred meters from the house when they found me at night." She paused to pat my head. "And now, you'd think this is my darkest hour, but I'm not scared at all, especially with you here. It's like you're taking me home, and isn't that what a wing leader is always supposed to do? Funny how that works, isn't it?"

I felt her breathing weaken and slow. "I'm so sick of all of this," I said. "Every day it's another bullet, another friend—family. We kill one of theirs. They kill one of ours. And for what?"

"To protect what we have and the ones we love."

"I know, but that doesn't make me any less weary. And thinking about Rademacher makes it worse. He could have killed us both, but didn't. Who does that?"

"A man sick of war."

I nodded. "Or a man touched with madness. I'm not sure which I believe. He never struck me as either when I met him."

"My head is floating. Do me a favor?" she asked.

"Of course."

"Sing to me," she said. She coughed, laughed, and hit me on the top of my head. "Because I'm so awful, the least you could do is serenade me once and show me how it's done."

I lifted my head off her shoulder. My stomach tightened. Any requested performance made me nervous, but a final one made my anxiety a thousand fold worse. I tried to think of something to sing to her, something meaningful and from the heart. Something she could listen to, relax to, fall asleep to. And that is how I settled on a lullaby.

Sleep, my darling, sleep, my baby,
Close your eyes and sleep.
Darkness comes; into your cradle
Moonbeams shyly peep.
Many pretty songs I'll sing you
And a lullaby.
Pleasant dreams the night will bring you . . .
Sleep, dear, rock-a-bye.

Muddy waters churn in anger,
Loud the Terek roars,
And a Chechen with a dagger
Creeps onto the shore.
Steeled your father is in gory
Battle . . . You and I,
Little one, we need not worry,
Sleep, dear, rock-a-bye.

My voice carried through the air like an angel consoling the frightened and lost. The entire room had quieted by the end, and when I was finished, I noticed Alexandra was asleep.

She never woke up.

Chapter Twenty-Six

I SAT IN that chair for countless hours, even when the bed was empty and later occupied by someone else. The halls filled with the wounded, and I learned a bomb had taken out the 895th Rifle Regiment HQ the day before and survivors were still being brought in. I eventually gave up my seat to a recent amputee who had no other place to rest.

Waiting gave me a lot of time to reflect. I'd been so hung up on the idea that being a good fighter pilot was my only path to happiness and self-worth that it took Alexandra's death to make me realize I was chasing an illusion. What I'd been longing for since that last flight with Martyona was acceptance, not from others— certainly Alexandra and Klara gave that to me—but from myself. And no amount of Luftwaffe dead by my hands would grant me that. As depressing as all that sounded, for the first time I had a glimmer of hope I could heal. It wasn't that I didn't want to defend my home, I did, but I did that because of circumstances. What I was choosing at this point was to find a way to be comfortable in my own skin, scars and all. But with a war raging, I knew that would be far easier said than done.

During that time, I took no food, and the only drink that passed my lips was due to the soldier who drove me back to Rakhinka airfield the next morning holding a canteen to my mouth and tipping it up. Most of it wetted my jacket, but what liquid did find its way to my parched throat was soothing.

When the dawn's light crested the horizon, I found myself sitting in my cockpit at the end of the runway, waiting to fly home. No one was there to hug me and tell me to come back safe. No one told me where I went, they would go. I had no God. No enemy. My only company was loneliness.

"Little Boar, this is Badger," the radio said. "Repeat, you are cleared for takeoff."

Mindlessly, I pushed the throttle forward. The plane picked up speed, and for a split second, I thought about letting my feet off the rudder. Without any corrective input, the plane would spin itself off to the side, and with luck, would take me in the crash. But those thoughts were born from frustration and anger. I wanted to live. I also wanted to keep my squadron's reputation intact. I definitely didn't want to be known as that Cossack girl from the 586th who left a dreadful mess. Silly, I know.

I was in the air and making my first turn toward Anisovka when I looked left and saw column after column of smoke rising from Stalingrad. Instead of continuing my course home, I entered a steep, spiral climb until I was just under the cloud layer.

"Little Boar-"

I flipped the radio off. Anything they said would cloud my thinking. I made a slow circle of the area, my eyes fixed toward the city. The fighting still raged, and I had to laugh at my own pity. Those dying for gains in the street literally measured in houses, if not rooms or even meters, would laugh at me being this distraught over the loss of one friend—sister in arms or not. How many had each of them seen killed? Hundreds? Thousands? More to the point, when had they stopped counting? I couldn't imagine, nor did I want to.

But I could imagine something. Gerhard Rademacher's 109 would be over those skies, looking to pounce on the Red Army Air. I checked my gauges one last time to ensure there were no surprises and put the plane on a direct course for Stalingrad. I wanted to find him, engage him, and put a close to it all, one way or another.

On the east bank of the Volga River, I spied countless Red Army artillery batteries firing into the city. Stalingrad rocked and burned with a violence second only to Mount Vesuvius's wrath on Pompeii. Even from three kilometers up in the air I could see the fighting was as fierce as ever. The battle in the skies looked non-existent. Not a single Luftwaffe could be seen anywhere.

"I know you're up here," I mumbled. "Somewhere."

Paranoia set in, and I weaved my plane to check my six. He had to be around, watching me, waiting for his opportunity to attack and put me in the grave as he had done to all the girls before me.

I clenched my jaw with frustration and popped above the clouds, thinking he might be flying high. Over the white cotton tops, all I could see was a beautiful blue winter sky with me as its sole occupant.

I eased back the throttle until I was on the verge of a stall so when I slid open the canopy it wouldn't jam. The cold air roared into the cockpit, blasted my face, and stung my cheeks and nose. My palms ached, and I knew it wouldn't be long before they became excruciating.

I leaned out the cockpit as best I could, hoping to catch a glimpse of Rademacher's plane. "Where the hell are you?"

My scream never had a chance against the wind and engine, not that it mattered anyway. As I slid the canopy back into place, I knew he wasn't around. Then I realized I didn't want a dogfight with him. I only wanted a confrontation where I could understand him to make sense of all his actions. Sadly, that was the one thing this war would never provide.

I turned the plane north-northeast, pushed the throttle forward, and entered a shallow dive. I skimmed my belly a few meters above the Volga's surface and followed the river all the way back to Anisovka. Along the way, I wondered what people would say to me about Alexandra's loss, Klara's words especially.

Then I wondered where the hell God was in all of this. Was there a method to His madness as to why He never stopped the killing? I turned the question over in my mind, and the more I did, the more I found hope in Alexandra's words. Maybe God was brushing the world's teeth and things would become clear on the other side of life. I had nothing else to grab on to.

"Little Boar, this is Den," the tower at Anisovka said when I neared. "You are cleared to land. Welcome home."

I swore under my breath. The operator's voice was so . . . upbeat. I wasn't expecting a total breakdown on their end, but acknowledging my flight was returning minus one would have been appreciated.

Once down, I taxied to my plane's parking spot. Klara directed me into place with slouched shoulders and a blank stare. The spot was roomier than last I saw it. The space next to it, Alexandra's, was empty, and the sight of it hit me in the gut like a cannon.

I killed the engine and slid back the canopy. Even on the ground, frozen air stung my face, and I loathed to get out and face the regiment. I slumped forward and whispered, "God help me."

An arm snaked across my back, and Klara's cheek pressed into mine. "I'll help you."

I sank into that touch of warmth, something my soul craved. I grabbed and squeezed her tight, dying for a bit of goodness to cling to. I pulled her into the cockpit, and she looked up at me, laughing first, then horrified she'd done so.

"Sorry," I said, not moving one bit to help her out of her awkward position. It was a good thing she was small. We barely fit in the cockpit together. "I'm a mess."

"I know," she said. "I've been worried about you since Gridnev told us about Alexandra. I almost thought you wouldn't come back on your own."

"What else did he say?"

"He said the two of you fought bravely and saved many lives, and that she's left a hole in his heart that will never fill."

His words were kind, but deep down, I wish he hadn't said them, at least, not yet. "So he gave her service already," I said, angry at him that he'd done so already and at myself for being so petty. "I would have liked to have been there."

"He said a few words. Maybe there will be more later."

"No. That's all she'll get. That's all anyone gets."

My eyes dried out and stared at nothing in particular for a few moments before Klara reached up and brushed back my hair. She pulled her hand back and said, "You should let me up. I might kiss you and everyone will see."

"I might let you."

That was all the encouragement she needed, and I fell into the intimacy of her intoxicating embrace and cast aside the world.

We parted, and Klara gently wiped her mouth. "People will start paying attention soon if we don't go."

"I don't care anymore," I said. My words drew a puzzled smile from her. "What's the point in hiding anything if we can already die at any moment? That's not living. That's waiting for Death."

"I don't know what to say," she said, looking frightened and hopeful. "But if it's the same to you, I don't want my neck stretched."

I ran my fingers through her hair and gave her a playful tug. "I could think of something to do with it, later. But right now, my legs are falling asleep."

I helped her out of the cockpit before getting out of the plane and sliding off the wing. I wouldn't call my movements lively, but they were several steps away from the grave mood I'd been in.

Perhaps I'd survive Alexandra's loss after all. That said, I still wanted things to be over. The flights. The war. The killing.

Klara looked down at the wrench she was carrying and toyed with it as we walked. Something was on her mind, but I could tell what she said next wasn't what she was thinking about. "Gridnev said he wants to see you as soon as you land—for the official after-action report."

"I know," I said. "They told me on the radio before I landed."

"Also, the Commissar was poking around your dugout while you were away."

My blood turned to ice. "Why?"

Klara shrugged. "I'm not sure," she said. "I imagine he was looking for anything he could use against you."

I almost didn't ask. I was afraid she'd think I was using again, even though I wasn't. But I was really terrified that he'd found the syrette I'd tossed in the oil drum. "What did he find?"

A hint of confusion flickered in her eyes. "Nothing I'm aware of. Why? Could he have?"

I exhaled. "I'm tired and paranoid he'd plant something, I guess."

Klara chuckled. "I know he doesn't like you, but I don't think he'd stoop to that."

"I hope not, but I need to report in. I'll talk to you later," I said, before starting for the command post.

A few paces into my walk, she called out to me. "I never hated her."

"What?"

"Alexandra," she said. "I never did, but I know you think so."

My thoughts split into a hundred different directions. Could I talk about this? Did I want to? How could she ever say otherwise? "You never treated her well." As much as I loved Klara, saying anything else felt like it would betray my wingman. "You two were practically at each other's throats."

"I might have been jealous of all the time you two spent together," she said.

"Might?"

"I was. I was," she said. Her voice picked up tempo and fluttered in pitch as if she barely had control. "But that was before I had you, before we-" She stopped and shook her head. "It doesn't matter. All I want you to know is in the end, I was thankful you had her."

I couldn't help but snort. Some of Third Squadron's ground crew were walking the airfield nearby, and I worried they were about to see me lose my mind. "I'm sorry. This is a little much for me at the moment."

"You don't have to believe me. I wouldn't," she said, "but it's true. As much as I wished I had as much time with you as she did, she always looked out for you. She always brought you home safe. And that's all I ever wished for."

The newly formed lump in my throat made my reply near impossible. "She died for that wish, and all I could do was sing for her before she was gone." I sucked in a breath and steeled myself. "I'm going to report in."

Klara let me go, though I could tell by her pained expression she didn't want me to leave. The couple of hundred meters to the command post seemed as if it stretched out to a full kilometer. The noise of Anisovka muted in my ears and the bustle was reduced to blurred movements in the corners of my vision. My mind was shutting down in anticipation of having to relive the day before in agonizing detail.

Gridnev was waiting for me outside, his leather flight jacket zipped up and goggles around his neck. "Come in, Nadya," he said, holding the door open for me. "This will only take a moment. I'm taking some of the boys from Third Squadron up for some training."

I nodded. My muscles relaxed as I stepped through the threshold and thanked God for the small favor. "I'll try to write it up quickly so you can sign and be on your way, comrade major."

I sat down at the chair by his desk and looked at the map on the wall. Battle lines around Stalingrad were scribbled all across it. The German army had a firm foothold there, that much was clear, and the Romanian armies looked to be dug in and protecting the flanks. The war looked as it always had on first glance, but as Gridnev rifled through some papers and I studied it more, I noticed a buildup of Soviet forces to the south and northwest of the city.

"Is something going on, comrade major?" I asked, eyes fixated.

"With Stalingrad? Always." he said. He flopped a couple of pages onto the desk and pushed them my way. "I put this together based on what you told others at Rakhinka. Read, sign at the bottom. You're on light duty for today, but you're flying tomorrow. I know Alexandra was close to you, but I need everyone, every day, from here on out."

I barely heard the last two sentences. I was too busy reading what he'd put in my lap. It was the after-action report I was supposed to give. Normally, I'd give an oral report, type it up after answering any questions he might have, and then we'd both sign it together. Instead, this report had already been signed—and prepared, I assumed—by him. The contents were straightforward, accurate for the most part as to what happened on the escort. It said I earned two kills, but also claimed Alexandra had shot down two 109s and an He-111 before running out of ammunition and being forced to return to Rakhinka. And she had done all of that after being wounded.

As much as I wanted her to go home a heroine, it would be another lie I'd have to live with. I slumped in the chair. "This isn't right, comrade major. She didn't shoot down anything."

Gridnev arched an eyebrow. "Are you certain? I was under the impression you'd temporarily lost sight of her."

I nodded. "That's correct, comrade major."

"Then unless you saw something concrete contradicting this report, I'd like you to sign at the bottom."

I took the pen he offered and looked down at the line begging for my signature. A few simple strokes of the pen would grant Alexandra one last set of honors, I knew, and no one would be the wiser—especially with Gridnev's approval. Morality aside, putting lies to official reports was a severe crime, and I didn't understand why Gridnev would risk such a thing. Then again, the report would likely never be challenged. Still, my gut tightened. "Why?"

"Because she deserves the honor for all that she's done," Gridnev said. "And her parents could use the extra comfort knowing their girl died valiantly protecting Stalingrad and had something to show for her sacrifices."

I pulled the report closer. I wanted to sign and give Alexandra the recognition she deserved. She may not have shot down a couple of fascists that day, but she was no less heroic in my eyes. I longed for people to talk about her fondly for generations, and this gave it to her. She'd be an ace. One of the few pilots to have five confirmed kills in aerial combat—a female one at that.

"I can't," I said with a heavy sigh. "It's not the truth, and she'd have my head if she could if I did such a thing. Honesty was always the most important thing to her."

Gridnev smiled and took the report. He crumpled it up and tossed in a nearby box. "How is this one then?" he asked, reaching in his desk and handing me a new document.

I looked it over. The report was sterile, a simple account of an uneventful escort followed by an interception of German bombers. It credited me with victories over an He-111 and a Bf-109. Alexandra's loss was a line near the end, and like the first one, Gridnev had already signed it at the bottom. I detested how little attention she'd been given, but signed the paper without objection. "This one is accurate, comrade major."

He tucked the form back into a folder. There was a hint of pride in his eyes, accented by the smile on his face. "You may go, Nadya, and do as you please for the rest of the day. Thank you."

I stood, bewildered at what had happened. I started for the door, but stopped after a couple of steps and turned back toward him. "Why the two reports?"

"I wasn't lying about what I said of Alexandra," he replied. "But there are some who would have liked you to sign the first document and those reasons were not good ones."

"Petrov . . ." The Commissar's name slipped by my lips without thought. My eyes widened at the spoken accusation, but they found nothing to be fearful of in Gridnev's look.

"Your intuitions serve you well, Nadya," he said. "I told him you'd never lie, even to benefit another. But I'd leave this exchange—even the false report—unspoken from here on out if I were you. I don't want him or anyone else thinking you didn't sign the original report because I tipped you off."

"Of course, comrade major."

I should have been happier to have sidestepped Petrov's little trap. There was no telling what he wanted to do to me had he caught me making false reports. The truth of the matter was, however, there was no telling what he'd try next.

Chapter Twenty-Seven

A ZIS-5 TRUCK idled near my dugout. White smoke from the exhaust hung in the air, making clouds that reminded me of those I'd been in the day before. A driver waited inside the cab, drumming his fingers on the steering wheel as he absently stared at the entrance to my earthen home. A few moments later, a soldier came out of the dugout with a stuffed burlap sack over his shoulder and a large book in his arm. Alexandra's book.

"What are you doing?" I yelled, running up and planting myself between the soldier and the waiting truck.

The young private jumped. He looked himself over with a perplexed expression on his face as if some grave breach in his uniform of winter coat and pants was about to send him to the stockades. "Junior Lieutenant Makunina's items are being sent to her parents, comrade pilot," he said. "Major's orders."

I snatched the copy of War and Peace he carried like a hawk plucking a fish from water. "This isn't going."

"The Major was explicit," he stammered. "Everything goes."

"This does not go," I said.

"The book has her-" The soldier hesitated. His face paled and his voice trailed as he finished his thought. "It has her name in it."

At that point I realized my left hand had tightened around the handle of my revolver at my side. I let go of the firearm, but kept the intensity in my voice and stare. "This book stays."

The poor boy shifted the sack on his shoulders, and thankfully for the both of us, he didn't argue any further. "Yes, comrade pilot."

I fumed as he hopped in the truck and left, all the while clutching Alexandra's book against my chest. It was all I had left of her and I'd be damned if I was going to let anyone take it from me. I headed inside the dugout and cringed at how hollow it felt when I looked at Alexandra's bunk. Without her personal affects around, the place seemed alien, even more so when I noticed Bri and the mutt had taken refuge under Alexandra's bunk together. I wouldn't have called them friends, but I assumed their mutual hatred of the cold drove them to a cease fire.

Needing a distraction, I sat on my bunk, opened her book, and thumbed to the first chapter. I had to shift in order for the light outside to reach the pages and see well enough to read:

Well, Prince, so Genoa and Lucca are now just family estates of the Buonapartes. But I warn you, if you don't tell me that this means war, if you still try to defend the infamies and horrors perpetuated by that Antichrist-

"So, Junior Lieutenant, it seems you've taken to strong-arm robbery now."

Given the line I was reading, Commissar Petrov's arrival couldn't have been any timelier. He stood at the entryway of the dugout, looking at me as hungry as ever. He also held an air of smugness about him, one that said he'd finally gotten what he'd been long searching for.

"I don't have time or energy to guess what you're talking about, Commissar," I said, barely remembering to interject some proper formality into my reply.

"You know exactly what I'm talking about," he said as he closed the distance between us. "If you're going to lie, try not to sweat so much. We both know you stole property from the deceased, with a gun, no less."

I stood with the strength of a saint accused of blasphemy and kept the book behind my back and out of his reach. "The book is mine."

"No, Nadya, it's not," he said, drawing a thin smile. "The inscription on the inside clearly states it was Alexandra's, and now it belongs to her family."

My eyes narrowed, and I wanted nothing more than to pull the man apart, limb from limb. "You've got no authority here, and I don't care what the hell you think you know."

He struck me on the side of the head with his fist. "I assure you, I have plenty of authority, and this goes beyond a mere book," he said as I reeled from the blow. As I recovered, he held out his palm. In it was the scorched and slightly melted remains of the syrette I'd tossed into the oil drum the other day. "Recognize it? I missed it yesterday, but this morning I had the inkling to look around one last time. I'm glad I did."

"It's not mine."

"How predictable," he said, chuckling.

My mechanic stepped in, stopping just inside the threshold, confusion splayed across her face. "You wanted to see me?"

The Commissar turned and held the syrette out for her to see. "What can you tell me about this?"

Klara's eyes flickered to the needle, and her mouth hung open for a couple of heartbeats before responding. "I-I don't know what to say."

Petrov snickered. "I think that's all you needed to say," he replied. "The only thing at this point I should consider is whether or not you're her accomplice."

"No. She didn't-I mean, it could be anyone's. Alexandra's even." With every stumble Klara took, I could feel the graveness of the situation worsen. I'm sure she could too since she fidgeted with her hands and couldn't find a place comfortable to stand.

"I'd considered that possibility, Klara, when I first found it," he said. "But logically, it's much more likely to be Nadya's. Alexandra would have never stolen from us. And that's why I wanted you here, so I could see your reaction. You're as guilty as she is and will suffer the same."

I leapt forward. "I stole it. Not her. She had nothing to do with it."

Petrov smirked. "As if I'd believe you two lovers have any secrets between the two of you. I'm going to enjoy keeping you both alive as long as I can."

I replied by driving the palm of my hand into his nose. A soft crunch filled the air. Blood splattered across my hand and sprayed on the ground. He stumbled back and fumbled for his pistol.

"Don't you dare!" I yelled, drawing my own sidearm and pointing it at his chest.

"You filthy little coward," he said. "Drop that weapon right this instant or so help me I'll have you tortured for a month before your body gives up its ghost."

"I'm the coward? I'm the coward!" I screamed, backing toward the exit. "I dance with Death every day while you sit behind the lines trying to be important!"

Petrov drew his weapon. I pulled the trigger. My ears rang from the blasts of two distinct shots. Smoke lingered in the air and filled my nose with the smell of gunpowder. The Commissar screamed in pain, clutching his bloody right hand with his left. His pistol laid on the ground, several paces away. Klara retreated with wide eyes and a slew of mutterings.

"You shot me!" Petrov started at me, but froze when I snapped out of my trance and leveled my revolver at his head. "You've only sealed your fate at this point."

My body shook, and it was all I could do not to break out into a run. Dogfighting Luftwaffe seemed a thousand fold safer at this point, but like any fur ball, I knew I had to keep my wits about me and stay one step ahead if I was going to survive. "I'll be the one deciding what my fate is."

My hand cramped, and the all-too-familiar fire built in my palm and worked its way down my arm. I backed, knowing I had to get out of there before my burns betrayed me.

"Oh what I'm going to do to you," he said, grinning. "If you had any sense, you'd turn that gun on yourself."

I gritted my teeth. Sweat dripped into my eyes, and I kept the weapon trained on his chest as I continued to leave. "Don't even think about moving," I said. "I can still use it on you."

"Nadya! Don't make it worse!" Klara shrieked, grabbing my shoulder from the side.

I'm glad I had the sense not to turn, for as I shrugged her off, Petrov started for me. My eyes staying locked on him were the only things that kept him at bay. "Hold still, damn you!"

Petrov shifted his gaze to Klara. "Comrade Rudneva, stop this turncoat. She's trying to kill me. She's trying to kill us all."

"Shut up!" I said. "You're the only one trying to kill anyone around here. You've had it out for me from the start."

Petrov ignored my words and stayed focused on Klara. "She hates the Motherland, hates us all. She's the same as her father who fought with the White Army. Stop her now and I'll see you're never punished for her crimes."

"No," Klara said, her voice barely a whisper. "Tell me he's lying."

I hesitated, horrified that he'd learned my family's past. As my shoulders fell and my jaw dropped, a wicked grin spread across his face. In that instant, I realized he'd bluffed, but it had worked.

"See, Klara, it's true," he said with a triumphant gleam in his eyes. "She's from a family of traitors and a traitor herself. Why else did she shoot me? What more do you need? Take that gun from her and take your place in history."

"Klara, you know me," I said, stepping back. My hand was cramping so badly I thought the muscles would tear themselves apart, so I shifted the pistol from my right hand to my left and hoped using it with that one wouldn't matter at close range.

Petrov charged faster than a bull stuck with a branding iron, driving his shoulder into my chest and sending his hands after the revolver. We tumbled out of the dugout. The weapon fired once more before being knocked from my grasp.

Petrov landed on top of me. I clawed his eyes and left smears of blood on his face. He grabbed me by the hair, but his grip faltered. He opened his mouth to say something, but all that came out was a bright red bubble. Petrov fell to the side, and I scurried out from under him.

Klara was at my side before I even realized the commissar was dead. "Nadya," she said, her eyes fixed on Petrov's body. "What have you done?"

I caught myself on my knees and panted. "I had no choice."

"No. No. This isn't right," she said. "How could you do this?"

"How could I? How could I not!" I yelled. "God, Klara! That psychotic ass was going to kill us both!"

Women and men from the entire regiment appeared, many with guns. Gridnev ran toward us as well, sidearm in hand. At that moment, I knew I'd be executed before sundown.

Chapter Twenty-Eight

I SAT ON the straw mat in the box, rubbing my ankles. I was grateful the fetters that had been on them the first day had been removed, but my skin was still sore even though eight days had passed. Truth be told, I was surprised I was still in the box at this point and not dumped in a shallow grave, but I didn't regret what I'd done. I was glad to have stood up to Petrov, and if I were to die, at least I'd die true to myself and not hiding. Thankfully, Klara would escape it all. I only hoped whatever was in store for me wouldn't be visited on my parents as well.

I spent some time thinking about Alexandra's comment about God brushing teeth as well. Even though she'd been far from a religious scholar, let alone a leader or believer, the more I turned her idea over the more it made sense to me—or at least, gave me hope. Maybe things we saw as awful were necessary for growth for reasons we'd never understand this side of life. It still wasn't a perfect answer, but I felt it had possibilities.

I took to my feet when I heard some talk near the door. By my best guess, it was still a few hours away from whatever scraps they'd feed me for dinner, but it sounded as if the guard was debating with someone on whether or not he was allowed to let that person in. The door opened, and Zhenia walked in. On top of the flight jacket, gloves, and goggles, she wore a look of concern and helplessness.

"I'm taking Klara up for an escort soon," she said. She kept a few paces away, though I suspected it was not by her choice. If I had to wager, she was on the verge of crushing me in a hug. "I thought you should know since she'll be flying your plane."

"It's hers now?"

Zhenia nodded. "Likely, yes. But we're also getting replacement fighters soon. They might give her one of those, but I suspect not since she worked on yours and knows it better than any."

The news didn't surprise me. I'd figured Gridnev would do such a thing. In another time, another life, I'd have been jealous. Now, I only wanted to be sure she'd live through the war when clearly I wouldn't. I would've liked one last kiss with her as well, but if wishes were horses. "Is she ready?"

"She's too afraid to pull G's," Zhenia replied. "She thinks she'll blackout and crash, which is bad in a dogfight. But she's a natural at anticipating her opponent's maneuvers. I'd hate to be in her sights once she gets over her fears."

I laughed. "That doesn't make me feel better."

"Well this should then. The Luftwaffe have almost disappeared over Stalingrad."

Shock hit me harder than Petrov had hit my cheek. "Why?"

"We're not sure," she said. "The British and Americans have made big gains in North Africa. We think the bulk of the Luftwaffe in the area have been reassigned to help that front."

"It's about damn time our allies drew them away," I said. "I have half a mind to think they waited this long on purpose."

Zhenia snorted. "You're far from alone on that thought. Regardless, despite Hitler's early advances, with so many countries pushing against him now, his industry will never keep up. Mark my words, the Luftwaffe will stay overstretched until his country is in ruin. With luck, Klara will have good experience by the time she encounters her first real dogfight."

"I hope so."

"One last thing," she said. "I want you to know none of the other girls believe anything Petrov said about you."

I smiled. "You have no idea how much I needed to hear that."

The door opened again, and this time it was Gridnev who entered. Where Zhenia had come to me with concern on her face, he came with irritation and weariness. Thankfully, he didn't seem to mind that Zhenia was in the box with me. Perhaps he'd given her clearance before, something I'd considered likely, given that the guard had let her in. "See to your duties, Zhenia," he said, throwing her a glance. "Nadya and I have matters to discuss."

When she left and shut the door, I decided to get right to the heart of things. There was only one reason why he was here. "When's my trial?"

"The twenty-fourth of December. You get to sit here for a month."

My eyebrows arched. This was the second bit of news I hadn't expected whatsoever. "You mean rot. Why so long?"

"Things are . . . happening on the front," he replied. "Oddly enough, we can't spare the time or manpower for a trial since the brass wants upper officers not connected to any of this to preside." He sighed and shook his head. "And then there's the absurdity of the entire situation. A respected pilot and a decorated commissar get into a fight and one ends up dead. That doesn't look good no matter how the pieces fall. Brass wants this dealt with neatly, quietly, if that's even possible. I dare say they don't know what to do."

I seized the moment like a starving dog being tossed a scrap of chicken. "I shot in self-defense. He would have killed me if I hadn't."

"I believe you, but the only other person there was Klara, and she says it all happened too fast for her to make sense of it," he said. His face turned grave. "And then there's the burnt syrette. I know you said he planted it, but the brass is sending an interrogator to see how truthful you are and to test your loyalty. I presented your side as best I could, but they weren't convinced of your innocence. I think my words are the only reason you're still alive."

My throat tightened, and I could feel the strength in my legs wane. At least it seemed Klara had kept quiet about the syrette. I guessed she was hoping that it was an old one, and it was, but from her point of view, I knew she couldn't be certain. God, that had to be eating her alive, trying to decide whether to stay true to me or her country. All of that, however, was secondary to my feelings about an interrogation. "I'd rather be dead."

"For your sake, so would I," he said. "However, that doesn't change anything."

I slumped against the wall. "What will become of me?"

"It depends on your questioning," he replied. "I doubt anything good. If there's anything I can do for you in the meantime, I will."

At first, I didn't give much thought to his comment as I considered it a passing politeness and nothing he could make good on. When the current state of the war popped into mind, I thought I'd take a shot at something, even if it seemed impossible. "You could let me fly one last time. I'd like to go up with Klara if I could so she could see who I really am, before my wings are clipped forever—before I'm beaten and killed. I don't want to die with her thinking I'm a drug addict and a thief."

Gridnev chuckled. There was even a touch of life in his eyes. "I don't either, but I don't think that will be possible. Innocence will only come from your interrogation."

Refusing to be dissuaded, I pressed the idea. "Something big is going on, yes? Surely you need every pilot and plane available."

Gridnev folded his arms and drummed his fingers. I thought for a moment he wasn't going to say anything on the matter but was proven wrong when he replied. "There's a counter offensive about to be launched and details are on a need-to-know basis, but yes, we need everyone for it, which is why your trial has been pushed so far back."

"Let me fight," I begged. "Let me fly one last time. Let me prove to those who would judge my character who I am."

"Putting you in a plane given the severity of your charges is begging for trouble for both of us," he said. "Whatever they have in store for you would be visited upon me and my family tenfold if you took the opportunity to escape."

"I won't," I said, repulsed at the idea. "Order Klara to shoot me down if I try."

Gridnev cracked a half smile. "We both know she never would."

"It won't come to that," I said, feeling the opportunity slip away. "I'm a single kill away from becoming an ace. Can you imagine the pressure they'd be under to side with me if I came back with my fifth victory?"

Gridnev rubbed his chin. "You make a point. Public opinion alone could save you. I suspect Marina would fight for you tooth and nail."

"Then get me cleared for one last mission. What's the worst that could I happen? I'd die and this would all be over." When I could still see the reluctance in his face, I played my last card. "You owe me. I saved your life."

"That you did. That you did," he replied. He paced slowly around the room, mulling his options under his breath. "Okay, Nadya. I'll see what I can do. No promises. We strike in three days. You'll know by then one way or the other."

I lost my composure and grabbed him in a tight hug. "Thank you!"

Gently, he pushed himself free. "No promises," he reiterated while holding up his finger. "And not a word of this to anyone."

* * *

On the third day after Gridnev left, my stomach was queasy with anticipation of his return. Despite the cold, my aching arm, and constant nightmares of Alexandra's death, hope sprang in my soul that I'd be set free to fly once more. God, it would feel so good to see Klara again, not to mention fly alongside her. It was as if I had an angel behind me, whispering words of comfort and joy even though a bleak future loomed. The day wore on and my spirits fell, and those angelic words of comfort seemed to be more and more demonic words of torment.

When I woke the fourth day, I continued down my spiral of hopelessness. However, after my banquet of stale bread and chilled water I tricked myself into believing I'd counted the days wrong. That comforting delusion lasted a few hours. The reality was our forces had launched their counterattack, and since Gridnev hadn't come for me, it must have gone well.

I went to sleep after sunset, wondering if they'd let me write one last letter home. I also wondered if I even should. My family could be judged guilty by association. No matter how innocent my words would be, those letters could be labelled as code.

I woke at a knock on the door. Someone cursed on the other end at the stubborn lock. Convinced it was a firing squad sent to dispatch justice, I hid off to the side, ready to pounce.

"It's me, Nadya. You can relax," Gridnev said as he entered. Despite it being in the late hours of the night, he was dressed for command. That wasn't surprising given he'd probably been coordinating assaults for the last day and a half. This must have been the first break he'd gotten.

"Apologies, but I'm going crazy in here," I said. "How'd the counterattack go?"

"It hasn't," he replied. "Operation Uranus has yet again been delayed thanks to logistics and manpower."

I reflexively sucked in a breath, hopeful this might mean something good for me, but braced myself otherwise. "Does this mean . . .?"

"Yes, you're flying. Our assault launches in the morning. You'll be escorting Il-2 Sturmoviks when they hit enemy lines," he said, handing me a folded map. "Should be light resistance in the air, perfect for Klara's first combat mission."

I took a moment to study the flight plans scribbled across the paper. Klara and I would be meeting a flight of four Il-2s east of Mikhaylovka, shortly after dawn. From there we would be heading south, across the Don River, and striking Romanian gun emplacements protecting the flanks of the Germans and then a depot. "Seems straightforward," I said, looking up. "What's the catch?"

"These are high-priority targets, Nadya," he said with deadly seriousness. "The guns are out of range of our own. If they don't get knocked out, there's no telling how many of our men they'll kill. Every last one of them has to be destroyed. We have to have this drive succeed if we are to cut off the German 6th Army and put Hitler on the defensive. You will help knock out all those emplacements or die trying. Understood?"

"Understood." I paused when I noticed a glisten in his eye. "What aren't you telling me?"

His voice lowered. "Your interrogation is scheduled the day after tomorrow. It's to last at least a week, assuming it doesn't kill you."

My mind fogged. My tongue stuck to the roof of my mouth. Though the techniques that would be used against me were more than enough to frighten anyone—beating, burning, tearing, and breaking anything and everything—the most fearsome thing I had to think about was how any confessions would be used against my family. Perhaps it would be best if I died on this mission after all.

"What if I run?" I asked.

"They'll go after your family as co-conspirators against the State, and they'll hunt you down for the rest of your life. I understand the NKVD are already on their way to watch your parents."

"Why are you telling me this? You'll share my fate if they find out."

"Because I know what it's like to be scrutinized by them over false charges," he said. "Anyone who's saved my life deserves to know what's in store. Come back an ace, however, and I think you can avoid everything. The only problem with that is I don't know if there will be any Luftwaffe for you to engage."

Chapter Twenty-Nine

AN HOUR BEFORE sunrise, after I'd finished studying the mission maps and memorizing every detail, I grabbed a small bucket of red paint, a brush, and a lantern. I brought all three to my Yak-1 and painted the cross of the Knights Hospitaller on the fuselage, a quarter meter behind the cockpit. My burns tormented me as I worked, but I looked at the pain as penance for all I'd done. Strangely, that idea made it bearable, almost welcome.

I felt emboldened with each stroke of the brush, for I wasn't only applying paint to the skin of the plane, but I was declaring who I was for all to see. As I'd said to Klara, a life hiding wasn't living. It was waiting for Death. I was done waiting.

A whisper in the darkest recess of my mind told me my whole life had been leading up to this point. Maybe madness was responsible, but the thoughts gave me purpose and excitement. And if I was going to meet my maker and have the opportunity to ask Him why the world was so broken, I wanted to be able to do so knowing I hadn't been ashamed of Him, at the end at least.

Once finished, I sat on the wing of the plane and raised the lantern to inspect my work. The lines on the cross were crisp, and

I was pleased I'd managed such a good job. I shut my eyes and envisioned the look on everyone's faces when they saw how my plane had changed—what statement it now made. I could even hear the gossip about how silly I must be to believe any god exists. So be it. I might be silly, even foolish, but I didn't care what others thought anymore. Maybe I'd even smooch Klara in front of a crowd for the hell of it.

By the time I'd put everything back, it was about a half hour to sunrise, which didn't leave a lot of time before we launched. I snuck across the airfield where Klara was getting ready in her fighter.

When I reached her plane, she was darting onto the wing and into the cockpit, stumbling as she did. I put a quick finger to my lips to hush the mechanic assisting her and jumped on top of the wing root. "Klara! Slow down!"

Klara nearly flew out of her seat. "Nadya! Are you trying to give me a heart attack?" she said with a death grip on the lip of her cockpit. "Can't you see I'm trying to get ready? Where have you been?"

"Painting."

"Painting what?"

"A little addition to my plane," I said with a huge grin.

Even in the low light, I could see her face sour. "Painted over my boar?"

"I'd sooner destroy a stained glass window than do that," I said. Though I wished otherwise, I knew something was bothering her, and I knew what that was. "I wasn't using again, Klara. I swear. My arm is in far too much agony not to be."

Klara's gaze drifted away from me. "I know what I saw."

"It was old." I said, pulling on her parachute harness to be sure it was secure. She didn't answer, so I tried a new approach. "Grill me when we get back. You'll see I'm not lying."

When I tried to lean in to give her a hug, she pulled away. "No, Nadya. I'm not going to let you muddle my thoughts," she said.

"They're clouded enough, and I need to be able to fly so I don't turn into a crater."

Though hurt, I nodded and backed off. "Fair enough. From here on out, it's all about the mission, and I promise to bring you home safe. Okay?"

I hurried back to my plane, wanting to tell her how much I loved her and her doubts about me were breaking my heart, but she needed time and space. I could only pray she'd get enough of both and realize I spoke nothing but the truth to her.

Climbing into my cockpit, I cast a worried glance to the east. An orange glow crested the horizon, and it meant I didn't have long to pre-flight everything. The mechanic who'd replaced Klara's role this sortie came from Third Squadron. Although I was sure he was a capable young man, it still made me nervous to have him responsible for my aircraft. Klara knew the intricacies of this plane. He did not. She'd put it back together after countless holes and explosions. He had not. So I triple checked it all.

I taxied on to the runway at the first glint of sun, ever hopeful the morning fog would not delay or cancel the flight. Those worries were largely unfounded, for our airfield was missing dozens of planes that had already been sent off on missions. Klara and I were some of the last scheduled to go.

At precisely 8:05, a single flare launched into the air, signaling that it was time for us to depart. Even this far behind lines, no one wanted to risk an early radio intercept on such an important day.

My mood lifted when I took off from the runway. I pulled back on the stick as far as I dared in eagerness to soar with the eagles. The plane's climb was steep enough to sour any veteran's stomach. It was a tiny miracle I didn't stall the plane and crash, but as this flight would be historic for so many reasons, I was going to enjoy every second. I also wanted to show off my cross, so I made a low-level barrel roll over the airfield for everyone to see.

"Little Boar, stop playing."

"Acknowledged," I replied, even though I didn't care in the least. I glanced over my shoulder. Klara saddled behind me about fifty meters to my seven o'clock. "On me, Klara?"

"On you."

Her voice was calm, focused, like she sounded when she was working on an engine or remounting a machinegun. It helped me relax as we traveled west. "Watch those skies," I said, despite needing to keep chatter non-existent. "I don't care how empty they look or how overstretched the Luftwaffe are. Only takes one to catch us off guard and ruin our day."

"Understood."

"Remember to keep your speed up in a fight, but don't be afraid of G's. And don't shoot until you're sure of the shot. Ammunition goes quick up here. If they don't see you and you're close, don't let off the trigger until you see flames."

Klara's laugh blasted over the radio, music to my soul. "You trying to teach me everything you know over the next ten minutes?"

"I'm only passing on tidbits that could save your life."

"Well, here's something I'm going to pass on," she said. "I hate this plane."

I chuckled at the unexpected remark and feigned a deep hurt. "What? We're flying the same one. You always said you loved my fighter."

"I do love your fighter. I hate this one. It's fresh from the factory and barely broken in," she said. "I don't know a thing about its personality."

"Guess you'll have fun discovering it," I said. "Be sure to give it a paint job that reflects it."

"Like your cross?"

Her tone was curious, but it held an edge of shock. "You don't have to have one if you don't like," I replied. "But I like my cross. It's from the Knights Hospitaller."

"I know what it is. Why do you want it?"

"I admire who they were," I said. "Their strength, their unwavering trust in God in a world that made no sense, and if I'm going into mortal combat, I think they're admirable role models."

"If you say." She sighed. "I wish you wouldn't have painted something so against the Motherland. People will wonder about you, but I guess it's your choice." The conversation died for a moment, and Klara picked it up before I replied. "Nadya, I'm sorry. I shouldn't talk to you like that. My nerves are getting the best of me."

"You're doing better than I did my first time. When we get home, you'll laugh looking back."

We zipped over the frozen landscape for another ten minutes before the radio crackled to life. It was the tower from Anisovka. "Little Boar, be advised, Code Siren has been ordered."

This was it then. The command to launch the attack had been given. I couldn't begin to imagine what was happening on the ground, but going by earlier talks with Gridnev, the response must have been on a massive scale like no other.

I rolled my shoulders and stretched both arms to loosen up for battle. Fog still blanketed the ground, and I wondered if the pilots we'd be escorting would be able to see their targets.

It wasn't long before we rendezvoused with Sparrow flight—the group of planes we were to protect—about twenty kilometers north of The Don. The Ilyushin Il-2s were single-engine, ground-attack fighters and a bane of the German armies. Each plane bristled with 23mm cannons and 7.62mm machine guns, as well as a rear gunner. On top of those, each also carried full racks of bombs. Truly they brought hell's fury to the battlefield, and their legendary toughness helped to ensure they'd wreak havoc on enemy lines and live to tell about it. They were more than enough to obliterate our targets, provided Klara and I could keep them alive.

"Glad to have you with us, Little Boar," their flight leader said. "Keep us clear and we'll do the rest."

Our flight crossed The Don shortly before nine. The fog had thinned, and the sight we were greeted with stole my breath. The Red Army swarmed the ground like ants with countless tanks and a thousand times that in men, all driving toward the Romanian lines. Fresh craters filled the landscape, a testament to an artillery barrage that had rained down on the enemy with the wrath of an angry god. Smoke rose from the earth and burning vehicles.

"Do you think anyone survived that?" Klara asked, her words mirroring my thoughts.

"I don't see how anyone could have."

We'd barely passed over our own troops when tracers leapt from the ground toward us. They appeared to bend away at the last moment, an optical illusion due to our speed and the gunners not adequately leading their shots. I brought my plane up a few hundred meters. There was no reason for us to be low at this point, and a lucky cannon shell would ruin our day like dynamite ruined a house of cards. "Popping up to cover."

My eyes scanned the area, searching for hungry Luftwaffe pilots. I also kept tabs on where we were headed with equal intensity. I suppose I should have left navigation to our targets up to the boys in the Il-2s, but with Gridnev's adamant statement that these guns had to be destroyed at all costs, I didn't want to leave anything to chance, including our escorted pilots getting lost.

"I can't make out anything," one of Sparrow's pilots said. "Where's their damn artillery?"

"Hard to say with all the fog," Sparrow Leader replied. "We should be having breakfast with the ground crews by now. Wide circle left. Little Boar, can you see anything up there?"

"Just anti-air," I said. Surely those guns would be near our targets. What else would they be protecting?

"I think I've got them. East, about four kilometers away," Klara said.

I turned my head right and found what she'd spotted. Underneath a small row of trees were at least six guns in a loose row at the top of a small hill. Next to them were trucks, and a little way off were some vehicles I assumed towed more anti-air. Even from a distance, the artillery looked imposing. I could only imagine what they looked like up close. The second I spotted them, all six fired. The flashes from their muzzles made me say a quick prayer for those who'd be receiving those shells.

I put my plane high and left of the Il-2 formation, proud of my wingman. "Nice work, Klara," I said. "Sparrow flight, do you have eyes on target?"

"Copy, Little Boar. We're starting our attack."

I watched the Il-2s make a tight circle near to the ground. I knew I should have been scanning the sky, but a morbid curiosity kept me engrossed on the Il-2s. "Keep watching the skies," I told Klara, figuring she'd be enough for the next few moments. "Can't afford to let any fascist pilots slip in now."

"I am. I am," she said. Her voice sounded irritated, as if I were a parent nagging her for the umpteenth time to tend to chores already being done.

The anti-air fire intensified as the boys made their run. One of the trailing Il-2s took a hit to the wing and then three more to the fuselage. Black smoke poured from its nose, and fire spread down its side. My gut tightened for the crew. The pilot kept his plane on course with the others, and I watched in equal parts awe and horror as all four planes dumped their ordnance on the Romanian forces. Sixteen explosions in all sent up large plumes of snow and debris.

Fragments of wreckage from the artillery were still in the sky when the damaged Il-2 disintegrated. My body numbed, and I banked to watch the fireball slam into the ground. I told myself the crew was dead long before it hit, but I didn't believe it. I'd been in a plane like that, and Death took its time.

I distracted myself by inspecting what was left of the Romanian artillery. The area looked as if God Himself had driven an angry fist into the land several times over. Craters marred the rise, and both guns and trucks were overturned and shattered. The only signs of life I could see were two men scrambling down the hill. "Sparrow, they're done for. I suggest moving on."

"Copy," Sparrow Leader replied. "Moving to secondary targets now."

Klara and I followed the Il-2s as they changed course. Our next target was a direct-support fuel depot. Prior recon had shown it had a pair of field guns near the fuel tanks. The twin 23mm cannons each Il-2 sported would make short work of such a soft target. With no German air to protect them, I pitied those on the ground as much as I hated their invasion.

"Little Boar, this is Stag. Luftwaffe is incoming from the south."

I cursed under my breath for foolishly thinking they'd never show up. They'd never leave us unchallenged, no matter how thinly spread they were.

"I don't see them," Klara said with a nervous edge.

"Sparrow, we're climbing to fifteen hundred meters, still escorting," I said as my plane responded to my desires. "Recommend not sticking around longer than we must."

"I agree, Little Boar. We'll dump and run."

I soon found the road we were to follow to the southeast. The depot was no more than a couple of minutes away. As the five of us sped toward our target, my eyes went back to the sky. It didn't take long to spot the yellow-nosed 109 shooting across the landscape.

"Vis on a Messer low, one o'clock," I announced to the others. "He's headed straight for us."

"Only one?" Klara said. "That doesn't seem right."

Her thoughts rang true, and I held off from intercepting his attack. "You're right. He's got to be bait."

"He'll be on us before we reach the target," Sparrow Leader said. "Deal with him one way or the other."

I nodded, knowing his words were as true as Klara's. The German at this point was a few of kilometers away, which would put him in a firing position in no time at all. With no other options,

I rolled right and throttled up, praying the jaws of whatever trap I was about to fly into weren't as bad as I feared. "Klara, stay with the others. Look for his wingman."

In seconds, the distance between me and the 109 closed to a few hundred meters. My thumbs mashed the triggers, but it was a hair too late. The German fighter cut left and pulled up, dodging my fire. I followed with my own climb, thinking to catch him before he brought his plane to bear on me, but when I was at the peak of my climb, I found his nose pointed square at my plane.

Flames erupted from his guns. Tracers danced around my plane before skipping off my canopy and leaving large cracks across its top.

I kicked the rudder pedals, sliding my plane out of the line of fire and rolled it at the same time so I could keep my eyes on my adversary. The muscles in my neck burned with fire due to a combination of me twisting in my seat and fighting high-G maneuvers at the same time. That pain was only second to the massive amount ripping through my arm. I didn't dare rest, however. If I did, I knew I'd be dead.

"Assist?" Klara asked.

"Negative," I replied. "Keep those Il-2s safe."

The German and I danced in the air. Each step we took was a lethal one should the other miss a beat. We ended up on course for another head-to-head pass, but this time when I rolled the plane upright, I slammed the stick forward and dove my plane to slip under his aim.

My body lifted in the seat and blood rushed to my head, causing my vision to redden. My plane slid under his, and as I chopped the throttle to pull up and stick on his tail, I saw the bright yellow eight painted on his plane. Once again Rademacher and I fought, and once again, his plane sported several more victories since last we'd met.

To my surprise, Rademacher didn't bring his plane around to re-engage. It only took a heartbeat to understand why. Our brief encounter had put him on the tail of Sparrow flight with me heading in the opposite direction. Though I circled my fighter as hard as I could without bleeding off all of my speed, I'd never catch him before he engaged Klara and the Il-2s.

"Klara, it's Rademacher. You're all that's between him and our boys."

Klara's fighter went vertical, climbing far above the Il-2s. Though she reacted quickly, her voice had concern. "Nadya, I still don't see his wingman."

"We'll deal with him when he comes."

Klara flipped her plane and dove toward the German ace. The maneuver set her up for a perfect attack, but before she fired, he side-slipped before issuing a perfect barrel roll, throwing her aim and forcing her to overshoot.

"Damn! Damn! Damn!" she shouted on the radio. "I should've had him!"

"Don't lose heart. We'll get him," I said, trying to sound hopeful.

I leaned forward in the cockpit, trying to make Rademacher's plane seem larger in my gun sight than it really was. At this point, his plane looked like the size of my pinky. I'd never land a shot on him from that range.

The Il-2s broke formation. Two turned left with the other going right. At first I thought it was because Rademacher was about to take them out, but then I saw a second 109 diving in from the clouds. It raked the solitary Il-2 with a vicious barrage of fire before veering off.

"Status?" Sparrow Leader called out.

"Leaking fuel. Gunner is hit," came the reply. "I'm not sure I can stay."

"Understood. Break and return home."

Sparrow Three cut a fast, low turn toward me and we passed by in seconds. As we did, I gave the pilot a quick salute, hoping it would ease his worries, but I don't think he saw it. Ahead, the remaining two Il-2s swung back on course while Klara and Rademacher entered their own dance together.

"Nadya, I'll be fine," she said, her voice wavering. "Get the other 109."

She must have known as much as I did she hadn't a prayer. Worse, Rademacher's wingman was circling over the Il-2s and was about to re-engage. Time ground to a halt when I realized I had a choice. I could try and save Klara, or I could try and save the Il-2s. I couldn't do both. I might not be able to do either.

"Hang on, Klara," I said, angling my plane toward her. "I'm coming."

"No. Finish the mission. Save the others."

"I give the orders, not you," I barked. There was no way in hell I was losing another friend, let alone my love. "We'll save them together."

I sped on, studying the dogfight as it unfolded, trying to feel what Klara and Rademacher were thinking. When I got within a few hundred meters, I chopped the throttle and pushed the nose down, anticipating the German ace's next maneuver.

My instincts proved true, and Rademacher slipped under Klara and dead in my sights. I hammered the triggers and peppered his wing. Not as much debris flew as I'd hoped, but it was a start.

"Little Boar, we need assistance!" Sparrow Leader called.

"Finish him, Klara," I said, banking my plane away and hoping the odds now favored her.

"Working on it," she replied.

My plane dove to where the two Il-2s weaved back and forth in an effort to dodge the 109's aim. Between their maneuvers and their rear gunners sending a lot of gunfire up into the air, the German pilot attacking them appeared to be having a lot of trouble lining up a good shot. Maybe we'd somehow all come home after all.

I caught up to them after a few seconds. When the Messer filled the ring on my gun sight, I sent a stream of death toward him.

Not a single round found its mark, but the German jinked a hard right. His sharp maneuver bled speed, and I easily made the high-G yoyo to compensate and fired again.

A portion of his right wing sheared off along with his aileron on that side. The plane rolled right and barely pulled out of a dive into the ground. The Messer shuddered back and forth. I'm certain the pilot was doing all he could to keep the fighter aloft. I saddled up behind him and fired off another long burst. The plane went down in a flaming heap.

Instead of a rise of elation at the kill, I felt a rise of bile and my soul wither. I'd executed someone who was no longer a threat. I could have let him go. I should have. Then I wondered what was wrong with me. Plenty of people had gotten over their issues about killing others, especially when it was the enemy. Then again, I wondered if that was something to even strive for. Maybe it was good for the soul, in a strange way, to always be revolted by such a thing.

"You're clear," I said, turning back to the Il-2s and clearing my eyes.

"Good kill," Sparrow Leader said. "We'll take it from here. Go send that other one straight to Hell."

I snapped my head around and saw Klara and Rademacher locked in rolling scissors a few kilometers away. Both planes were streaming at this point, which meant Rademacher had managed to score some hits on her. Hopefully, I could enter the fray before it was too late and the two of us could bring him down.

"Nadya," Klara said as I raced toward her. "He's on me tight."

My hands shook, but I tried to sound strong for her sake. "You're doing great. Keep moving."

"I don't know how much longer I can keep this up."

"As long as you need to."

"You're supposed to bring me home."

I cringed at the desperation in her voice. "I will. Few more seconds. I promise."

My hands tightened on the stick. Pain laced my arm and fueled my determination. But they were still a thousand meters from my position, and I could do nothing but watch their duel. God, why couldn't this plane go any faster?

Rademacher won their contest before I got in range. He hammered Klara's fighter, and her plane flipped upside down and went into a steep dive, streaming fuel, coolant and bits of metal. Rademacher didn't follow. Instead, he hooked left, keeping me from getting a shot.

"Klara, what's your status?" I asked as I followed my adversary. Despite the damage to his plane, it was all I could do to keep from overshooting as he threw my aim.

"Little shaken," she said. "I'm not sure how long this plane will last."

"Return to base. That's an order."

"A wingman does not leave her wing leader."

I hit the side of the cockpit with my fist, knowing arguing was useless. The only way we were both going home was to bring Rademacher down before her plane gave out or he blew us out of the sky.

Sweat built on my forehead and neck as Rademacher and I jockeyed for position. I took potshots here and there, but he seemed to slip away from my sights at the last moment every time. My burning hand made it difficult to compensate for his sudden movements.

I eased off the trigger as we went into a rolling dive. I knew my guns were running low on ammo, and I couldn't afford to miss anymore. When we pulled out of it, Rademacher was back on Klara's tail.

The fight wore on for what felt like hours. More than once I thought Klara had cleared Rademacher from her tail, only to realize he'd not only thwarted my aim, but he'd put himself into a better position to shoot her down.

"You've got to end this, Nadya," she said, her voice cracking. "My engine is overheating."

White mist no longer poured from her plane. Her coolant was gone, and the life of her engine could be measured in seconds. With no time, no options, and a thread of hope to cling to, I gave the one order I could think of. "Klara, lose some altitude and hammerhead. I can come around up top when you two stall."

It was a deadly choice that would kill her if it went sour, but what options did I have? I had to get Rademacher to stop moving to get the shot, and the only way I could do that was to use Klara as bait.

"You better not miss," she said.

Her plane rolled into a tight downward spiral with Rademacher following. As they went around, I pulled up and banked, setting myself up for a high attack where I hoped they'd be.

"Here goes," Klara said.

Her plane rocketed up and stood on its tail. Rademacher followed. Perhaps his fighter was more damaged than I'd thought and he needed a kill fast to even the odds. Whatever the reason, right as he was about to get a perfect sight picture on Klara's plane and blast it out of the sky, he lined up perfectly with my guns.

I was a lot of things that day: a daughter, a Cossack, a Christian, a thief, and a failure to two of the best female pilots I'd ever met. But one thing I wasn't going to be was the one responsible for not bringing Klara home.

I grinned with a devilish delight and hammered my triggers. My guns stayed silent.

Chapter Thirty

I WANTED TO die a hundred deaths rather than see Klara get torn apart. I cursed myself a thousand times over for running out of ammo, and with equal parts instinct and hate, I drove my plane into Rademacher's. He opened fire as my left wing struck his fuselage. Despite the violent collision, I managed to pop the latches to both the canopy and seat belt as my fighter tumbled in flames. I was immediately thrown clear.

Almost two thousand meters over the earth, I fell through the sky. Wind blasted my face and roared by my ears. I arched as hard as I could and pulled the ring to my rip cord. My parachute opened, snatching me upward and swinging my legs out in front of me. Sitting in the harness, I twisted in both directions to see what had become of Klara and Rademacher.

I found Klara's fighter above and behind me, making a wide circle around my position. I could hear her engine making a grinding, clanking sound. There was a loud bang, and a black cloud erupted from the nose of her plane. My gut tightened, fearing for her life.

"Land over there!" I yelled, waving my hands toward a level clearing a few kilometers away. Though the ground below me had few trees, it looked like it had enough small hills in it to be a dangerous place to ditch a plane. She must have had the same idea—I know she didn't hear me—and after half circle, she lined her plane up to make an emergency landing where I'd pointed.

I watched her plane glide overhead and remembered to bring my feet and knees together a moment before I hit the ground. Unlike the end of my first dogfight with Rademacher, this landing was softer thanks to the thick layer of snow.

My parachute fell on top of me, and it took me a few moments to get out from under it and untangle myself from the lines. Once I was clear, I undid my harness and drew my revolver. Off in the distant north, I could hear the constant booms of a large battle—one I knew stretched for hundreds of kilometers. I needed to get past it and back into friendly territory. As much as I feared the investigation into Petrov's death, it was still true that everything would be ten times worse if I were captured.

Rademacher was probably thinking how bad things would be for him if the Red Army broke through and caught him. The thought of him spurred me to scan the sky. I saw him coming down in his white parachute, about a half a kilometer away, wobbling like a slow-spinning top. I wondered if something was wrong with his parachute and if he'd survive hitting the ground.

I headed toward where he was landing, and he disappeared behind the far side of a rise. My feet sank deep into the snow with every step, making the travel at times both difficult and tiresome. As I blazed my trail to Rademacher, I questioned the wisdom in such a thing. He'd be armed and obviously had no qualms about killing people. Moreover, he'd be working his way back to his own airfield and wouldn't let anything or anyone get in his way—especially with the Red Army on his heels.

I considered avoiding him and taking the safer route to find Klara and get home. But my entire life on the southwestern front had revolved around him one way or another. I had to bring it to an end if it was the last thing I did. If I didn't do it for myself, I had to for Alexandra and Martyona. They deserved rest more than I deserved closure. And of course, I had to know why he did the things he did.

I crested the hill and found the German pilot lying on his back. He struggled with getting out of the mess of lines wrapped around his leg and lower torso. I ran up behind him, pistol raised and ready to shoot.

"*Hände! Hände!*" I yelled.

Rademacher's arms shot into the air. "*Nicht schießen! Nicht schießen!*"

I froze and couldn't help but crack a smile at the absurd situation. My orders had fully taxed my German vocabulary, and it wasn't as if he didn't speak Russian.

I eased around Rademacher and for the first time I got a look at the man who'd been trying to kill me—who'd killed my friends. He stared at me with eyes belonging to an innocent babe, not the devilish ones I thought they'd be. His thin lips, combined with a narrow chin and large, broken nose made him appear more comical than threatening. He wore leather gloves and a well-fitted fleece-lined jacket in near pristine condition with a white scarf. I was envious of the ensemble, for I still had my original, ill-fitted heavy winter coat and pants I'd been wearing since my first day of training. I looked like a hobo, a child at best, pretending to be a valiant and noble fighter pilot. He looked to be the real thing.

Rademacher was the first to break the silence. "Oh, it's you. I'd congratulate you on shooting me down, but I guess you rammed me. I didn't expect that."

"There's a lot I haven't expected when it came to you."

He looked up at his hands still held high. "They are tired. May I bring them down?"

"So you can shoot me?" I scoffed. "I think not."

"No, but if I may," he said. Keeping one hand high in the air, he slowly reached for the 9mm Luger at his left side. Using his thumb and forefinger, he took it out of its holster and flung it on the ground at my feet.

I picked up his pistol and stuffed it in my satchel, all the while keeping my revolver pointed at his head. "What makes you think I still won't kill you?"

"If you were going to you would have by now," he said. "But if you plan on taking me prisoner, go ahead and shoot me."

"You killed my friends," I said as memories of Alexandra flooded my mind. The gun shook in my hand and my voice cracked. "I should send you straight to Hell."

"I did," he said with a large, unexpected amount of remorse. "But you killed mine as well. Those men had lives, families, and friends, too."

"Maybe they should've thought of that before they invaded our land." My finger tightened on the trigger, my hate being barely contained. Looking back, I'm surprised the weapon didn't go off.

"They fought because they had to," he replied. "As do I. Surely you know what that's like. Stalin has killed millions of your people and invaded Poland, yet you defend him with your life."

"I'll never defend him. I defend myself and the innocent people you'd murder."

Rademacher shook his head. "I don't go after civilians, nor would I. It's why I fly fighters and not bombers. I decide who to engage, who to shoot. At least this way whoever fights against me has a chance." He shrugged and finished untangling the lines around his leg. "You and I are not so unlike. We both fight for madmen who would kill us as much as praise us, and why? Because we must."

I lowered the weapon. As much as I hated to admit it, his words had a ring of truth to them. He had no more choice in invading Russia as I had in defending her. I wagered some of the fascists enjoyed the conquest and wanted to see Germany rule it all, but that wasn't the feeling I got from him.

"So what now?" I asked, unsure what to do with all these new thoughts.

"We can part ways, or you can shoot me. But I won't be taken prisoner."

"No, I can't do that," I said. "You'll fight again and shoot down more of my friends."

"On my word I'll do no such thing," he replied. "I've been tired of this war since it began. Hitler never learned from Napoleon's mistake, never respected the vastness of Russia nor her mighty winters. He will lose this war, and I have no desire to be there when he does."

I smirked, certain I caught him in a lie. "You said you fight because you must. You'll fly the second they give you a new plane."

A loud explosion thundered through the air, and Rademacher looked behind me. "I don't think the Romanian lines will hold much longer," he said. "My superiors will assume I died on the ground if not in the air. Believe me, I've thought long and hard how I can make my exit, and now I have a chance, if you'll let me live."

"If I let you live," I repeated. His words resonated in my soul. I'd been sick of the killing as well, and if the roles were reversed, I'd be making the same plea. But, God, I wanted him dead. No, I wanted more answers first.

He pulled his ID tags from around his neck and tossed them at me. "Take them. Proof to your commanding officers that you won the day."

I picked the tags off the ground. They were oval with smooth edges and had three holes punched on the top and bottom. In the middle, printed twice, was his unit and a few other numbers I assumed identified him.

"Do you know how many planes I've shot down?"

I cocked my head at the unexpected question. He said it with such a flat affect he might as well have been asking if I knew how many brothers and sisters he had. "A lot, judging by the tail on your plane."

"Yes, a lot," he said. His face turned morose. "Forty-seven to be exact. You've gotten a few as well since we first met in August."

"You're number six," I said.

He smiled as if the number was something both to be proud of and pained over. "You've come a long way since then. Such a sloppy flyer our first fight. You still fire too soon and waste ammo. I knew your guns were dry when you set me up with your wingman."

"Why are you telling me this?"

"Because every night when I go to sleep, I see each kill I made over and over, and I sit there and think about how one day, when I meet my maker, I'll have to account for all the lives I took. Worse, should I ever be allowed to walk the streets of Paradise, I'll no doubt come face to face with those souls. I fear their look more than anything."

"Tell me something. Why didn't you ever shoot me down?" I asked. "You've had a few chances you've passed up."

"I told you, I'm tired of death," he replied. "You were no longer a threat when I let you go, and I didn't want my soul blackened any more than it already was." I don't know what my face did, but he paused for a moment and nodded. "You know that feeling, don't you? Executing someone who's helpless. It's a wound I fear I might never recover from."

"Yes. I know what that's like."

"So remember that then as you're deciding what my fate will be. Remember that if you shoot me now, you're one kill closer to becoming the man we both hate. I admit I want to live to see grandchildren and great grandchildren, but I don't wish my nightmares upon anyone. Spare yourself my conscious and let me go."

The wind picked up, biting my already frozen skin. Yet despite the harshness, I sweltered under my jacket as an internal struggle grew. I knew I was at a crossroads, a defining moment in who I was and who I wanted to be. The problem was, I still didn't know who I was, save being a girl far from normal and having to do and live through things no one should.

I wanted to stop it all, the insanity, the battles, but if there was one thing the war had taught me, it was that I could control little in this world. I couldn't control which girls lived or died. I couldn't control what aces I encountered, what missions I went on, what my own countrymen thought of me. I could, however, control my actions in this moment, and I knew whatever I did, I'd think about it to my last day. Did I want to be someone who traded in death or one who dared to believe in life? Thus far I'd known the foremost the best, and it didn't bring anything but misery.

Slowly, I holstered my weapon, though I was mindful to keep my distance. "Go," I said. "If peace is what you want, may God speed it to you."

Rademacher smiled. "Might I have your name before we part?"

"Junior Lieutenant Nadezhda Buzina."

"Well Junior Lieutenant Buzina, I'm pleased to meet you," he replied. "Though I do wish it had been under more agreeable circumstances. When this war is over, if you ever find yourself in Lucerne, feel free to find me. I plan on having the best butcher shop in the city. Or maybe a bakery. Or a good pub where people can relax . . . After all this, I could use a stiff drink. Regardless, I hope our next meeting will be more cordial."

"Switzerland?" I said with a laugh. "I doubt I'll be there anytime soon. It's a bit of a walk."

"All the more reason I should be going now if I'm to make it."

A single pistol shot ended the conversation.

Chapter Thirty-One

SNOW KICKED UP a few paces behind Rademacher. I spun around to find Klara a couple dozen meters away, limping toward us. Her left leg was bloody, but helped support her weight. She clutched her pistol with her right hand and kept it pointed at the German ace. The ire on her face said she'd unintentionally missed.

"Out of the way, Nadya," she said. "Let's finish this and get home."

"No," I said. "I don't want you to kill him."

She stopped, and her brow furrowed. "They'll be here soon. It'll be impossible to take him with us."

I shook my head and steeled myself for the inevitable confrontation. This was going to get ugly, and though I was certain Klara wouldn't understand, I had a fool's hope she would. "I'm not taking him prisoner, and I'm not executing a defenseless man. I'm letting him go."

"You can't be serious."

"I am." I glanced to Rademacher. While he looked thankful, tension stayed etched on his face. I doubt he had half as much confidence I could control the situation as I did, and the little I had was fragile. "Please, hear him out."

"I'm not listening to a damn thing he's said. He killed our friends. He tried to kill me. God, Nadya, how many times has he tried to kill you?"

"Too many," I replied. "But it's more complicated than I thought, or maybe it's simpler. I don't know. What I do know is he wants out of the Luftwaffe and out of the war. He's not a threat, and I refuse to kill someone who's surrendered. I won't be that kind of girl."

Klara looked at me incredulously. "Think, Nadya. Of course he'll say that. He'll say whatever it takes to save his hide."

"I will say whatever it takes," Rademacher said. "But I wasn't lying. If you let me go, I'll make my way to Switzerland and never fight again."

"Quiet! Speaking Russian won't win trust with me," she said. The barrel of her gun dropped, but only for a second. Her face twisted, and her eyes studied every centimeter of my body. "And why should I trust you, Nadya, especially after what Petrov said about your family?"

"He wanted me dead, Klara. He'd say anything to turn you against me."

"I saw your reaction, Nadya. I'm not stupid."

In that moment, I had a huge choice to make. If I lied, our relationship would continue to crack, possibly die right then and there. If I told her the truth about my parents, I had to believe she'd keep quiet, not only for my sake, but the sake of countless others. I hesitated, which I wasn't proud of, but I realized at this point she could've knifed me several times over before and hadn't yet.

"You're not stupid," I said. "My family fought with White Army. While I'm proud they stood up for what was right, I'm not dumb either. I have to keep it quiet or everyone will suffer the consequences. I hope you understand. But I swear on all that is dear to me, we're on the same side."

"And the morphine?"

"It was an old syrette. I tossed it in the oil drum to let it burn so I couldn't use it," I said. I took a step toward her, but when she didn't lower the weapon, I stopped, fearing she might actually use it on me. Tears welled in my eyes. "Klara, I love you. And if you don't believe me then you might as well shoot me right now because you're tearing my heart in two."

"I-" Her gaze drifted behind me, and everything happened so fast. There was a hail of gunfire. Rademacher grabbed me from behind, punched me in the lower back, and threw me to the ground. He leapt on me before I could move and had my pistol in his hand.

"Move and die," he hissed into my ear.

I froze, even held my breath. My eyes flickered to the side. An Opel truck idled at the rise of the hill. Next to it, three men stood wearing bundled uniforms and sloped helmets I'd not seen on either Russian or German troops. I guessed they were the Romanian allies of the Germans. Two of the men had Mauser rifles shouldered. The third held a submachinegun that looked like a PPSh-41. Its drum magazine and heavy barrel had a distinct look I could pick out from a hundred meters away. The fact that it was of Russian origin didn't hurt either.

I couldn't see Klara. As much as I didn't want to see her dead, part of me hoped she was to avoid a prisoner's fate.

Rademacher and the Romanians exchanged words I couldn't follow. It wasn't a heated exchange, but one filled with energy. He walked out of my field of view and fired a single shot. I presumed it was into Klara. I held back my tears as best I could.

He walked over to me once more, aimed my pistol at my head, and fired. The bullet struck next to my ear, and I jumped. He fired again. That shot struck a hair away from my skull, but I kept still. My ears rang, and the smell of gunpowder filled my nose. He dug into my satchel, took his Luger, and tossed my weapon on the ground before hurrying off.

Chapter Thirty-Two

FOR THE NEXT minute or two, all I can do is keep still and pray the Romanians don't come back to inspect Rademacher's handiwork. My shoulder burns, and my chest feels wet and sticky. Slowly, I look down and find the bloody hole in my jacket under my left collarbone. It's messy, but I figure I won't bleed out, at least, not soon.

I start to shiver in the snow and dare to glance around. Neither Rademacher nor the Romanians can be seen, and Klara is on her back in the middle of crimson snow.

I dash to her side, tripping over my feet as I come to her. Her eyes vacantly stare at the sky. Blood tinges her lips. Her chest rises and falls, but I don't think it will last. She needs a surgeon and a half-dozen miracles. I don't have either. But I do have hands, and I take hers in mine.

She tilts her head toward me, but she's looking far away. "Nadya?"

"I'm right here," I say, squeezing her hand.

"You know what?"

"What?"

"I'm sorry for doubting you," she says as her body eases into the ground. "And I'm sorry I got you shot."

"I'd go through all that and more if I could bring you home," I say, settling next to her. She whimpers as I pull her close and brush her hair from her face before kissing the top of her forehead. "I love you."

"I love you, too," she says. She sighs with content. "What did you sing for Alexandra?"

"A lullaby," I reply.

"I bet it was nice," she says. Her voice barely makes it to my ears. "Sing it for me?"

I grit my teeth. "No."

"I suppose I deserve that."

"I mean I don't think I'm able."

"Oh." Her body trembles, and I fear her last breath is almost upon us as she speaks. "You don't have to stay. More will come. Go while you can."

"If I do, I'll never be able to come back to you," I reply.

A smile forms on her face. "According to your god, I'm going to Hell. You'll never come to me there."

"Then He'll be in for a rude surprise."

I shut my eyes as her hand tightens. I wonder how long it would take to get back to friendly lines and what people would say when I returned not only as an ace, but with Rademacher's ID tags. I'd get commendations and medals. Maybe even a promotion. But I'll be damned if I'm leaving Klara, no matter how weak we become.

My head grows light, and all of creation feels distant, alien. I'm a stranger in it, and stranger still, I'm glad. It takes a few seconds to understand why: My time in this broken world is coming to an end, and I'm certain that's just the beginning of something new, something more wondrous and amazing, and maybe I'll finally get some answers. Most of all, I realize I'm happy because I feel my teeth are finally brushed.

"Klara?" I say, hoping she'll rouse one more time.

"Yes?"

"We're going home."

Acknowledgements

The list of people who helped shaped this to what it is today is enormous. Each and every reader that managed to get through draft after draft and provide invaluable and honest feedback will have my eternal gratitude, especially all those that helped nail down the intricacies of the time period, culture, and the Red Army Air.

I owe special thanks to both Therin Knite and Crystal Watanabe, two amazing editors who helped transform the text through various stages.

And most of all, I always owe the most to my wife, Mary Beth, who's read through more material than I can dream of and is still as supportive as ever.

About the Author

C.S. Taylor is a former Marine and avid fencer (saber for the most part, foil and epee are tolerable). He enjoys all things WWII, especially perfecting his dogfighting skills inside virtual cockpits, and will gladly accept any P-38 Lightnings anyone might wish to bestow upon him. He's also been known to run a kayak through whitewater now and again, as well give people a run for their money in trap and skeet.

About the Publisher

Tiny Fox Press LLC
5020 Kingsley Road
North Port, FL 34287

www.tinyfoxpress.com

CPSIA information can be obtained
at www.ICGtesting.com
Printed in the USA
LVHW090505021120
670439LV00001B/55